CHAOS IN MUDBUG

JANA DELEON

CHAPTER ONE

As she exited her hotel room, Jadyn heard the yelling downstairs and picked up her pace. Whatever was going on, she didn't take kindly to people yelling at Mildred, and was determined to see that it stopped. The hotel owner had basically given her a roof and a makeshift family without so much as blinking an eye, and Jadyn wasn't about to have anyone verbally abuse her—not while she was within earshot.

She hurried down the stairs and stepped into the lobby. A red-faced man she recognized as one of the hotel patrons for the past week stood at the front desk, his hands clenched at his side and potbelly heaving up and down from his heavy breathing.

"I'm telling you those venison steaks were stolen from my room last night. As well as the head I was supposed to drop off at the taxidermist on my way home. I killed that deer, and by God, the spoils of the kill belong to me!"

Jadyn stiffened. Deer season hadn't even started yet.

Mildred glared across the counter at him. "You hit that buck with your pickup. Stop making it sound like you're the John Wayne of deer."

Jadyn relaxed a bit as she approached the counter. "Is there a problem here?"

The man barely glanced at her. "Nothing you can help with, honey."

Jadyn stiffened again. "I beg to differ. You see, I'm the game warden, and I'd like to know why you didn't report the accident to me."

He turned and gave her a full-body look, then smirked. "What were you going to do—give the deer CPR? Maybe call a priest?"

Jadyn stared at him. "I would have inspected the deer for disease. It can spread to other animals and infect the meat. I might have called a priest *and* a coroner, if your disrespect at the scene was as big as it is now."

His face turned a shade darker. "Are you threatening me?"

"Since I don't have a time machine, no. But I'm reserving the right to do so depending on what you say next."

"You're all crazy. All I want is my deer steaks. They were in a cooler in my room. This morning, I checked to see if they needed more ice and they're all gone. Someone sneaked into my room and stole them, and that makes it the hotel's problem."

"Uh-huh." Jadyn glanced over at Mildred, who shrugged and mouthed "Helena." Jadyn held in a sigh. Mildred was probably right. Barring the existence of professional deer steak thieves, Helena was the only explanation that made sense. The only other person with a key to the room was Mildred, and Jadyn would bet her last round of bullets that the hotel owner hadn't taken up food theft in her later years.

"And the deer head?" Jadyn asked.

"Was bagged and sitting in ice in my bathtub. It's gone, too."

Which was much more disturbing.

Jadyn was positive Helena had stolen the steaks. The ghost had the appetite of twenty people and didn't think rules should apply to her, especially when it came to her acquisition of food. But what in God's name had she taken the head for? A better question was, did she even want to know?

A second later, a bloodcurdling scream rang out from the floor above them and a door banged against the upstairs wall. Footsteps ran across the overhead hallway, then down the stairs. They all turned to look at the stairwell. Finally, a middle-aged woman with a bad bleach job, clutching a tote bag and wearing a robe, ran into the lobby, then straight past them and out of the hotel, where she jumped into a late-model sedan and tore off down Main Street as if she'd seen a ghost.

Jadyn looked at Mildred, who shook her head.

Maybe something worse.

The man's jaw dropped. "Shelia?" he called out, but by the time he'd managed to form the word, Shelia was probably halfway to Miami. He whirled around, glaring at Mildred. "What the hell kind of hotel are you running?"

Mildred frowned. "The kind that's not charging you for your stay, with the understanding that you, your cooler, and any plastic that contained heads or meat leaves with you within the next hour."

"This is a joke."

"Not at all," Jadyn said. "I think the offer was exceedingly fair, but if you'd like to discuss it further, I'm happy to take the entire situation up with Louisiana Wildlife and Fisheries headquarters, or if you'd like to file a report about the theft, I'm happy to call the sheriff and let you explain the entire situation to him."

The man knew he was defeated. He gave both of them a dirty look, then whirled around and stomped up the stairs, muttering "stupid broads" as he went.

Jadyn waited until he was out of sight, then looked at Mildred. "I guess we should check out Shelia's room."

Mildred sighed and pulled a set of keys from under the counter. "Just one normal day—that's all I ask. Is that too much?"

"With Helena around?"

"You're right," Mildred said as she walked around the counter and headed upstairs. "I don't know what I was thinking."

Jadyn followed the hotel owner up the stairs and down the hall to the room that Shelia had fled. "Was Shelia with the deer killer?"

"Not in the same room, but apparently he knew her."

The door to Shelia's room stood wide open, so Mildred slipped the keys into her pocket, then paused to make the sign of the cross before peering inside. One look and the hotel owner yelled, "I'm going to kill her!"

Jadyn stepped past Mildred and into the room, needing only a second to process the scene in front of her and completely agree with Mildred's assessment.

The comforter and sheets on the bed had been thrown to the side, as if someone had jumped out of bed in a hurry. The set of antlers peeking out from under the comforter told the entire story. Jadyn walked over to the bed and threw the covers back, exposing the deer head, still partially wrapped in plastic.

"If that head bled on my new sheets, I'm going to kill her twice," Mildred said.

Jadyn grabbed the neck where the plastic bag was secured and lifted the entire thing from the bed. "It looks like the neck was covered with plastic. I don't see any stains, but for the record, I'd still kill her."

Mildred whirled around and stalked down the hall to the room at the back of the hotel that she'd "allocated" for Helena.

She pulled out her keys, unlocked the door, and flung it open as if she were robbing the place. Jadyn hurried into the room behind her, not wanting to miss the show.

Helena sat on the bed, eating a blueberry muffin and watching television. Even if Jadyn hadn't already known Helena was the guilty party, her cat burglar outfit gave her away. She looked up at Mildred and Jadyn wearing an innocent expression that no one bought for a single minute.

"You people don't knock anymore?" Helena groused.

Jadyn held up the deer head. "We had a free entry pass."

Helena stared at the head. "Oh."

Mildred put her hands on her hips and glared down at the ghost. "That's all you have to say for yourself? Don't even try to lie your way out of this. I already know you stole those deer steaks, and although it's totally wrong, at least I understand that one given your new career as an Olympic eater. But this?" Mildred pointed at the deer head.

Helena had the decency to look a little guilty. Very little.

Mildred sucked in a breath and her eyes widened. "*The Godfather.*"

Jadyn frowned for a moment, then put two and two together and realized Mildred was referring to the movie and not a real person. "There was a marathon on television a couple of days ago."

"Do you think this is funny?" Mildred asked.

"Well," Helena said, "given how she tore out of the hotel, yeah, I find it hilarious."

"I'm running a business here," Mildred said. "How am I supposed to maintain a decent reputation if a woman is out there claiming she awakened to the head of a dead animal in her bed?"

Helena shook her head. "She's not going to tell anyone. Neither is he."

"You can't know that," Mildred said.

"Sure I can. See, Deer Killer claims he came here to fish, but he was really here to bang Robe Runner, who is *not* his wife. He keeps a separate room in case his wife gets suspicious and checks up on him." Helena shrugged. "I figured they both deserved it."

Jadyn rubbed the back of her neck with her free hand, not about to admit that she sorta agreed with Helena, at least in principle.

"That's rich," Mildred said. "Helena Henry, in charge of ethics and morality. I don't suppose you've heard the one about cleaning up your own doorstep, have you? Well, you can start with Deer Killer's bathtub and Robe Runner's sheets."

Helena shoved the remainder of the muffin in her mouth and her cheeks puffed out like a chipmunk. "Youff a relf drag mately."

Jadyn mentally translated that to "You're a real drag lately" and wondered if Mildred would get it. Apparently she did, because she reddened and pointed her finger at the ghost.

"In the entire time you were alive, you allowed exactly two visitors into your home. If someone had moved into your property, then proceeded to destroy it while simultaneously running off your means of support and eating you out of house and home, you would have shot them and claimed self-defense."

Helena rose from the bed, gave Mildred a long-suffering look, then disappeared through the bedroom wall.

"I always know I'm right when she leaves without arguing any longer," Mildred said.

Jadyn studied the hotel owner for a couple seconds. "Out of curiosity, has there ever been a time when you've been wrong?"

"Ha! Not when it comes to Helena."

Jadyn stared at the wall where Helena had disappeared and frowned. When she'd first realized she was seeing and talking to a ghost, she'd fought believing it. But Helena wasn't exactly the kind of ghost you could brush off as active imagination or eyestrain. For all intents and purposes, Helena was as real to Jadyn as Mildred was. That was just plain weird, and something that confused her when she thought too long about it.

"What are you going to do about her?" Jadyn asked. "You can't live like this forever. For that matter, neither can she. I haven't known her for very long, but I can tell she's bored. That strikes me as a problem."

Mildred sighed. "You're right. It's something Maryse and I have been discussing. We have no way of knowing how long Helena will be here. She didn't even have much of a chance to get bored the last time, and she still managed to wreak plenty of havoc before she ascended. The thought of her hanging around for years makes me want to move to Alaska and not leave a forwarding address."

"Do you have any ideas?"

"Unfortunately, no. I think we need to approach this as seeking a permanent arrangement...at least until we know Helena's expiration date. But I have no idea what kind of permanent arrangement to make for a ghost. The fact that the ghost is Helena just makes the entire mess that much harder."

"I can see that." Jadyn hadn't known Helena when she was alive, but she'd heard enough stories to know that the woman had been hell on wheels then. Fortunately, she'd kept to herself more. Now that only a handful of people could see and hear her, she seemed determine to stick close, regardless of what it did to the quality of life for the living.

"It's getting harder to make up cover stories for the things she does," Mildred said. "I'm afraid she's going to get someone in hot water with the law one of these days."

Jadyn nodded. "If she were alive, I'd say she needed a job, a hobby, or a friend." Jadyn froze. "A friend. Maybe that's the answer."

"She already harasses everyone who can see her and everyone who can't. There isn't anyone left."

"Not a live friend. A dead one."

Mildred's eyes widened. "I understand where you're coming from in a very general sense, but I don't think you've thought it through."

Jadyn frowned. "Why not?"

"Because instead of a companion *for* Helena, *we* could get another Helena."

"Right! Wow. Dodged a bullet with that one. I'm not sure Mudbug could handle two Helenas."

"Not even the devil himself could."

Jadyn's cell phone sounded and she pulled it out of her jeans pocket, frowning when she saw Colt's name on the display. A call from the hunky sheriff would put a smile on the face of most of the women in Mudbug, but if you were the game warden and it was only 8:00 a.m., that call wasn't nearly as flattering as one might think.

"What's up?" Jadyn answered.

"I've got a situation in Miller's Cove. A shrimp boat washed up, probably from the storm last night. It's been beat pretty good and was half-sunk when Harley Koontz came up on it this morning."

"Any sign of the driver?"

"No. And it's not a boat I recognize, at least not offhand."

She grabbed the pad of paper and pen off the dresser. "Give me directions to Miller's Cove. I'll head there right now." She took down the directions and hung up the phone.

"Problems?" Mildred asked.

"A shrimp boat washed up in Miller's Cove. No driver in

sight and Colt doesn't recognize it."

Mildred's expression turned grave. "That storm last night was a doozy. If someone got caught out in it, he could have been blown some distance. There are fishing villages branched out in every direction at least a hundred miles. It could have come from any one of them."

Jadyn nodded. "Well, since it landed in the game preserve, it's my problem now."

"Be careful," Mildred said.

"Always." Jadyn headed out of the room, hoping the missing driver had abandoned his sinking boat and hitched a ride home. The stack of dead bodies that had piled up since she'd been in Mudbug was already bigger than she'd hoped to see in a lifetime.

Whoever said small towns were quiet and boring clearly had never lived in one.

———

SHERIFF COLT BERTRAND STOOD AT THE EDGE OF THE COVE, staring at what remained of the shrimp boat and wondering how much was left of the boat's captain. It was a thought better saved for later in the day and after he'd had coffee and breakfast, but unfortunately, he didn't get to choose. Equally unfortunate, the back portion of the boat that would have contained the name of the boat had been broken off, leaving the boat and Colt facing an identity crisis.

"You don't recognize it?" Colt asked, looking up at Harley.

Harley was fiftyish with a head full of silver hair that always had at least one piece sticking straight up in the air like Alfalfa. If you measured to the top of that sprig, Harley probably topped out near seven feet tall and weighed in at negative two. He had to be the tallest, skinniest person, with the longest limbs, that Colt had ever seen. He was, quite frankly, a walking scarecrow.

He was also a professional fisherman and tour guide and spent every waking moment on the water.

Harley stared at the boat and scratched his head, flattening the sprig with his finger, only to have a replacement pop up an inch farther along his part. "It's nobody from Mudbug. Bud Peterson has the same model, but he just replaced the floor in his a couple weeks ago—painted it some pansy-looking green color."

Colt leaned over to inspect the bottom of the boat. "Dark gray."

Harley nodded. "A man's color."

Colt hadn't seen Bud's unfortunate color choice for his boat floor, and he hoped Harley's opinion on the matter never made it to the surly fisherman. Bud would snap Harley in two like a twig.

"Could be from one of the nearby villages," Harley suggested. "If he shrimps the Gulf or the channels closer to New Orleans, I wouldn't cross paths with him often, if ever."

Colt nodded. He'd already figured that was the case. "Were you out last night?"

"Yeah. I was fishing out Buford Point way when I saw the storm brewing. Came in a bit earlier than predicted, but isn't that the way it always goes? I'd packed up most of my stuff an hour earlier, figuring the weather would screw me out of another hour like it always did, but I still caught the front end of it before I made it back to town."

"It was moving that fast?"

"A good clip. I was doing twenty miles an hour or so, faster when I got a straightaway, but it moved in quicker than I could run through the channel. Probably a good forty-mile-an-hour wind blowing southwest pushing it. "

Colt sighed. "Which means this boat could have traveled fifty miles or more by drift alone, and just during the storm."

Harley nodded. "That sounds about right."

Colt heard the engine of Jadyn's jeep before it rounded a corner and emerged from the woods. She parked next to Colt's truck and headed over, giving Colt a wave as she approached.

Colt held in a second sigh. The sight of Jadyn St. James in jeans, a T-shirt, and hiking boots, wearing no makeup and with her long dark hair in a ponytail, sent him to a mental state he hadn't experienced since high school. Without a single bit of effort on her part, she was the sexiest woman he'd ever met. He'd been fighting his attraction from the moment he laid eyes on her at that first crime scene, but stubbornness had finally given way to desire and he'd kissed her.

He wasn't sure what he'd expected from it. Maybe he'd been hoping that it would feel all wrong, and then he could apologize for his presumptuousness and things could go back to normal. Normal for Mudbug, anyway. But instead, that one kiss had terrified him. And that was something a Southern man did not admit, especially when he was the sheriff.

Fortunately, he'd had to leave the next day for a law enforcement conference that had lasted a week. He'd hoped the time away would clear his head of Jadyn, but instead, he found his thoughts constantly drifting back to her—during workshops and dinners, and even in his dreams. On the drive back to Mudbug, he'd finally decided it was time to put up or shut up. Either he believed all women were bloodsucking vipers like Maria or he believed a woman could be good-looking and capable, and still be warm-blooded.

This was the first time he'd seen the very warm-blooded Jadyn St. James since he returned from the conference. And aside from the problem the wrecked boat presented, Colt was almost relieved that their first meeting would be over business.

Working a job together was a much better way to ease back into interaction with Jadyn—get him on firm footing until he could decide how to approach the elephant in the room.

"Morning, gentlemen," she said as she stepped up.

Colt introduced her to Harley, whose eyebrows lifted when he caught the "new game warden" part, but he was smart enough to keep any opinions he had on the matter to himself.

"You thinking it got caught in the storm?" Jadyn asked.

Colt nodded and recounted the conversation he and Harley had about the wind speed and direction.

Jadyn blew out a breath, and Colt knew she'd already processed the variables and come up with the same conclusions he had. That was another thing—Jadyn was smart, which made it impossible to dismiss her as just another good-looking broad.

"Can you put out a request for any missing persons bulletins for the surrounding areas?" she asked him.

"I'll put it on the wire and make some phone calls as soon as I get back to the office."

"Great. I'll give Marty a call and see if he can get this out of the cove and towed to his shop. Maybe I'll be able to find something in it that tells me who it belonged to."

"Hell," Harley said, "if the guy's missing, surely someone's looking for him."

"Really?" Colt asked. "If you went missing, how long before someone would know?"

Harley frowned. "Well, now that I think about it, I guess wouldn't no one know until I missed a fishing tour. Yeah, I see your point. Hey, maybe I should get one of them girlfriend things...so's she could set up an alarm if I didn't come home."

Colt smiled and clapped Harley on the back. "I think you should get right on that. I bet there's a girlfriend thing just waiting for you to show up and sweep her off her feet."

Jadyn's lips quivered and Colt could tell she was trying not to smile.

"How about you?" Harley asked, giving Jadyn the once-over. "You got a man?"

Jadyn's lips and the rest of her froze and her eyes widened. "Me? No, I'm not in the market for a man."

Harley nodded. "You go for women. I figured as much, being that you have a man's job. Oh well, guess I'll have to check out Pete's tonight. Bet I could hook me a good one there."

Jadyn's mouth dropped open as though she was going to respond, but she must have decided it was pointless, or safer, because a second later, she closed her mouth and pulled out her cell phone. "I'm going to give Marty a call and head back to town. I'll let you know if I find something on the boat. Nice meeting you, Harley."

"Nice meeting you," Harley said and shook his head as he watched her walk back toward her Jeep. "Damn shame about the woman thing. I bet she'd look good in a cast net and rubber boots."

Colt grimaced. "Yeah, it's the bedroom outfit of choice for men all over the world. Listen, I best get going. I appreciate you reporting this."

"'Course," Harley said, but his gaze was still on Jadyn, probably mentally dressing her in different fishing equipment.

Before he could offer up another ensemble, Colt headed for his truck, giving Jadyn a wave before she pulled away. With any luck, the shrimper would be having coffee and cussing at his insurance adjuster. Colt gave the boat one last glance before climbing into his truck.

The thing was, Mudbug hadn't seen luck in a long, long time.

CHAPTER TWO

JADYN'S HEART POUNDED IN HER CHEST AS SHE DROVE DOWN the narrow dirt road that led back to the highway. But her uptick in pulse had nothing to do with her missing boat captain and everything to do with Colt Bertrand. Since her arrival in Mudbug, her job and Colt's had been intertwined, forcing her to spend more time with him than she was comfortable with.

Colt was everything a red-blooded Southern woman wanted in a man and probably more than most could handle. He was gorgeous to look at, built like an athlete, smart, hard-working, and one of her personal requirements, deadly. The last thing she'd come to Mudbug looking for was a man, but Jadyn could no longer deny her attraction for the sheriff.

The last time their jobs had crossed paths, things had ended in a gun-slinging showdown that had almost gotten them both killed. Then Colt had kissed her and despite the lack of bullet wounds, Jadyn was certain she'd been shot. Just not a flesh wound.

Her heart, on the other hand, had clenched as though it was in a vise. Then he'd left almost immediately for a conference and she'd spent the past week watching reruns on television and taking cold showers. Colt certainly knew how to get to a woman. That one kiss had marked the moment she'd given up completely on pretending she didn't want Colt Bertrand in every way possible.

But was it worth the risk to go for it?

Granted, if things didn't go the way she wanted, the only casualty would be her ego. But romantic rejection was the worst kind of ego bruise. Jadyn would be the first to call herself tough, but she was still human. Wanting someone who didn't want you back was the worst kind of suckage.

And that was the crux of the issue—Colt seemed to blow hot and cold. At times, Jadyn was certain of his interest. It was as if it were written in bold lettering across his face. Then just when she thought he was going to make a move, he'd retreat. She supposed she could give him the benefit of the doubt on this last one, as he had to attend the conference for his job. It wasn't his fault that they had a showdown with the bad guy and then he had to leave for work.

She frowned. But had he kissed her because it was an emotionally charged moment in which they'd almost died? Or had he kissed her because he wanted to kiss her? She'd hoped when he returned from the conference she'd be able to tell, but so far, he'd been back two days and the only contact he'd made with her was over the mystery boat.

Maybe he's tired.

That was certainly possible. Those professional conferences were often exhausting.

Maybe he changed his mind.

She sighed, certain that somewhere between "he's tired" and "he changed his mind" was the truth. The question was, which direction did the truth lean toward—ultimate bliss or decided embarrassment? More than anything, Jadyn wished she could get the answer to that question without putting herself out there. Without risking ultimate humiliation.

If she were a normal girl, she'd have a group of crafty girlfriends with clever ideas, just like the ones she saw on television shows. They'd be able to draw Colt's feelings out of him without him even knowing and with no exposure for Jadyn. But she was far from normal. And although she could quite happily—and surprisingly—claim a group of girlfriends, she wouldn't put Mildred, Maryse, and Helena in the "crafty" club, especially when it came to men.

Which left her with sticking her neck out or waiting. Patience had never been one of her strong suits, but then neither had volunteering for a beheading. She sighed again as she pulled in front of the café. She didn't have to make a decision right now. In fact, the worst time to make a decision was before you'd had coffee.

As she hopped out of her Jeep, Maryse bounded up the sidewalk waving and looking more like a teenager than the brainy scientist she was. Jadyn couldn't help but smile. As a botanist, Maryse was a serious professional, but once she left the lab, she exhibited a tiny bit of immaturity that translated to playful and passionate. With most women, it would be an annoying combination, but with Maryse, it was sort of charming. Probably because it was genuine.

"Jadyn!" Maryse called. "Are you going to have breakfast? I desperately need a cinnamon roll, or I may not make it through the day."

Jadyn smiled. Sometimes Maryse and Helena were more alike than either of them would be willing to admit. "I'm definitely having breakfast, but I'll leave the life-changing cinnamon rolls to you."

"Don't tell me you're still watching what you eat." Maryse

rolled her eyes as they walked into the café. "I can't think of anything more depressing than counting calories."

"That's because you're blessed with one of those fat-repellent bodies," Jadyn said, a bit grudgingly. Since she'd arrived in Mudbug, Jadyn had watched Maryse consume more calories in one sitting than a lumberjack did in a week, and yet not a single extra pound ever appeared on her.

Maryse grinned as they slid into their regular booth in the back corner and gave their breakfast order to the waitress. "Luc says I talk it all off."

"Maybe when he gets home, but you're alone all those hours in the lab."

"I sing. Loudly. And I dance. Last week, the pest control guy caught me doing the samba with a push broom."

Jadyn laughed. "I would have liked to see the look on his face."

"Oh, it was classic, especially after I told him I'd been this way since the last time he sprayed."

"That's awful! And hilarious. Did you give him a heart attack?"

"He got all flustered and started assuring me the chemicals they use aren't toxic."

"So what did you say?"

"Nothing. I straddled the broom and started riding it around the lab like it was a stick horse. I swear he might have made two squirts of that stuff before leaving."

A clear mental picture of Maryse riding the push broom flashed through Jadyn's mind, and she couldn't help but envy her cousin's spirit. "I bet you were hell when you were a kid."

Maryse sobered and shook her head. "Not at all. I was mostly a drag. My mom's dying shook me up. I mean, I had Mildred and Sabine, but..."

A wave of sympathy washed through Jadyn. "They weren't your mother."

"No. And then I hooked up with Hank—biggest mistake of my life, but I guess I wouldn't be where I am now if I hadn't married him. Helena couldn't have left me the land, giving me enough income to fund my own lab, and Luc would have never come to Mudbug, and I would have missed out on the best part of my life."

The expression on her cousin's face when she spoke about Luc never ceased to tug at Jadyn's heart. Her cousin and the sexy DEA agent were so obviously enamored with and completely perfect for each other that it was almost depressing. No matter how hard she tried, Jadyn couldn't imagine herself in that level of bliss with a man. Perhaps it was a state of existence limited to only a few lucky ones.

"I'm really happy for you," Jadyn said. "God knows, you've gone through a rash of crap to get to where you are now."

"Did someone call me?" Helena popped through the café wall and into the booth next to Maryse.

Maryse nodded. "Jadyn said 'rash of crap.' That must be what tipped you off."

"Cute," Helena said. "You two aren't going to rag on me the entire time I'm here, are you?"

"That depends," Maryse said, "on how long you're staying. And are you wearing...is that Hello Kitty pajamas?"

It took Jadyn a couple seconds to figure out that Maryse was right. The fabric was stretched so tightly across Helena's more than ample body that it had been too distorted for her to recognize, but now that she looked closely, that burst of pink was indeed a bow.

"Can't you at least make them the right size?" Maryse asked.

"Don't you think I've tried?" Helena groused. "I practiced for hours last night, but never could get them in a larger size."

"Maybe they don't exist in a larger size in real life," Jadyn suggested, "so you can't make them appear."

Helena frowned. "Hmmmm. That's an interesting thought. I'm going to have to test that theory later."

Maryse stared at her in dismay. "I can't wait to see what kind of trouble that will bring."

"You're ragging again," Helena said.

"And I'm not done," Maryse said. "What the hell were you thinking, stealing meat and putting a deer head in someone's bed? That's awful, Helena, even for you."

"I just spent the last thirty minutes paying for it by doing laundry and scrubbing the bathtub with bleach. The fumes almost made me pass out."

"Ha," Maryse said. "If only it were that easy."

"I don't know why everyone is being so pissy about it," Helena groused. "He was a lousy cheater anyway, just like Harold."

Maryse's expression softened a little, and Jadyn remembered what her cousin had told her about Harold Henry. Helena's husband had made a career out of banging cheap women in even cheaper motels, causing Helena to adjust her will and leave him one single item of inheritance—the fleabag motel where he'd spent most of his cheating time. A prenuptial agreement prevented Helena from divorcing him without paying him a fortune, and she had been determined that he get nothing, even if it meant dying before he did just to insult him.

Jadyn figured, even if Helena had long since ceased caring about Harold, it had to cut pretty deep that the person you married had that much disrespect for you. So she guessed a little sympathy was in order. If she'd been in Helena's situation, she might have been tempted to do the same thing. Not saying she would have, but she understood the temptation.

"Okay," Maryse said, "I'll give you a pass on this one, but only because he was a lying, cheating bastard and she was a floozy. But Mildred gets to make up her own mind on this."

"Fair enough," Helena said. "So what's up?"

"Nothing you'd understand with me," Maryse said. "How's the swamp holding up, Jadyn?"

"The swamp appears to be fine, but it may have claimed a victim. A fisherman found a shrimp boat washed up in one of the coves this morning, probably from the storm last night. The planking with the boat name is torn off and no sign of the boat captain, but we're hoping he bailed and hiked it home."

Maryse frowned. "I know most every boat around here. We could go to the cove after breakfast and I could take a look."

"You're not supposed to be in the swamp unless absolutely necessary," Jadyn pointed out.

"I know." Maryse sighed. "But this is getting old really fast. All my research is delayed because I can't get fresh specimens. I'm practically unemployed until I can get back in the bayou."

For the past couple weeks, Maryse had been working out of two rooms at the hotel, in an attempt to ease Luc's mind. One of the drug-runners he'd taken down was out of prison and gunning for the men who'd sent him there. He'd already made one personal attack on a DEA agent's family, so Luc had asked Maryse to limit her work to well-lit, occupied places. Jadyn knew being housebound, or hotel-bound, was putting a serious crimp in Maryse's usual routine. Until she'd met Luc, her cousin had lived alone in a tiny cabin on the bayou that could be reached only by boat. For Maryse, being in the swamp wasn't just part of her work. It was therapeutic.

"All that aside," Jadyn said, "I'm having Marty tow the boat to his shop, assuming it's possible, of course. If you wouldn't mind taking a look at it there, I'd appreciate it."

"Of course," Maryse said, perking up a bit.

Jadyn knew the restlessness her cousin felt. Even something as small as looking at a boat could make the difference between feeling as if you'd done something relevant that day or feeling as if you'd wandered around accomplishing nothing.

She glanced over at Helena and frowned. Maybe that was the ghost's problem. Could it really be as simple as she didn't have a purpose? Jadyn looked at the ghost. "Do you think you can check at the beauty salon and see if anyone's talking?"

Helena's eyes widened. "Me? You want me to help with an investigation?"

"If you don't mind. Women talk about things that don't necessarily make it to the police. For all I know, this guy could have a wife who thinks he ran off with the babysitter and isn't reporting him missing."

Helena nodded. "But she'd tell her best friend, who'd blab to someone else. That's smart. I'll check the beauty shop and the antique stores—see if I can find the usual gossips. If anyone's husband is missing, they're sure to be talking about it."

"Great," Jadyn said. "Thanks."

The ghost looked so pleased with herself that Jadyn almost felt guilty. Why hadn't she thought of it before? Mildred and Maryse had known Helena before she was murdered, when she was rich and essentially useless. She totally understood why they might not make the leap to Helena wanting to feel needed. If Jadyn had known her before, she might not have latched onto that idea either.

A loud crash in the kitchen made them all jump and swivel to look in that direction. A couple seconds later, one of the cooks came stomping out of the kitchen and behind the bar.

"I can't work this way," he said to the woman at the register. "There's no bacon in the freezer. It's your responsibility to place the food order, yet twice this week, I've run out of basic ingredients."

Immediately, Maryse and Jadyn turned to look at Helena. The ghost stared at them for a moment, then put her hands in the air. "I swear, it wasn't me."

Helena was as close as one came to a professional liar, but Jadyn hadn't known her long enough to know her tells. Maryse, on the other hand, could smell the ghost lying from another parish. She took one long look at Helena, then looked over at Jadyn and shook her head.

"I ordered five pounds of bacon," the woman argued. "I took possession of the order yesterday and did the inventory myself. The bacon was right there in freezer number two where it belongs."

"Well, it's not there now. So either you're crazy or the bacon's walking."

"Then the bacon's walking. Maybe you should have this conversation with the other cooks."

The man's face turned red. "Are you accusing one of my employees of stealing?"

"Unless that bacon grew legs, that's exactly what I'm doing. Figure it out, because Sally's not going to be happy if her food cost doubles and profits don't."

The cook spun around and headed back into the kitchen, the swinging door flapping in a frenzy behind him.

"That was pleasant," Jadyn said.

"Freda is no pushover," Maryse said. "Willie can get as angry as he wants, but if she says that bacon was in the freezer yesterday, I guarantee you it was."

Helena nodded. "Freda's practically a military commander. I always thought she was scary."

"Agreed," Maryse said.

Jadyn stared at the kitchen door. "I wonder who took it."

"Probably someone who works in the kitchen," Maryse said.

"That makes the most sense, but five pounds of bacon. That's a lot of breakfast."

"Or fishing bait. Catfish like it."

"Really?" Jadyn said. "You learn something new every day."

The waitress appeared and slid their breakfast plates onto the table. Maryse had two cinnamon rolls and hot chocolate. Jadyn had opted for the healthier and far less sexy egg white omelet with mozzarella and spinach. Helena took one look at Jadyn's plate and made a face.

"You don't have to worry about anyone stealing your food," Helena said. "Maryse's on the other hand..."

"Don't even think about it," Maryse said and held the fork above the ghost's approaching hand.

"I'll give you half of the deer steaks."

Maryse frowned and Jadyn could see her cousin wavering. *Steak* was the magic word with Maryse.

"Half of one," Maryse said. "But you have to take it and leave."

Helena rolled her eyes. "Of course. What do you take me for—an idiot?"

"Don't answer that," Jadyn said.

Maryse cut one of the cinnamon rolls in half and put it on a napkin. Helena scooped it up and disappeared back through the wall without a sound. "Hopefully, we can finish the rest of breakfast in peace," Maryse said.

"I still haven't gotten used to seeing her pop through walls," Jadyn said. "I mean, I see a whole person, and God knows, she's as annoying as real people."

Maryse nodded. "She's the most annoying person of all.

I've seen her do the wall thing a million times, but there's still that couple of seconds when I wonder if it's not going to work and I'm going to have to dream up some absurd cover story."

The door to the café opened and two middle-aged women walked in and sat at a table near Jadyn and Maryse. One of them was clearly upset.

"I'm telling you, Bernice, I don't know what this town is coming to. Murder, drugs, chop shops...and now this thing with my laundry."

"You're sure someone stole it?" the other woman, Bernice, asked.

"Well, I think I should know what I hung outside, and I'm certain only half of it was there when I went back to take it in. I could handle the towels and the cotton blanket, but the quilt really hacks me off. My grandma made that quilt."

Bernice shook her head. "Sharon Simmons said someone took two packages of shrimp off her back porch yesterday. She'd put them out there to thaw and not twenty minutes later, they were gone."

"If Colt Bertrand doesn't get this town under control, I'm not voting for him again. I thought someone younger would be more educated on crime and such, but things are only getting worse. When you can't even hang out your own underwear without fear that someone will make off with them, well I just don't know what to say about that."

"That's weird," Maryse said.

"I take it Mudbug doesn't usually have much petty theft of random food and laundry?" Jadyn asked.

"Not that I've ever heard of."

"Do you think Helena had anything to do with it?"

"I can't see a good reason why. Helena can throw deer steaks on a grill, but she doesn't know how to cook shrimp. She's never had to know. And she would never use someone else's linens. She bitched night and day about cooties until Mildred finally bought her new sheets and towels for her room at the hotel."

Jadyn frowned. It could be a coincidence that those things and the missing bacon had all happened recently, but as a rule, Jadyn didn't like coincidences. In her experience, things that appeared to be linked usually were. "Do you think all the troubles will cause Colt to lose the next election?"

Maryse bit her lower lip. "I'd like to say no, but the reality is, small towns can be funny places. One day you're the hero, and the next day everything bad is your fault. I was hoping things would settle down to the point of boredom, and everyone would forget all the bad stuff, or at least push it to the back of their minds."

"How long have things been happening?"

"I guess the first wave started when Helena was murdered and came back. That was over a year ago, but we had a rash of bad for a good while. Then, except for your basic small-town stuff, almost a year of quiet, until..."

Jadyn cringed. "Until I came to Mudbug."

Maryse shook her head. "Until Helena returned."

"But there's no way she could be at the root of the last month's trouble. We know who the bad guys were in all those situations, and some of the crimes exposed were going on long before Helena was murdered."

"I know. It's not logical to pin it on her. But until someone proves otherwise, I'm convinced that Helena is the harbinger of doom. She shows up, and everything goes to hell in a handbasket."

"So what's the solution? I mean, you helped her ascend before, but this time is different. This time, she wants to be here."

Maryse sighed. "Whether we want her here or not."

"You know earlier, when I asked Helena about spying at the beauty salon?"

"Yeah. That sort of surprised me."

"It was an idea that crossed my mind." Jadyn explained her theory to Maryse.

Maryse scrunched her brow. "Do you think it could really be that simple?"

Jadyn raised one eyebrow. "How bored are you right now?"

"I'm ready to set myself on fire for some entertainment."

"Exactly. And you've only been sorta dormant for a couple of weeks. Helena's been at this for well over a year."

"You may be onto something." Maryse stared out the window for a bit, then looked back at Jadyn. "Okay, we'll try it. But we have to give her things to do that won't cause even more trouble."

"I'm not even sure what that would be."

"Nothing around food."

"Naturally. What else?"

"She tends to play practical jokes when she doesn't like someone."

Jadyn shook her head. "That seems a limiting rule, since I'm not sure she likes anyone."

"Good point. Maybe we should have her patrol the swamps."

"No good. She won't walk and I'm not letting her drive a boat again."

"God forbid. Well, I don't see any straightforward option. The beauty shop thing was a good one. We might just have to play it by ear."

"We might have to make stuff up."

Maryse grinned. "I've never been above lying for the general good."

"Then we have a plan."

CHAPTER THREE

I<small>T TOOK ONLY A MINUTE FOR</small> M<small>ARYSE TO DECIDE SHE DIDN'T</small> recognize the shrimp boat. Marty, the garage owner, had managed to drag the mangled boat out of the cove in one piece and tow the entire mess to his garage, where he'd parked it in the end slot.

"Sorry," Maryse said as she stepped onto a ladder and peered inside. "I've seen this same model, of course, but not with red stripes or this color decking. Unless someone in Mudbug got a new boat in the last couple of months, I don't think it belongs to a local."

"I appreciate you looking," Jadyn said.

Maryse stepped off the ladder. "I wish I could have helped."

"You did help. I'll concentrate my search on the villages surrounding Mudbug instead of wasting time polling the locals." She reached into her duffel bag and pulled out a pair of plastic gloves.

"You want me to help you search it?" Maryse asked.

Before Jadyn could answer, the door at the far end of the

garage swung open and Colt walked inside. Maryse grinned and winked. "Never mind," she said. "You've got this."

Maryse skipped off across the garage, singing a hello to Colt as she passed. He glanced back, then shook his head as he stepped up to the wreckage. "What's she so happy about?"

"Nothing in particular," Jadyn said. "But I'm pretty sure Luc is at the bottom of the majority of her good moods."

"You may be right. I don't ever recall her skipping when she was hooked up with Hank Henry. In fact, back then Hank did all the skipping—skipping out on bills, skipping out on responsibilities, skipping out on his wife."

Jadyn nodded. "I've heard some of the Hank horror stories. It's hard to reconcile those stories with the man he is now."

"He's definitely made changes for the better, and God knows, no one expected him to. If you'd told me a year ago that Hank Henry would be a productive, responsible, married man about to be a father, I would have laughed myself into heart attack range."

"Maybe there are still miracles after the New Testament."

"I hope so. We might need one to figure this out." He pointed to the boat.

"I take it you didn't find any missing person reports?"

He shook his head. "I called all the local law enforcement offices myself and explained the situation. They're all going to pay a visit to the docks and ask around, but as of this morning, none of them have had a report or heard any gossip about someone's boat sinking."

Jadyn felt some of the tension leave her back. "I keep forgetting that he may have bailed and made it home. For all we know, he could be sleeping off the six-pack he consumed last night after sinking his boat. And all of us are out looking for someone who isn't missing at all."

"That's definitely the best-case scenario."

"Then why do I always gravitate to the worst?"

He stared at the boat for several seconds and frowned. "Maybe because worst case is all you've experienced since you've been here."

"I suppose that's true, in a work capacity anyway. But the rest of it has been better than I'd ever imagined it could be."

He raised one eyebrow. "Really? Do tell?"

Jadyn felt a blush run across her chest and up her neck. She hadn't meant to make such a personal statement, but now that it was out, she had no choice but to explain. "I guess I was thinking about Mildred and Maryse. When I first arrived, I expected polite because that's the Southern way of anyone raised with some manners, but they took it way beyond that."

"They treated you like family from the moment they met you."

Jadyn stared at him, slightly surprised. "Yeah. How did you know?"

He shrugged. "I've known them my entire life. Maryse, for all her recent skipping and singing instead of talking, is one of the most practical women I've ever met. And she has absolutely no verbal regulator. If she's thinking it, she says it. So if she's saying she likes you, bet your butt she does."

Jadyn grinned. He definitely had Maryse down perfectly.

"If Mildred likes you," he continued, "she's going to try to take care of you. More so in your case because you're Maryse's family and Mildred practically raised Maryse after her mom died."

"I suppose you're right, although it feels odd to be mothered. My own mother wasn't all that into it."

"Well, be flattered that Mildred wants the job. She doesn't suffer fools well and is a great judge of character. It speaks highly of you that she wants to be involved."

Jadyn felt her face redden with the words.

Colt grinned. "You're blushing. Good Lord, woman, don't you know how to take a compliment? Surely you've gotten your share."

Jadyn tried to think of something to say, but nothing came to mind that didn't make her sound more pathetic. She could only hope that Colt found her blushing charming and not sad. That would be the death blow. No woman wanted the man she was attracted to feeling sorry for her.

"I guess so," she finally managed.

Apparently sensing her discomfort, he changed subject. "So are you ready to do a search?"

She held up her plastic gloves. "You want a set or are you merely an observer?"

Colt took the gloves from her. "I'll observe when I retire."

She grabbed another pair of gloves and they climbed into the boat. "I figured we should check the storage compartments first...see if there's any paperwork."

Colt nodded. "I'll take the cabin," he said and ducked into the tiny cabin at the front of the boat.

Jadyn pulled the cushion off the back bench and checked inside, but all she found was netting and an anchor. She put the cushion back in place and checked both the storage bins in the floor, but both had sustained large holes so only items too big to fit through the openings still remained. She moved to the storage in the driver's column, hoping this was where she got lucky, but when she opened the cabinet door, the only thing she saw was straight through to the concrete floor of Marty's garage.

"Any luck?" Colt asked as he exited the cabin.

"Not even a scrap. The column storage and floor storage are both broken through. If any paperwork was there, it's long gone now. What about the cabin?"

He held up a hat. "This is for a high school in one of the larger villages about twenty miles from here."

"Well, I guess that's a place to start."

As they climbed out of the boat, Marty walked up and greeted them. "Sorry I couldn't get over here when you arrived. My mom called all in a snit and I thought I'd never get her off the phone."

"Anything wrong?" Colt asked.

Marty waved a hand in dismissal. "She's ranting about someone stealing tarps and gasoline out of her garage."

Jadyn frowned.

"Did someone break in?" Colt asked.

"Probably wouldn't have to. I'm always telling her to keep the door locked, but I don't think she does half the time. But it's nothing to worry about. The way mom's mind is going, chances are she didn't have gas or tarps in there. Last week she was harping about someone stealing her clothesline. Now, I ask you, why in the world would someone go to the trouble of stealing a cheap piece of metal wire?"

"Was the clothesline missing?" Jadyn asked.

"Yeah, but it could have popped and sprung off into the swamp. Mom's property backs up against it. That's far more likely than someone stealing it."

Jadyn nodded, but after what she'd heard at the café that morning, she wasn't as ready to dismiss his mother's claims as he was.

Marty waved at the boat. "I had to use some tie-downs to hold the back end together, but I'm pretty sure I got it all out...everything that was attached when it was in the cove, anyway. I scanned the area for the pieces that broke off, but didn't see anything except an oar handle."

"You did a great job," Jadyn said. "I didn't realize how much of the bottom had broken off until we searched it."

33

Marty nodded, but Jadyn could tell he was only half listening. His gaze was focused on the back part of the boat where the siding that would have contained the boat name had been ripped off. He narrowed his eyes on it and frowned.

"Is something wrong?" Jadyn asked.

"What?" Marty swung around to face her. "No. I don't think so. I mean...I don't want to tell you something wrong."

"If you see something off here," Jadyn said, "I'd love to know, even if it's just a feeling. Usually those bad feelings are our subconscious mind locking onto something that our conscious mind hasn't processed yet."

Marty scratched his head. "I don't know about all that. I was just thinking that the damage on the back of the boat looked funny."

"Funny how?"

"Well, if we assume the boat got caught in the storm and tossed about, then the back end must have slammed into something to break out those planks."

"That's what we're thinking," Jadyn agreed.

"But the thing is, the splintering on the back looks like the back was broken from the inside out." He studied the back of the boat once more and ran his finger across one of the broken planks. "Never mind. The more I think about it, the dumber it sounds. That couldn't possibly happen in a storm."

He looked back at them. "I'm going to lock up for lunch in about twenty minutes. If you need to stay longer, I'll give you a key."

"I think we're done," Jadyn said, "but thank you for everything. And remember to send me an invoice for the tow."

Marty waved a hand in dismissal. "I'd rather wait and bill the tow and storage all at one time. Hate doing paperwork. No sense doing it twice." He headed across the shop toward the office.

Jadyn looked over at Colt, who was studying the back of the boat and frowning. "You thinking what I'm thinking?" she asked.

Colt nodded, his expression grim. "If someone deliberately tried to sink this boat, it doesn't look good for our boat captain."

"We need to find out who he was. We may never find a body, but until we know who he was, then we have no way of knowing who would have wanted to harm him."

She pulled out her cell phone and snapped some pictures of the boat, then sent them to Colt. "If you can give me a list of the villages in the order you think they should be covered, I'll get started now."

"You kicking me off the job?"

"No! I mean, if you have the time to help, I would definitely appreciate it, but I don't want to presume anything."

"I've got some time, and I'd rather get a handle on this before tongues start wagging."

Jadyn instantly recalled her conversation with Maryse about the security of Colt's sheriff position, and she understood exactly why he wanted to get to the bottom of things. If this turned out to be a crime, people wouldn't be happy waiting for answers, especially if it meant a killer was on the loose.

"That would be great. Unless you see any advantage to covering them together, we can split them and cover twice as many. If that's all right with you."

"That's fine. I need to know if this man is sitting at home somewhere, bitching about his boat, or if he's gator bait. I'll go get started on that list. Drop by in twenty minutes or so and I'll have that and a good map for you."

He headed across the garage toward the exit. Jadyn stared at the boat a couple seconds more before heading after him.

Finding out the identity of the missing boat captain was definitely the priority. But if he was gator bait, the job was just starting.

Was the wreck a horrible accident or an intentional act?

That was the one question Jadyn hoped she wouldn't have to answer.

———

DOWNTOWN WAS SO CROWDED WITH ANTIQUES SHOPPERS that Jadyn had to park a block down from the sheriff's department. She had barely exited her Jeep when she heard yelling. She looked across the street and saw two women standing outside the beauty salon.

Uh-oh.

Jadyn recognized the woman in the doorway as Millicent, the owner of the salon. She was always accosting Jadyn and trying to get her to come in for a haircut. Jadyn wasn't hung up on her looks, but she'd seen enough people with odd haircuts exiting Millicent's shop to send her to New Orleans for her hair styling.

The woman yelling at Millicent cinched Jadyn's decision to never, ever let the beautician touch her hair. Yelling woman was in her mid-fifties and had probably gone to get her hair styled and gray covered. It was covered all right, but Jadyn wasn't about to believe that the bright purple the woman now sported was what she'd asked for.

"You did this on purpose," the lady with the purple hair yelled. "You're a miserable cow, and I swear I'm going to sue if this doesn't come out."

"I put the same color on your hair that I always do. You saw the bottle. The only reason your hair would turn that color is if you put something else on it yourself. And given how cheap you are, I bet that's exactly what happened."

Two insane women arguing on the street wasn't exactly her job responsibility, but given that Jadyn had sent Helena to the beauty shop, she was afraid she might be ethically responsible for the situation. But as she was about to step off the sidewalk and cross the street, someone jostled her from behind and Helena shoved a bag of popcorn in her hands.

"Hold this," Helena said. "It would probably look weird if the bag was floating on Main Street, but a good show always deserves popcorn." She grabbed a handful and stuffed it in her mouth, her cheeks puffed out like a chipmunk. She was still wearing the Hello Kitty pajamas but was now sporting military boots instead of slippers.

Jadyn narrowed her eyes at Helena. "What role exactly did you play in this show?"

"Who, me?" Helena did her best to look innocent but she managed to look about as benign as a serial killer.

"There!" Jadyn heard a woman yell down the sidewalk and turned to see a large middle-aged woman pointing straight at her. The fact that the woman looked completely deranged and was dragging a small boy as she stomped toward Jadyn was more than a little disconcerting.

"You evil bitch," the woman said as she stepped in front of Jadyn, wagging her finger in her face. "How can you steal popcorn from a child? What the hell is wrong with you?"

"Uh-oh," Helena said and disappeared through the wall of the general store.

If it were possible, Jadyn would have followed Helena straight through that wall and shoved the entire bag in her mouth until she choked. Instead, she put on her surprised face and tried to come up with a decent cover story.

"I'm sorry. Some kid ran by—almost knocked me off the

sidewalk—and dropped the bag as he went by. I was going to throw it away."

The woman narrowed her eyes, trying to determine if Jadyn was lying. Finally she looked down at the boy. "Is this the woman who stole the popcorn from you?"

He sniffled. "I told you. It was the Invisible Man."

She blew out a breath, clearly exasperated. "You and those damn comic books." She snatched the popcorn out of Jadyn's hands and went off in the other direction, the boy struggling to keep up with her pace.

Jadyn shook her head. The poor thing didn't have a chance with that mother.

The shouting across the street increased in volume and Jadyn turned just in time to see Purple Hair grab hold of Millicent's bangs and pull her down to the ground. Millicent was up in a second and launched at Purple Hair like she was playing tackle for the Saints. Jadyn hurried across the street, now certain Helena was at the bottom of the hair fiasco.

She grabbed Millicent's arm and yelled at the two women, who were now rolling around in the street, but they were too angry to listen. A crowd had already formed and every second the yelling continued brought more people out of shops to see what was going on. The last thing Colt needed was store owners fighting with customers right in the middle of Main Street. Even though he had absolutely nothing to do with this fray, she knew some people would find a reason to lay the blame on him.

Desperate for a way to stop the two screaming banshees, she spied a water hose at the edge of the beauty shop. Before she changed her mind, she grabbed the hose and turned it full blast on the two women.

The shrieks increased a thousand times in volume and pitch when the cold water hit them. Immediately, they released each other and struggled up from the street, their gazes locking in on Jadyn. They were both drenched from the spray and had dirt and tiny flecks of asphalt clinging to every inch of their clothes and skin. But Purple Hair was in even worse shape.

A mass of the offending dye had run straight off her hair and onto her face, neck and top, leaving her looking like an extra on *Barney & Friends*. She glanced down at her outfit, then glared at Jadyn.

"Look what you did!" she yelled. "You ruined my shirt. I'm going to sue."

"You're not going to do anything of the kind." Colt's voice sounded across from her, and Jadyn peered around the two women to see him stepping through the crowd. He gave both women the once-over and shook his head. "You two ought to be ashamed of yourselves."

"Me?" Purple Hair said, her eyes widening. "She's the one who did this to my hair."

"I did not do that," Millicent said, clearly digging in her heels. "The chemicals reacted to something different on your hair or in your body."

"Regardless," Colt said, "that doesn't excuse you fighting like children."

Purple Hair threw her hands into the air. "What the hell am I supposed to do? I can't walk around like this. My hair looks like an eggplant."

"I'm sure Millicent will work with you until your hair is back to a normal color." He looked over at the angry beautician. "Right?"

His expression clearly indicated that the only correct answer was "yes." Millicent gave him a grudging nod, and Jadyn wondered if Purple Hair wouldn't be better off shampooing her hair nonstop for a couple of days rather than allowing Millicent to put more chemicals on it.

"Show's over!" Colt yelled. "Everyone get off the street and back to your own business."

The crowd began to disperse, mumbling as they left. Purple Hair and Millicent gave Jadyn one final dirty look, then stalked back into the beauty shop. Colt looked over at Jadyn, his lips quivering, and finally the smile broke through.

"I can't believe you hosed them down," he said.

"Well, logic and yelling weren't exactly effective, so..."

He nodded. "Sometimes, a cooling-down period is the best thing for everyone involved. I was just finishing up that list of villages when the beauty brawl broke out. Do you want to go over it now?"

Jadyn put the hose back against the beauty shop wall. "It's probably best if I get out of sight for a bit."

Colt grinned as they started down the sidewalk to the sheriff's department. "I hope you don't need a haircut anytime soon."

"I'd borrow Mildred's Weed Eater before I set foot in there."

He laughed. "A solid plan."

Shirley, the day dispatcher, looked up from her desk as they walked inside the sheriff's department. Jadyn gave her a wave.

"Who won?" Shirley asked.

Colt pointed to Jadyn. "She doused them with the water hose."

The dispatcher brightened. "I should have gone with you. That would have been worth the walk to see."

Colt shook his head. "Remember the pleasure you feel right now before your next hair appointment. You're always talking about that karma stuff."

Shirley put her hands on her hips and frowned at Colt.

"Even if I were unemployed and without a car, I swear to God, I'd hitchhike to New Orleans with a busload of devil worshippers and sweep floors for payment before I'd let Millicent touch my hair."

Jadyn leaned over and held up her hand for Shirley to give her a high five. The dispatcher slapped her hand and gave her a satisfied nod. "At least someone else in this town has some taste."

Colt rolled his eyes. "This is not your cue for another speech about how I need a haircut." He waved at his office. "Let's get going."

Jadyn grinned at Shirley and followed Colt back to his office. She knew the dispatcher's constant opinions on his life aggravated him. Likely, it made him feel that he was still the same child that Shirley babysat when he was a little boy. But Jadyn found it kinda sweet, in an annoying mothering sort of way.

She felt the same about Mildred. She loved that the older woman had taken her in and genuinely cared about her, but it also felt strange and sometimes slightly claustrophobic. In her case, she simply wasn't used to older adults taking an interest in her life outside of how it affected their own. In Colt's case, she guessed it was a manly man thing.

Colt closed the door behind them and she took a seat in front of his desk. He sat next to her and pulled a sheet of paper and a map of the area toward them. She glanced over at him and felt a slight blush run up her chest. In this case, Jadyn completely disagreed with Shirley. Colt's a-bit-too-long, slightly wavy dark locks were as hot as the two-day stubble on his jaw. The man belonged on a poster for Sexy.

"Here's the list of villages," he said and pointed to the piece of paper. "That isn't all of them, of course. There's probably more out there that I haven't heard of than I have, but those are the ones big enough to support a shrimp house."

Jadyn nodded. "So we check with the shrimp houses first and see if anyone recognizes the boat as one of the fishermen they buy from."

"Exactly. Pricing varies a bit among the buyers, but not so much to make it worth a trip too far away from where he lives. Otherwise, he'd eat up the profit gain in gas." He pointed to the map. "Given the path of the storm as it moved inland, I only covered villages to the east of Mudbug. So that leaves us ten shrimp houses to cover."

Jadyn studied the map for several seconds, gauging the distance between the villages. "Great," she said finally. "If we split up, we should be able to cover them all today."

"I think so. If either of us gets a lead beyond the shrimp house, then we check in and decide whether or not to double-team the lead."

"Perfect."

"I'll make a copy of these and we can get going."

Jadyn rose from her chair as Colt gathered the map and list. She followed him to the door, where he stopped and turned to look at her. "If you run into problems, even something small, or something doesn't feel right, I want you to call me. You've got good instincts. If you are uncomfortable with someone or something, then there's probably a reason for it."

Jadyn felt a blush creep up her face at his compliment. He stared so intently at her that she completely lost her voice, managing only to nod.

"When we're done," he said, "maybe we can grab a bite to eat and exchange notes."

He said it casually, like one law enforcement officer inviting another to beers after work, but Jadyn could hear an edge in his voice that told her the invitation wasn't nearly as casual as

Colt was trying to make it sound. And even if she'd been obtuse and completely missed that sign, the constriction of her chest would have been a dead giveaway.

"Sure," she said, hoping she sounded remotely normal. "After a day of talking to fishermen, I'll probably be dying for food and a beer."

He smiled. "Give me a call when you're on your way back to town. Unless something comes up first, of course."

He exited the office, made copies, and filled Shirley in on their plans for the rest of the day.

"I'll call if I get a line on a missing persons report," she said. "You two be careful."

"It's just a wrecked boat," Colt said.

The dispatcher raised one eyebrow. "That's exactly how trouble starts around here."

Jadyn followed Colt out of the sheriff's department, glancing back at Shirley as she closed the door behind her. The dispatcher was staring out the window toward the bayou and frowning. It was an unsettling sort of frown.

Jadyn didn't blame her. Nothing about this situation felt right.

CHAPTER FOUR

TAYLOR BEAUMONT LOOKED ACROSS HER DESK AT THE distraught woman sitting in front of her. One hand held the tissue Taylor had just passed her. The other clutched a Fendi handbag that Taylor knew was part of a recent collection and cost more than she'd made last year with her detective agency. The diamonds on her fingers and around her neck were probably worth more than she'd ever seen her entire career.

"I'm sorry to be such a mess." The woman, who'd identified herself as Sophia Lambert, patted the corner of her eyes with the tissue, careful not to smear her mascara.

"Don't worry about it," Taylor said. "If people's lives were perfect, they wouldn't need me."

Sophia sniffed again and nodded. "I suppose that's true. You've probably seen more than your share of weeping women."

"I've seen a few. Please tell me how I can help you?"

Taylor had been intrigued by Sophia as soon as she'd walked into the agency. Everything about her screamed old money, and Taylor was rarely wrong when it came to old money. What intrigued Taylor most was why Sophia was here, when she could have easily afforded the poshest private investigators in New Orleans.

"I want you to find my husband."

Taylor's interest flew a million times higher. A wealthy disappearing husband was the sort of thing movies of the week were made of. Which brought her right back around to why Sophia had chosen Taylor's single-person, fairly green operation over the big agencies with tons of experience and lots of resources.

"How long has he been missing?" Taylor asked, figuring she'd get the business out of the way first, then get to the bottom of why Sophia had picked her.

"Well, technically twenty-nine years, but it's a bit complex."

Taylor froze, her pen poised on the tablet. "You might need to start at the beginning."

"Of course. I know it sounds strange, and well, it is strange." She blew out a breath. "I guess I should start with the explosion."

"Whatever you think," Taylor said.

"Okay. My great-grandfather started the first rubber refinery in the state, and every generation increased business and branched out further with the scope of what we do. One of our manufacturing plants uses highly flammable liquids for production. My husband, Sammy—Samuel Perkins—worked at one of the chemical plants as an operations director."

"So you met Samuel through your family's business?"

"Actually, we met at a bar in New Orleans, but my family still doesn't know that. They all think we met at college. The funny thing is Samuel never even went to college. His family was quite poor and he'd been working construction when I met him." She gave me a mischievous grin. "I might have lied to my family about his credentials to get him a job at the plant, but he was so smart and good at the work that no one ever checked."

"No harm, no foul," Taylor said.

"That's exactly what I thought! Anyway, my father was an engineer and far more interested in the inner workings of the machines than running the business, so he was quite happy to leave a lot of those decisions to my Sammy, who single-handedly brought us into the twentieth century by installing computers and automating systems. He was what they call an early adopter." She frowned.

"Tell me about the explosion."

"No one's quite sure what happened. Sammy said he needed to talk to my father, and the secretary told him that my father had left for one of the power buildings near the bayou twenty minutes before. Sammy left the office, presumably to talk to my dad. Twenty minutes later, the power building exploded."

"Your father and Sammy were inside?"

She nodded. "The security cameras didn't capture the area in front of the building, but they showed both of them entering the security gate that led to the dock and the power area. The explosion was so strong they never found any...they couldn't..."

"They didn't find the remains," Taylor finished.

Sophia sniffed again and shook her head. "Before the firemen could even get the fire out, it started raining—one of those downpours that southern Louisiana is famous for—and a lot of the debris washed into the bayou. They searched the wreckage and the bayou for days, but never came up with anything concrete."

"Except that neither man returned home."

"No."

"So what do you think I can find, all these years later, that the firemen didn't discover during their investigation? My chance of locating something containing DNA almost thirty years later is practically nil."

Sophia's eyes widened and she sat forward in her chair. "But that's just it—I'm not sure he's dead."

Taylor stared at her for a couple of seconds, trying to make the same leap, but couldn't quite get there. "Let's just assume he could have lived through the explosion. Why didn't he come home? And where has he been the last thirty years?"

Sophia nodded, beginning to look a bit excited. "I saw this special on television, about people who'd been in horrible accidents and wandered away. Everyone thought they were dead, so no missing persons reports were filed. They were all rescued by Good Samaritans and nursed back to health, but not a single one of them knew who they were."

"Amnesia?"

She nodded. "A couple of them started to remember as time passed, but several never remembered a single thing about their previous life. In every case, it was a chance meeting with someone who knew them before that exposed the truth."

Taylor leaned forward, trying to keep up with Sophia's leaps. "And someone who knew Sammy before saw him recently?"

Sophia beamed. "I think so. My friend Norma was doing some work with one of the local literacy organizations, delivering donated books to children in the villages southwest of here. She said she saw a man on a shrimp boat that was the spitting image of my Sammy. Only older, of course."

Taylor sat back in her chair and tapped her pen on the desk, not sure how to proceed without completely dashing the woman's hopes and not sure she had the tissues to handle it if she did.

"I can understand why you'd want to believe that Sammy somehow managed to live through the explosion," Taylor said, "but none of us have any way of knowing what Sammy would look like today. It's far more likely the man your friend saw reminded her of Sammy but he was someone completely different."

"I'm well aware of how crazy this sounds. It's exactly why I didn't go straight to one of the big detective agencies. People talk, and the last thing I need is rumors circulating that I've lost the plot. I'm the CEO of Lambert Enterprises now. I can't afford loose talk. The board of directors is just looking for a chance to get me out and anyone with a penis in. Sorry for the crassness of the statement."

Aha, Taylor thought. Sophia's seemingly odd choice now made perfect sense. "No, that's all right. I've been left behind in the penis wars a couple of times myself. I know what you're up against."

She stared out the window, considering Sophia's story. She didn't think for a moment that Sammy was still alive, but if Sophia wanted her to make sure, what did it hurt? She could definitely use the business and if she did a good job, and Sophia wasn't too disappointed, she might get some clients out of the deal.

Suddenly, a thought occurred to her and she looked back at Sophia. "Did you remarry?" If the one in a million chance happened to pan out and Sammy was still alive, Taylor couldn't help but wonder if there was a Mr. Sophia in the picture who wouldn't be nearly as happy with the news.

Sophia looked down at her hands and twisted a large diamond around her ring finger. "I came close a couple of times, but it wasn't right. No one's ever been right since my Sammy."

The forlorn look on Sophia's face tugged a bit on Taylor's

heart. She always tried to keep her personal feelings out of her work, but the thought of Sophia pining for Sammy for almost three decades was the sort of thing made-for-TV movies were written about.

"I can pay extra," Sophia said. "Double whatever you normally charge."

"That won't be necessary. I'll take your case, Ms. Lambert, but only if you understand a couple of things—one, shrimpers usually cover a wide area depending on where the product is, so despite the fact that your friend saw this man on a specific dock, he could live miles away. It could take a lot of hours to locate him, *if* I can locate him at all."

"The money isn't the issue, and I understand the vastness of the task."

Taylor wondered if someone like Sophia Lambert ever really accepted failure in others to provide her with what she wanted, but as long as she paid her bill, Taylor was willing to deal with some dramatics when things didn't turn out the way Sophia wanted.

"Two," Taylor continued, "if I find this man, and by some miracle he turns out to be Sammy, I can't force him to meet with you. I will provide you with a means to locate him, but I can't make him engage."

"Of course you can't."

Taylor pulled out a contract and jotted down her hourly rate and a deposit. "Then I think you've found your detective," she said and pushed the paper across the desk. "I'll need the deposit to get started. I'll provide you a report every three days along with an itemized list of hours and expenses, unless I find something sooner."

Sophia didn't even glance at the contract before signing and pulling out her wallet. "I hope cash is okay. I don't want anyone to know..."

"Cash is fine. Do you want a receipt?"

"No. I trust you."

"Great. Then the only other thing I need from you is a picture of Sammy. I can have someone age it. It's not an exact science, but it gives me a little something to go on."

Sophia perked up. "Oh, I forgot to tell you." She reached down and picked up a manila envelope that she'd brought in with her. Carefully, she pulled a sheet of paper out of the envelope and handed it to Taylor. "My friend is a somewhat famous artist. She's even been commissioned to paint royalty. She drew the man she saw."

Taylor only had to glance at the drawing to know just how good the artist was. Every line, every tiny detail was so perfectly depicted that it looked almost like a black-and-white photograph. If Sophia's friend was as accurate with the details as she was talented with her drawing, then this picture should be easily recognized by anyone who knew the man from the dock.

"Let me make a copy," Taylor said. "You'll probably want to keep the original...at least for now."

Sophia looked relieved. "Yes, that would be great."

Taylor made the copy and handed the drawing back to Sophia, who rose from her chair and held out her hand. "I really appreciate you taking this case," Sophia said. "I know it's going to be a long, boring job that probably won't lead to anything, but if I didn't try..."

Taylor shook her hand. "I understand. I'm going to get you answers. Not knowing is always worse." A fact that Taylor understood all too well.

"Yes, it is. I look forward to your reports." She gathered her purse and exited the office.

Taylor watched as she walked past the front window on the sidewalk. She'd implied that she'd taken the case in order to give Sophia closure, but that wasn't really the case. The reality was that something about Sophia and her story set off a tingling feeling in the bottom of her belly. A feeling that she'd learned the hard way not to ignore.

Something important was going to happen, and this case was the beginning of it.

———

JADYN WAS JUST ABOUT TO CLIMB INTO HER JEEP WHEN SHE heard Helena's voice behind her.

"I can't believe you gave the popcorn back to that woman," she complained.

Jadyn glanced around to make sure no one was standing close enough to hear and pointed to the passenger's seat. "Get in. I'm not going to stand around Main Street talking to thin air."

"I'm not thin air."

"Don't I know it, but since no one else can see you, that's exactly what it would look like I'm doing. In the Jeep. Now. I need to talk to you."

"Fine, fine. Jesus, you're getting as bitchy as Maryse and Mildred."

"I wonder why."

Helena rolled her eyes and hefted herself into the passenger's seat. Jadyn backed up and pulled away. As soon as they'd driven out of downtown and were on the vacant highway, Jadyn looked over at Helena.

"I've seen you do some pretty bad things, and heard about even worse, but stealing food from a child is an all-time low."

"It was just popcorn. She could have bought him another."

"You heard that woman. That popcorn was probably the nicest thing she's done for that boy in the past year."

Helena's belligerent expression shifted to a slightly guilty one. "Okay, so maybe it was mean. But that's not why I did it. I just really love popcorn, and I wanted something to eat while I watched the fight."

"I'm glad you brought that up. Let's talk about the fight."

"Uh-oh."

"*Uh-oh* is right. What did you do?"

"How come you always assume I had something to do with it?"

"Oh, I don't know. Maybe because you always do?"

Helena huffed but didn't have the grounds to argue. "Can I help it if the people in this town make me so angry I want to slap them? I suppose I could have popped both those old biddies in the mouth with a wet towel, but wouldn't that have been a bigger problem?"

"Even if you were alive and visible, you can't just go around popping people in the mouth because you don't like something they say. Otherwise, you'd spend an enormous amount of time hitting people and then even longer sitting in jail."

Jadyn knew everything she said was probably going in one ear and out the other, but she felt a little guilty that she'd been the one to send Helena to the beauty shop in the first place. And now, God help her, she really wanted to know what the women said that set Helena off.

"What did they say?" she asked finally.

Helena was staring straight out the windshield, arms across her chest, and wearing her almost permanent pout.

"Helena?" Jadyn said.

"What? Oh, they were talking crap. Maryse came out of the hotel and walked past the shop. Millicent said as how she didn't know what a man as handsome as Luc saw in a tomboy like Maryse. Said it looked like she cut her hair with nail clippers."

The implication that Maryse wasn't good enough for Luc definitely got Jadyn's back up, but as she'd watched Maryse do exactly what Millicent suggested just last week, she couldn't work up indignation over the hair comment.

"Okay," Jadyn said, "I agree that was rude and would have made me mad, too."

"Oh, it didn't stop there. The other bitch said apparently you'd gotten all the looks in the family but it didn't do any good as you seemed content to tromp around the bayou in men's clothes and wear your hair in a ponytail like a six-year-old."

"Blue jeans are men's clothes? Since when?"

"Since forever if you ask some of the idiots who live here. Anyway, then Millicent said as how she'd offered you a discount for a cut and style but you'd turned her down. The other idiot said bad taste must run in the family and they both laughed like hyenas."

"So what did you do exactly?"

"I emptied the bottle of hair dye that Millicent normally uses and refilled it with the purple-tinted one. They both look white coming out of the bottle."

Jadyn struggled to remain irritated, but after what Helena had told her, it was hard. "What they said was bitchy and rude. And if I'd heard it, I would have told them off. I get that you don't have that option, but when you do things like this, it could cause trouble for Colt. People will think he can't control the town, especially with everything that's happened lately. There's an election coming up..."

Helena's eyes widened. "Crap. It would be just like that narrow-minded bunch of sheep to vote him out over things he couldn't control." She sighed. "I'll try harder. I swear, I held off as long as I could, but bad-mouthing you and Maryse is a sure-fire way to put me in the red."

"Maryse and I can take care of ourselves."

"Maybe so, but I don't have many people left on this earth that I can talk to. If anyone is going to hurl insults about the two of you, then by God, it's going to be me."

Jadyn sighed. Just when she thought she was making progress, the ghost brought her back down to reality.

"Now that we got that settled," Helena said, "where are we going?"

"We're going to visit some shrimp houses in nearby villages and see if we can get an identity for our boat captain."

Helena immediately perked up, convincing Jadyn even more that she'd been correct when she made that boredom call. "Cool!" Helena said. "I love a good mystery. What do I get to do?"

"You are going to be my eyes and ears after the fact," Jadyn said, the idea just occurring to her.

"What do you mean?"

"When law enforcement asks people questions, they don't tell the truth a lot of times. Sometimes it's because they are covering for somebody, sometimes it's because they don't want me to accidentally discover something else they're involved in, and sometimes it's simply because they don't want to be involved with the law no matter the cause."

"But where do I come in?"

"When I finish questioning people, you stay behind and see what happens. Maybe they talk to someone else in the room. Maybe they make a phone call. Then you report back to me and I try to decide if it has something to do with my case or not."

"That's a smart idea. I used to always talk about people once they'd left the room."

Jadyn looked over at the ghost. "You don't say?"

Helena waved a hand in dismissal. "Whatever. Come talk

to me when you've lived here a year and tell me you don't talk about people behind their back. I'll wait."

Jadyn didn't even want to think about dealing with Helena for another year, at least not as she was doing now. If the ghost wouldn't or couldn't leave earth for her otherworldly home, then things were going to have to change. Already Luc had offered Maryse a transfer to anywhere in the country. After her kidnapping, Raissa had resigned from her position with the FBI and was dead set on going back to college for interior design, claiming she'd never heard of draperies killing someone. Zach had also resigned and had opened a business specializing in security systems in New Orleans. They were already looking for a townhome in the Garden District.

Granted, Jadyn would be shocked if Maryse ever agreed to leave Mudbug. Mildred was here, as was her work. And Sabine was perfectly happy with her cabin in the swamp and her business on Main Street and more than happy with her husband, Beau, who seemed as content as his wife. But the strain of covering Helena's shenanigans was starting to show on all of them, especially Maryse and Mildred.

"What's with the boots?" Jadyn asked, forcing her mind to shift from a depressing subject to something that didn't matter.

"I tried switching to tennis shoes to steal the popcorn but something went wrong. Now I can't get my slippers back."

"Probably just as well, since we're going to shrimp houses. The boots will have better grip. I don't suppose you'd consider changing the outfit to something more appropriate for the boots?"

"No way. Pajamas are my new uniform. I can't believe I never knew how comfortable they are."

The question of what Helena wore before to sleep in hovered on the tip of Jadyn's tongue, but her fear of the answer kept her from voicing it. She turned the Jeep into a parking lot and pulled up in front of the first shrimp house on her list.

"Here's hoping this is quick and easy," she said.

"That would be a first," Helena said.

Unfortunately, Helena's prediction turned out to be true. They covered three shrimp houses without so much as a nibble—before or after Jadyn left. No one had heard rumor of a missing fisherman and no one changed their story after Jadyn left the building. Some mused over what might have happened to the boat captain, but according to Helena, no one seemed interested beyond basic curiosity.

"How many more are on the list?" Helena asked.

"I have six and Colt has five. He took the ones farther out, so it evened out better to give him one less."

Helena nodded. "That boat didn't materialize from thin air. Someone's got to know who it belonged to."

Jadyn turned onto the road leading to the fourth shrimp house on her list. "Colt said this shrimp house is one of the biggest in the area. Maybe we'll get lucky."

She pulled up in front of the building and parked, then headed inside. The front doors opened to a warehouse area with boat slips leading inside and unloading areas on each side of them. Two of the slips were occupied by fishermen, unloading ice chests full of fish onto the dock. The fishermen and the dock workers gave her curious looks as she walked toward the office in the corner of the building, but at least they managed to hold off the catcalls that she'd received at the last three stops.

Inside the office, two beefy men in their mid-fifties stood behind a desk, both their faces flushed slightly red. Their heads jerked around when Jadyn tapped on the door and poked her head inside.

"We're busy right now," one of the men said, shooting her a dirty look. "Come back later."

She pulled out her identification and flashed it at them. "I'm busy, too. Jadyn St. James," she said and extended her hand.

The surly guy's eyes widened as he shook her hand. "Game warden? I'm Peter Vincent." He pointed to the other man. "This is my brother Bobby."

"Everything about our place is up to code," Bobby said as he shook her hand. "Take a look around if you don't believe me."

"That's not why I'm here." She pulled out her phone and stepped closer to the men. "Do either of you recognize this boat? A fisherman found it in a cove near Mudbug this morning. Looks like it got caught in the storm, but the damage left no way to ID the boat or the missing captain."

Both men narrowed their eyes and leaned over to look at her phone as she scrolled through the pictures. When she got to the last one, Peter shook his head.

"I don't recognize it. I'm not saying he's never sold here, but he's not a regular."

Bobby nodded. "It looks vaguely familiar, but then, it's so torn up, I could be wrong. Like Peter said, if he's sold here before, he's not a regular."

"Thanks," Jadyn said. "I'm going to talk to your dock workers before I leave. I won't be long."

"Of course," Peter said.

Jadyn pulled a business card out and handed it to him. "If you hear talk, even gossip, of anyone missing, I'd appreciate a call."

He glanced at the card, then slipped it into his pocket. "Sure."

Jadyn turned around and cut her eyes at Helena on the way

out the door. Helena nodded and remained in her spot next to the doorway. Something was off in that room. Clearly, the two men had been having a disagreement when she'd walked in, and maybe that was all there was to it. But Jadyn needed to be sure. Hopefully, they'd launch straight into whatever was creating all the tension and Helena would manage to get the story straight when she repeated it.

She crossed the warehouse to the docks, frowning when she saw that the two boats that the dockworkers had been unloading earlier were pulling away. No fishermen had been unloading at the previous three shrimp houses, and she'd hoped to show her pictures to these men before they left. She chided herself for not stopping to ask on the way in, but professional protocol always called for talking to owners or management first before talking to employees. In the future, maybe she'd have to consider a lapse in professional courtesy.

"Hello," she called out as she stepped up to the dock. Both men gave her a wary look.

"I'm the game warden in Mudbug," she said, figuring they weren't going to speak unless she asked a direct question. "We had a shrimp boat wash ashore this morning in one of our coves, and I wanted to see if either of you recognize it."

They looked at each other, then both nodded, so she stepped closer and showed them the pictures. When she was done, both men straightened up and shook their heads.

"Looks sorta like Stumpy's boat," one man said, "but he was in here this morning getting gas, so can't be him. Don't know anyone else that has that framing."

The other guy was staring at the bayou, frowning.

"Can you think of anyone?" Jadyn asked him.

The guy jerked back to attention. "What? No, it's not someone I know."

She glanced back to see Helena exiting the office and

handed a business card to the first man. "If either of you hear something about a missing boat or fisherman, I'd appreciate it if you gave me a call. Even if it's just a rumor."

They both nodded and she turned around, motioning to Helena to stay behind. Jadyn walked slowly across the warehouse toward the exit. The dockworkers weren't arguing, but the same cloud of tension had hung over her entire exchange with them.

She glanced back and motioned again to Helena, who was moving at what could only charitably be called a fast stroll. If the ghost didn't get a move on, they'd be done talking before she got there.

In hindsight, telling Helena to hurry wasn't a good idea.

CHAPTER FIVE

As Jadyn reached for the exit door, she turned back to look just as Helena broke into a jog. She made only two steps toward the dock when her combat boots changed back to slippers. She hit the fish-covered deck, sliding as if she'd landed on ice. Jadyn sucked in a breath and prayed as she barreled, out of control, toward the dockworkers, waving her arms in circles.

When she passed through the workers without incident, Jadyn's breath came out in a whoosh, but she'd relaxed too soon. A second later, Helena hit the pile of fish and went solid, scattering the catch all over the dock. The two dockworkers whirled around and scrambled for the fish that were tipping into the bayou. Helena flopped around in the heap, floundering like one of the redfish and creating a bigger mess. Every time she rose part of the way up, she lost her balance and went sliding back into the pile, sending even more of the catch sliding toward the water.

"Help!" Helena screamed. "They're going to eat me."

"Grab those," the first dockworker yelled, pointing at a group of fish headed toward the edge of the dock. The second dockworker scrambled for the runaways as the first dock-worker tried to push them back into a pile with a push broom. But all he succeeded in doing was pushing the fish over Helena.

"I'm suffocating!" Helena yelled.

Jadyn clenched her hands and hesitated a couple seconds before opening the door. No matter how much she wanted to help, she simply couldn't wade into the fray with the two dock-workers right there. What possible excuse could she give for getting into the middle of their work?

"Jadyn!" Helena yelled as she flopped around once more. "I can't breathe. I'm going to collapse."

A couple of fish slid over the edge and into the bayou, and one of the dockworkers bailed into the bayou after them. Jadyn made the split-second decision to pass off her interfer-ence as help and rushed over to the pile. She pushed two large redfish back to safety and yanked Helena out of the pile while the other dockworker was leaned over the edge of the dock, collecting fish from the worker who'd taken a dip.

She went to the edge and grabbed one of the slimy catch as the worker handed it up to her and carefully tossed it back where the rest of the fish were scattered across the warehouse floor. The door to the office banged open and Peter and Bobby came running out. Jadyn straightened up and glanced back to see Helena stomping through the wall of the shrimp house.

"What the hell is going on here?" Peter asked.

"I don't know," the first dockworker replied. "We were just standing there and it's like the pile of fish exploded. All of a sudden, they were sliding everywhere. Some went into the bayou and we went after them."

Peter looked at Jadyn, obviously skeptical of the dockwork-er's explanation. "Did you see what happened?"

"No, I was on my way out when I heard the commotion. I

came back to help."

The second worker climbed back onto the dock. "Maybe one of 'em was still alive and flopped the pile loose."

Jadyn watched Bobby to see if he was buying it. The fish she'd grabbed was pretty frozen. She seriously doubted any of the pile could thaw and spring to life, but given that the dock-workers couldn't see Helena, she supposed it was the only thing they could come up with.

Bobby looked at the fish. "Whose catch was this?"

"Leonard's."

Bobby's jaw tightened. "Did you get them all?"

"Yes, sir."

"You're sure? I've told you time and again not to let Leonard's fish sit on the dock."

The man nodded, but Jadyn could tell he wasn't sure at all. Leonard must be a piece of work if they were afraid of shorting him payment on a couple of fish. Probably a better idea was to just pay him for a couple more than what they had and call it an operating cost.

"Then get these fish in crates," Bobby said. "And stop stacking the piles so high. You're supposed to be crating as you go."

Peter looked at Jadyn. "There's a sink and soap near the exit door. I'm sure you don't want to walk around smelling like redfish all day."

Although it was framed as concern, Jadyn knew a dismissal when she heard one. "Thanks," she said and headed to the sink, where she attempted to scrub the offending fish smell from her hands. She could feel Peter's gaze on her as she walked out the door minutes later.

Helena was standing next to the Jeep, staring down at her ruined pajamas. Jadyn could smell her from twenty feet away.

"This probably isn't going to come out," Helena said.

"No shit," Jadyn said. "You're wearing ghost pajamas. Can't exactly drop those off at the dry cleaner."

Helena's expression shifted from irritated to dismayed. "Darn it. Sometimes I forget things...you know. When I'm with people who can see me, it's almost like I'm really alive."

"For those of us who can see you, you may as well be. Stop grousing like a child. Just wave your arms or wiggle your nose or whatever and change them out for a clean pair."

Helena brightened. "Oh yeah!" She closed her eyes and wrinkled her forehead and Jadyn waited, but after several seconds, the smelly, stained pajamas still remained.

Helena opened her eyes. "It's not working."

"What do you mean it's not working? That's not an option."

Helena threw her hands in the air. "What am I supposed to do? It's not like there's a set of YouTube videos on how to be a ghost."

"You're not getting into my Jeep with those smelly clothes. I'd be sick before we made it a mile."

Helena clenched again, her face turning red with the effort, but not so much as a thread changed. "I can't do it. It's like I'm constipated."

Jadyn held in a groan. *This is what you get for trying to solve Helena's problems and make her useful.*

"Take them off," Jadyn said.

"What?"

"See if you can pull them over your head and take them off."

Helena's eyes widened. "All I have on under this is underwear and a sports bra."

Jadyn cringed. "I'll have to manage."

"*You'll* have to manage? What about me? I'm not going gallivanting around in your Jeep in my underwear."

"No one can see you but me. I'm the only one who suffers here, but I think the fish smell would be worse."

Helena put her hands on her hips and glared. "You *think*? Well, I used to *think* you were the nice one out of the bunch, but I *think* I've changed my mind."

"As long as you change your clothes along with it, we're good."

Helena clenched once more and a vein popped out on her forehead. A couple seconds later, her breath came out in a whoosh. "It's no use. I'm broken."

"Then take off the pajamas or stay here. I have a job to do and can't stand here all day waiting for divine intervention."

"Do I have to?" Helena whined.

"You've got one minute and then I drive away, and if you try to get into that vehicle in those clothes, I will shoot you." Jadyn knew the bullet would pass right through the ghost, but gunfire always terrified her.

"Fine. You're the one who'll have to live with this."

"Don't I know it," Jadyn grumbled.

Helena pulled the offensive pajama top over her head, exposing the pink-and-black zebra-striped sports bra. Jadyn said a silent prayer that the underwear didn't match but she hadn't even gotten to the "amen" before Helena pushed the pajama bottoms down, bent over, and gave her a tent-sized view of the matching bikini underwear. She supposed she ought to just be happy they weren't G-string.

"What do I do with them?" Helena asked.

Jadyn looked down and frowned. Sure enough, the pajamas were in plain view. "How is that possible?" Jadyn asked. "You created them out of thin air, and they weren't visible before, but when you took them off, it's like they became real."

Helena shrugged, jiggling her stomach rolls. "I'm just winging it."

Between the missing fisherman, the impending maybe-sorta-a-date dinner with Colt, and the odd vibes she picked up from Peter and Bobby, Jadyn already had more to think about than she could process. Trying to figure out Helena's invisible then visible clothing situation would have to wait until she had far more time, energy, and patience.

"Just toss them somewhere that no one can see," Jadyn said.

Helena picked up both garments, straightened back up, and flung them onto the roof of the shrimp house. Jadyn shook her head and climbed into the Jeep. A couple of seconds later, Helena hoisted herself into the passenger's seat and Jadyn's eyes watered.

"The fish must have leaked through the pajamas," Jadyn said. "I have no idea how it's possible, but you still stink. How in the world can a ghost take on an earthly smell?"

"I'm not taking off my underwear. Everyone has a line and that's mine. Besides, this is all your fault anyway...telling me to hurry. I don't *do* hurry."

Jadyn grimaced. As if the scene in her passenger's seat wasn't bad enough already, Helena had to go throwing even worse disasters into her mind. "Then ride in the back."

Helena stared. "Seriously?"

"Either you ride in the back, or I have to stop every mile or so to get ill. I need you downwind."

"Then take me back to Mudbug."

"I don't have time. Work? Missing person? Any of that ringing a bell?"

Helena stood on the passenger's seat, then attempted to slip between the front seats and into the back, but halfway through, she got wedged in between, her pink-and-black-clad butt perched right in Jadyn's face.

"Help me," Helena said. "I'm stuck."

"You have got to be kidding me."

"Do I look like I'm kidding?"

"Then get ready to push because I'm only doing this once. On three." Jadyn turned in her seat so that she could get better leverage, then lifted her hands in front of Helena's rear and tried not to cringe.

"One. Two. Three!" Jadyn planted her hands on Helena's butt cheeks and shoved as hard as she could. Her hands sank a good inch into the flab before she got results, but finally, Helena popped out from between the seats and fell onto the floorboard in the back. She flailed around a bit but managed to crawl onto the seat.

Finally, she huffed and crossed her arms across her chest. "With the way you're treating me, I shouldn't even tell you what I overheard."

Jadyn perked up. "Did Peter and Bobby say something after I left?"

"Oh, they said plenty. Mostly about someone named Leonard, who Bobby thinks is a problem, but I meant the two guys with the stinky pile of fish."

"What did they say?"

"One said the boat looked like Clifton's. The other said Clifton's boat didn't have flooring that color. The second guy accused the first guy of being color-blind. Then I hit the fish and that was it."

Jadyn glanced at the fish house and saw the pajamas starting to slide down the tin roof. She needed to get out of there before she raised any suspicion. She put the Jeep in gear and headed across the parking lot. As she turned onto the road, she looked to her left and saw Bobby exiting the shrimp house, slamming the door behind him. The pajamas lost their last grip on the edge of the roof and plopped right onto Bobby's head.

Helena set up a howl as Bobby whirled around, pulling at the offending garments and only managing to wrap them tighter around his head. Jadyn floored her Jeep and sped away, determined to be out of Bobby's line of sight when he got the pajamas off his head.

When she got to the junction of the road and the highway, Jadyn pulled into a convenience store parking lot and stopped at the far end.

"Are you going to get me a snack?" Helena asked. "I might be able to forgive you a little if you bought me Twinkies."

"No." Jadyn pulled out her cell phone and called Shirley. "I need to see if you can track down an address for me. I only have a first name—Clifton—and he probably lives somewhere near Pirate's Cove."

"Let me take a look," Shirley said. A couple seconds later, she said, "There's a Clifton Paschal near Sinful, but he's ninety-two and disabled. Probably not our fisherman."

"Anyone else?"

"Just a sec...one more. A Clifton Vines. Fifty-three."

"What's the address?"

"Box 65, FM 1168."

Jadyn grabbed a pen out of her glove compartment and jotted down the address on her map. "Great, thanks."

Jadyn hung up the phone and located the farm road on her map. "It's not that far away, but with all the winding roads, it's probably a twenty-minute drive."

"I'm not traipsing naked through the swamp."

Jadyn sighed. "You bitch more than any twenty people, you know that? I'm going to start calling you Queen of Complaints."

"Oh, I see. I'm the problem. So you wouldn't complain if you were parading around in broad daylight wearing only your underwear?"

"If no one could see me, I'd consider it an expedient way of getting out of doing laundry and be happy as a lark."

Helena shook her head. "The longer I'm around you, the more I can tell that you and Maryse are related."

"I'll take that as a compliment. Look, I need to get a water, so I'll pick you up some Twinkies, but that's the last I want to hear about this. No one would be happier seeing you clothed than me. Maybe while I'm in the store, you can figure it out."

Jadyn hopped out of the Jeep and went into the store. She pulled a cold bottled water from the cooler and grabbed a package of Twinkies on her way to the register. A couple minutes later, she strolled back to her Jeep, where she took one look at Helena and promptly dropped the package of Twinkies.

Helena still wasn't dressed, but her outfit had changed. A giant, sparkly crown rested on top of her head and a white sash with red letters across it proclaimed her "Queen of Complaints." The ensemble was polished off with the silver scepter she clutched in her left hand.

Helena looked over at her and if looks could kill, Jadyn knew she'd be six feet under. "Not one word," Helena said.

"But?"

"Ssssh!" Helena held up a hand. "If I could fix it, I would."

"So take it off."

Helena threw her hands in the air, pushing the scepter to the sky like she was commanding rain to fall. "I've thrown this thing on the ground at least ten times." Before she even finished the sentence, she flung the scepter past Jadyn and it shattered on the concrete, but when Jadyn looked back at Helena, another perfect scepter had taken its place in her hand.

Jadyn looked down and saw the package of Twinkies resting in the remnants of scepter jewels. She grabbed the package and handed it to Helena. "Will Twinkies make it better?"

"Doubtful." Helena snatched the Twinkies from her hand, then looked over her shoulder. Her eyes widened and she climbed over the back of the Jeep.

Jadyn turned around to see an older man pulling a bass boat putting fuel in his truck. "What's wrong?"

"Everything is wrong, but I just found my ride off the crazy train. That man lives in Mudbug. I'm going to hitch a ride back to town with him, and you can keep tromping through foul-smelling fish houses and looking for missing men or whatever else you want to do. But I am officially clocked out of police duty for the day."

With that, she stomped across the parking lot and heaved herself over into the bass boat. Jadyn waited until she sat up, then climbed in her Jeep and pulled away. She didn't have the time or inclination to argue Helena out of her ghostly hitchhiking. Not to mention, she could go about her job more focused and with less issue without the stubborn, unhappy ghost along for the ride.

She pulled to a stop at an intersection, grabbed her cell phone, and pressed in Colt's number. It went straight to voice mail, which might mean he was on the phone but more likely meant he was outside of the service area. She left him a quick message about Clifton Vines, gave him the address, and headed for Clifton's house.

If Clifton was the owner of the wrecked boat, Jadyn hoped she'd find him on his front porch, drinking beer and complaining about making an insurance filing, but she didn't count on it.

Counting on things turning out well was a recipe for disappointment.

CHAPTER SIX

MARYSE WALKED OUT OF HER HOTEL LABORATORY ROOM AND almost ran into a maid. The rather large potted rosebush she carried in front of her was to blame. It was so tall and full that Maryse could barely see where she was going. It would probably be a good idea to set the pot down and check the staircase before she attempted to go down it.

By carefully sidestepping, she managed to make it down the stairs without incident and carried the plant to the front desk, where she hefted it up on the counter. She heard some movement behind the plant and stepped to the side to see Mildred rising from her stool to peer around.

"What in the world?" Mildred asked. "I thought you were working on something for a cosmetic company?"

Maryse frowned. "I'm supposed to be, but if I can't get into the bayou to collect plants, I'm stuck. Theory only takes you so far before you have to test it."

Mildred gave her a sympathetic look. "I know this is hard on you, but you're doing the right thing. If Luc was worried about you, then he wouldn't be a hundred percent while he's working."

"I know. Why do you think I agreed to this without complaint?"

Mildred raised one eyebrow.

"Okay, without my normal amount of complaint."

"I'll give you that," Mildred agreed. "So what is this?" She pointed to the bush.

"You don't recognize it? It's the rosebush from your porch."

Mildred stared. "The dead bush?"

"Dead according to you. Lacking in the proper care and treatment according to me. Since it didn't appear that you were going to do anything with it, I decided to try an experiment."

Mildred fingered one of the leaves. "I can't believe it. It's at least twice as big as what it was before it started the death march. And I've never seen more than two blooms on it. Now it's covered with them."

Maryse grinned. "It will dress up the porch a lot better now. Think we should go see?"

"Definitely!"

Maryse lifted the pot from the counter and exited the hotel as Mildred held the front door. "I was thinking on the end next to the rocking chairs," Maryse said.

"Perfect." Mildred pushed the rocking chairs back a bit to allow Maryse to slide by with the pot, then watched as she lowered it next to the rocking chair at the end of the porch.

Maryse stepped back to stand beside her and admire the rosebush. "I probably shouldn't brag about my own work," Maryse said, "but it really is pretty. I can do a yellow one for the other side if you'd like."

"Oh, that would be lovely."

A horn honked farther down Main Street and they both turned around to look.

One of the locals had his hand out his truck window,

waving at them. "Looks great!" he called and pointed to the bush.

"Thanks," Maryse managed to choke out, but her attention was focused on the man's bass boat, and its single occupant.

Helena sat in the captain's seat, her crown and scepter glistening in the afternoon sunlight. The white sash almost seemed to glow against her pink-and-black undergarments.

"This cannot be good," Maryse said.

Mildred, who'd been staring slack-jawed, finally managed to close her mouth. "I...well... Good Lord, I don't even know where to start."

As the boat drew alongside the hotel, Helena hopped off the captain's seat and headed for the side, waving the scepter in the air.

Mildred's eyes widened. "She's not going to try to jump, is she?"

"Either that or summon lightning. I think I saw that fancy wand thing do that in a movie once."

Helena stepped over the side of the boat and onto the fender, waving her arms around to balance.

"Maybe she's trying to fly," Maryse suggested.

Mildred cringed as Helena jumped from the fender and hit the street with a thud. They stared for several seconds, but the lump didn't so much as twitch.

"What do we do now?" Maryse asked. "It's not like we can run into the street and drag off an invisible person."

Mildred bit her lower lip and stared anxiously at Helena. "We have to do something," she said but as she started to step off the porch and onto the sidewalk, Maryse grabbed her arm.

"Wait. She's moving."

They watched as Helena rolled over onto her back and groaned. Maryse heard an engine roar and looked over to see a UPS truck heading down Main Street, directly toward Helena.

"UPS is early today!" Maryse shouted, causing Mildred to jump.

Helena jerked her head around to see the truck barreling at her and jumped up from the ground faster than Maryse would have thought possible. She ran for the hotel, screaming the entire way, and dashed right past Mildred and Maryse and through the lobby wall. A second later, the UPS truck sped by.

Mildred looked at Maryse. "Should we go inside?"

"I'm afraid to."

Mildred nodded. "There is that."

———

BECAUSE OF THE STORMS, JADYN HAD TO BACKTRACK A couple of times to find alternate routes where the roads were blocked by debris. With all the delays, it was almost an hour before she turned onto the path that led to Clifton's house. As she turned into the driveway, she noticed there was no vehicle parked in front of the tiny cabin.

She made her way to the front door and rapped on it. The cheap wood made a hollow sound and shook as she knocked. "Mr. Vines?" she called out. "I'm the game warden in Mudbug. If you're here, can you please come out?"

She leaned against the door and listened, but couldn't hear any movement inside. Heavy curtains were drawn across the front windows, blocking any opportunity to peer into the house. She leaned back, figuring she'd knock once more, then circle the house to see if she could find a place to look inside.

As she finished her third hard rap, the door popped loose and swung open an inch. She pushed it open a couple inches more and called out again. "Mr. Vines. My name is Jadyn St. James and I'm the game warden in Mudbug. I'm going to enter your house. Please show yourself if you're inside."

She paused a couple seconds, then pulled out her pistol, pushed the door open, and stepped inside.

The front room was an open living room, kitchen, and dining area. The furniture was old and worn, but looked sturdy enough. The inside of the cabin was surprisingly clean compared to the other bachelor residences she'd entered, especially the commercial fishermen. Clifton's dining table, kitchen counters, and coffee table were also clear of lures, nets, weights, fishing line, and the many other things she expected to see.

A single door rested on the back wall of the kitchen next to the refrigerator. It was the only door she saw, so she figured it must lead to the bedroom. So far, nothing about the cabin set off alarms, but she couldn't ignore the uneasy feeling she had. Lifting her pistol into ready position, she crept toward the door and stopped in front of the refrigerator, listening for movement on the other side of the wall.

The low hum of the refrigerator was the only sound she heard.

She slipped around the refrigerator and gently turned the doorknob. As she pushed the door open, relief passed through her when the hinges didn't squeak. She peered around the doorframe and into the room, but it was empty. She made quick work of checking the closet and the tiny bathroom, but there was no sign of Clifton Vines.

She reached up to touch a bath towel hanging over the shower door. It was dry, as was his toothbrush, and the sink was completely free of water droplets. She went back into the kitchen and did some looking around, but found the same thing. No signs of recent use. If Clifton Vines was alive and well, he must have been gone from his house for a while.

She looked around the room and blew out a breath. Nothing she'd found here gave her any cause for immediate alarm. For all she knew, Clifton could have left this morning for his boat and be unloading his catch at one of the shrimp houses as she stood there.

So now what?

Her cell phone's ringing jarred her out of her thoughts and she saw Colt's name on the display before she answered.

"Sorry," he said, "but I just got your message. Cell phone service has been crap most everywhere I've been today. Any luck at Clifton's place?"

"Not really," she said and gave him a description of what she found, or the lack thereof. "I was about to search the cabin...see if I can find a photo of the boat maybe, but I wasn't sure of jurisdiction."

"The game preserve extends into that area, but I'm not certain if Clifton's cabin lies within the perimeter. I'll head over that way. If Clifton returns home and gets bent because we're tossing his place, I can always claim probable cause on a missing persons case. If he doesn't have anything to hide, it shouldn't be that big a deal."

"I'm beginning to wonder if there's anyone who doesn't have something to hide."

"Welcome to my world. I'm about twenty minutes out from where you are, coming in from the north. Go ahead and start looking around."

"Yep," she said and slipped the cell phone back into her pocket. In twenty minutes, she could probably disassemble the entire cabin, given its size. By the time Colt arrived, she'd likely be done with her search and taking a nap.

She glanced around and decided to start with the living room. The coffee table and the two end tables both had drawers. Maybe she'd find a photo shoved in one of them. She started with the coffee table but found only matches and old receipts. The end tables didn't provide anything other than a television remote and batteries.

The few kitchen drawers and cabinets held only kitchen items, and the tiny pantry revealed nothing but canned goods and cereal. She was just about to move into the bedroom when she heard a stick snap out back. Immediately, she pulled out her pistol and pushed the curtains of the kitchen window over just far enough to peek outside. The cabin backed up to the swamp, with a small clearing of mostly weeds that stretched about ten feet from the back wall of the cabin to the tree line.

She couldn't see anything moving in the brush or the trees, but that snap had been loud enough to carry through the cabin walls and definitely hadn't come from a twig breaking. Which meant none of the smaller swamp inhabitants had caused the noise. Something larger was lurking outside, but what?

She eased open the back door and looked outside. From this perspective, she had a better view of the weedy backyard and saw it contained only an old ice chest and a rusted metal chair. The swamp was equally still, with only the very tops of the cypress trees moving in the light breeze.

The gunshot caught her completely by surprise.

The shot boomed through the swamp, splintering the thin cabin wall and leaving a hole. She sprang back inside the cabin and dropped to the floor. What the hell? No vehicles had driven up to the cabin or she would have heard them, so it wasn't likely that Clifton had returned home. But what possible reason could anyone else have to shoot at her?

To throw the shooter off her location, she crawled into the bedroom and crouched in front of the back bedroom window, barely shifting the curtains to the side to see out. She scanned the tree line twice but couldn't see movement or shadows, then something moved in her peripheral vision. Immediately, she locked in on the black shadow sitting ten feet into the tree line and twenty feet diagonal from where she hid.

Standoff.

He knew she was inside and she knew he was outside. If he was going to make a move, it would have to be soon. Cell phone service was fine here and she could call for backup. The shooter had no way of knowing that backup was already on the way. He also had no way of knowing what her skill level with a pistol was, but she was sure he'd seen the weapon when she looked outside.

Trying to approach the cabin from the swamp left him a sitting duck, so her best guess was that he'd open fire on the cabin and hope he hit her. She scanned the cabin, looking for anything that would make a good barrier, but she didn't see anything that would withstand bullets. She glanced back outside, but the shadow was still in place.

Momentarily, she considered running for her Jeep, but the shooter would easily make it around the cabin and have a clear shot at her driving off. It was too risky with so little distance between them. She looked out the window again and sucked in a breath when a wide ray of sunlight shone where the shadow had been. Where did he go?

A second later, she heard a vehicle pull up in front of the cabin. The bedroom didn't have a window facing the front of the house, so she had to go back into the kitchen to see who had arrived. It could be Clifton, or Colt, or more backup for the shooter.

She crawled back into the kitchen and eased up the side of the cabinets until she could peer out of the window above the sink. Her breath rushed out when she saw Colt's truck parked next to hers. Then she heard footsteps on the steps outside and he stuck his head inside.

She motioned him inside and down and he slipped into the

cabin, immediately crouching below the windowsill next to the front door. She hurried into the living room, careful to stay hunched over below the windows, and crouched beside him.

"What's going on?" he asked, his pistol already drawn.

Jadyn explained about the shooter and the shadow in the swamp.

"But he's not there now?"

"No, but I didn't see where he went."

Colt frowned. "We can try flanking him—one of us on each side of the cabin. But if he's moved from the back, he'll have a clean shot when we exit the cabin."

"What are the other options? We can't sit here all night."

"I could call for backup, but it would take them at least an hour to get here."

"Exactly. Which would give him plenty of time to shoot up these thin walls. I think we have to make a move."

"Okay, then follow me out. I'll go around to the right. You go to the left. Stay low and yell if you see something move."

Jadyn nodded and followed Colt out the front door. Before she even made it down the steps, they heard a boat engine roar to life behind the cabin. Colt took off for the swamp and Jadyn rushed behind him. He barely slowed when he hit the tree line, pushing his way through the brush as he ran in the direction of the racing boat motor. When they burst out of the trees at the bank of the bayou, Jadyn saw the back of a bass boat disappear around a corner about fifty yards ahead.

———

THE SHOOTER SPED AROUND THE CORNER, THEN DIRECTED his boat down one of the narrow channels. He cut the engine and rowed along with the tide, using the channel to double back toward the cabin. When he reached the end of the channel, he jumped onto the bank and made his way through the narrow strip of land until he could see across the bank.

The man and woman were both still standing there, but not for long. Seconds later, they moved away from him, no doubt returning to the cabin.

What did they know?

That unanswered question was the only thing that had kept him from raining bullets down the side of the cabin. But what if his suspicions were wrong? Killing someone would only up the heat, and things were already sweltering.

He'd thought he had the perfect plan with the perfect backup plan, but things were proving to be outside of the expected scope. Years of living within a well-oiled machine appeared to be unraveling in a matter of days. He needed to be patient and smart...adjust and change things so that he came through it all with everything he planned on.

And he'd planned on a lot.

CHAPTER SEVEN

COLT CURSED AS THE BOAT SLIPPED OUT OF THEIR VIEW. "I didn't get a good look at it."

"Me either."

"What in the world is going on?" Colt asked. "Do you have any idea why someone would take a shot at you?"

Jadyn thought about her last shrimp house visit and frowned.

"What?" Colt asked.

"It's nothing, really. Nothing more than a feeling." She explained what she'd seen at the last shrimp house. When it came to Helena's role in things, Jadyn explained it as her lingering and managing to overhear the part about Clifton and the arguing between Bobby and Peter.

She shook her head when she finished. "Taking a shot at me seems a drastic action to take when they don't even know what little I overheard."

"Yeah, it's a bit extreme, but I'm not sure I like the alternatives any better."

"You're thinking if someone sabotaged Clifton's boat, they

may have come here looking for him or something else and found me instead."

Colt nodded. "I haven't liked the look of this from the beginning, and every little thing that happens sends me leaning more and more toward thinking some big trouble is going on behind all of this."

"Me too. But any of the stops I made today could be the one that set someone off. Some people are better at hiding things than others."

"Unfortunately true. Did you finish searching the inside of the cabin?"

"No. I was just about to move into the bedroom when I heard the shooter out back."

He blew out a breath. "Then let's do that and head out of here. There's a diner on the highway about ten miles from here. We can stop there and ask about Clifton."

Jadyn's stomach rumbled.

Colt smiled. "And maybe grab a bite to eat."

"Sure," Jadyn said, trying to brush off her embarrassment. Stomach-rumbling probably wasn't the most attractive look to guys.

Jadyn's mind whirled as they headed back to the cabin. Had she been in the wrong place at the wrong time, and the shooter had mistaken her for Clifton or someone else? Was it really that simple? Or had her questions at the shrimp houses stirred something up that she couldn't yet put her finger on?

As they rounded the corner of the cabin to the front, an older man with silver hair and a shotgun stepped from behind Colt's truck, the shotgun leveled at them.

"Who are you and what do you think you're doing here?" he asked.

They both lifted their hands. "Are you Clifton?" Colt asked.

"I asked you first."

"I'm Sheriff Bertrand, from Mudbug. This is Jadyn St. James, the game warden. We're looking for Clifton."

The man narrowed his eyes at them. "Show me some ID. And no funny business."

They both pulled ID out of their pockets and held them up. The man stepped a bit closer, then lowered the shotgun. "Sorry about that," he said, "but there's been some break-ins around here lately. Last one hit an eighty-year-old woman with a lamp, and she fell and broke her hip. Can't be too careful."

"I understand," Colt said. "So are you Clifton?"

"No. I'm a friend, of sorts."

"What do you mean?" Jadyn asked.

"I mean, Clifton don't have friends. More like acquaintances that he sometimes drinks a beer with."

"So why are you here, Mr....?" Colt asked.

"Dagget. Warren Dagget. I'm here because Clifton didn't show up to pick up the new nets he ordered from me. He was losing money every day trying to keep the old ones patched. He was supposed to show first thing this morning. I've called several times but never got an answer. Then I remembered the break-ins and thought I might ought to check things out."

"That's a neighborly thing of you to do, Mr. Dagget," Colt said, "but if there's vandals around, it's also a dangerous one."

Dagget frowned. "Did something happen to Clifton?"

"We're not sure," Jadyn said. "But maybe you can help us." She pulled out her phone and approached Dagget. "A fisherman found this boat washed up in a cove this morning with no way to identify it. We've been trying to find the captain and followed a shrimp house lead here."

Dagget looked at the pictures as Jadyn scrolled through them. "It could be Clifton's boat. I don't remember the floors being that color, but it's been years since I seen inside. He's probably painted since then. It's the same model as his."

"You're sure?"

"I'm sure it's the same model, and I'm sure Clifton didn't show up for the nets he's been calling about every day for the last two weeks they was on back order. You don't think...I mean, if you found the boat..."

Jadyn looked back at Colt, who shook his head.

"I have to be honest. It doesn't look good," Jadyn said. "Is there anyone who would know if Clifton left town? Does he have a camp nearby?"

Dagget shook his head. "No camp that I'm aware of, and no one he would check in with. Hey, wait, he usually has dinner at the diner on half-price chicken-fried steak night. That was last night. You might want to ask around the diner."

"Thanks," Jadyn said. "We had already planned on stopping there."

"Do you know where Clifton sold his catch?" Colt asked.

"Last time he said anything about it was a couple months ago. Said he'd heard the shrimp house in Pirate's Cove was paying a premium for redfish. Vincent Brothers, I think it's called, but when I asked later, he said it wasn't the case. Best I know, he was mostly selling to the shrimp house in Frederick's Bayou."

Jadyn nodded. Frederick's Bayou was one of the three shrimp houses on her list that she hadn't yet gotten to. "I don't suppose you know the name of his boat?"

"Sure. It's the *Houdini*."

"That seems an odd name for a shrimp boat."

Dagget nodded. "I thought so too and said as much. Clifton said he wanted the boat to work magic and named it accordingly. He was a strange man. Nice, but strange."

"This is probably an odd question, but when I was inside, I didn't see any photos. I don't suppose you have a picture of Clifton?"

"No. Like I said, he was a private kind of guy. Didn't go to backyard BBQs or other things that you might snap the random photo at."

"I understand," Jadyn said. "Do you still want to take a look inside?"

"Don't see the point. I've never been inside before so I wouldn't know as anything was out of place. You're already on the job, and there's nothing I can do at this point."

"Okay. We appreciate your help."

"If you don't mind, I'd appreciate a phone call when you find something out. I probably knew Clifton better than anyone. That ain't saying much, but he was a good guy. Worked hard. Never tried to short anyone. Never had a bad word to say, really."

"Sounds like the kind of man we need more of," Jadyn said.

"You got that right." Dagget hoisted his shotgun onto his shoulder. "I best be going. If you need me, I'm at my store most days. Dagget's Hardware in Pirate's Cove."

"Thank you, Mr. Dagget." Jadyn watched him climb in his truck and turned to Colt. "Let's take a look at that bedroom and see what we find."

"You mean, like a good reason to sink a man's boat and open fire on people in his house."

"Yeah. Exactly that."

———

MARYSE KNOCKED ON HELENA'S HOTEL ROOM DOOR. "YOU have to come out sometime or I'm coming in."

"Then stop that annoying knocking and come in," Helena said, "because I'm not leaving here like this."

Maryse looked over at Mildred, who removed the master key from her pocket and unlocked the door. Maryse pushed it open and stood back, allowing Mildred to walk inside. She made it two steps inside the room before drawing up so short that Maryse walked right into her back.

Maryse stepped around Mildred and stared. "What happened?" she asked.

Helena's outfit had been horrifying when she'd made her tumble and mad dash from the bass boat, but things had gotten even more confusing during the hours she'd been locked in her room. The crown was gone, but had been replaced by a turban with a giant emerald on the front. The pink-and-black sports bra and underwear were still in place, but now, she also sported the pink suit jacket she'd been buried in. The slippers were long gone and had been replaced by something so odd, Maryse had to step closer to get a better look.

"Are those Gene Simmons's boots from KISS?" Maryse asked.

"I don't know," Helena wailed. "I was trying to put on normal clothes, but I couldn't concentrate. The harder I tried, the worse it got. The only good thing I managed was this hot chocolate." She held up a giant Styrofoam cup.

Mildred grabbed a sheet of paper from the dresser and scanned it. "You were watching television, weren't you? *Aladdin, Fifty Best Hits from the '70s*...your mind is so jumbled with all this input that you can't manage a cohesive thought."

"I guess that explains this, then." Helena lifted her arm. The scepter had been replaced with a tennis racket. "There was a special on Billie Jean King on earlier."

Mildred shook her head. "I am about to say the most ridiculous thing in the world, but I think you're stressed. What, exactly, you have to be stressed about, I have no idea. But all this mind clutter you're describing is anxiety. I don't think you're going to be able to get things right, or almost right anyway, until you calm down."

Helena frowned. "You're saying I need a shrink?"

"Unless we find one that can talk to the dead, that's not exactly an option," Maryse said.

"Right," Helena said. "I guess that means I have to talk to you guys."

Maryse stared at Mildred, feeling slightly terrified. "Maybe Sabine would be a better option. She's all Zen and patient and sympathetic."

"No way," Helena said, as she jumped up from the bed, spilling her hot chocolate all over Mildred's new linens and rug. "She'll try some voodoo stuff on me...like putting me into a jar or bringing demons out to torment me into submission."

Mildred sighed. "You've been reading those Curse Keepers books again, haven't you? I swear, I'm going to send Denise Grover Swank a dry-cleaning bill."

"You know those books are fiction, right?" Maryse asked.

"Yeah, that's what you say," Helena argued, "but most people believe ghosts are fiction too, yet here I am."

Maryse started to reply, but for once, Helena had produced a sound argument. "That's beside the point. I'm going to call Sabine and you're going to talk to her. She will not make you a genie or whatever else you have cooked up in that strange mind of yours. But we have to get to the bottom of this. It was bad enough when you only got things right part of the time, but now you're batting zero."

"Fine," Helena said, looking completely defeated. "But can we do this soon? I don't like being trapped in here. It's sorta like a tomb."

"I'll call her now," Maryse said.

Mildred's hotel rooms were actually far better than the standard chain fare, but Maryse knew exactly how Helena felt.

Despite her neat little laboratory setup down the hall, she felt trapped like Helena.

The only difference is that her situation couldn't be resolved with counseling.

———

COLT WAS TIRED, CONFUSED, AND MORE THAN A LITTLE frustrated by the time he pulled up in front of the diner. The day had been filled with questions that seemed to have no answers. Dagget had provided them with their best lead, and that was completely accidental from being in the right place at the right time.

Or the wrong place, if he took the shooter into account.

He'd tried to control his emotions when Jadyn told him about her close call. As far as he could tell, she'd taken the near miss in stride and was more concerned about getting answers than what might have happened if the guy had been a better shot. He admired and respected her ability to keep her mind in the game, but he'd be lying to himself if he didn't admit that his heart clenched when he saw the hole in the cabin wall and realized exactly how close the bullet had been.

It was that feeling, of not being able to protect someone he cared about, that had kept him from acting on his attraction to Jadyn. But every day, he found something else unique and wonderful about her. Then something like the shooting happened and reminded him of all the bad possibilities that existed given her profession.

He wasn't being sexist, he told himself. And that was honest enough. He had no problem with women in whatever capacity they elected and were qualified for. Where he had trouble was imagining *his* woman in a dangerous capacity. Then he thought about all the women married to law enforcement and military and he felt like a wuss. Maybe women *were* the stronger of the species.

Besides, look how well marrying a civilian worked out for Luc.

The thought had lingered in his mind ever since he'd found out about Luc's no-swamp edict to Maryse, who normally spent most daylight hours out among the bayous and weeds. Luc had probably never expected his work to follow him home and threaten his wife, and yet, now Maryse was holed up in the hotel all day, and she was no part of the law enforcement community.

So what was the answer? Quit his job and become a bank teller? Up his home security system, put bars on the windows, and get a Rottweiler? No matter how many times he processed the circumstances, he got back around to the same cold, hard facts—no one was safe. Not really.

Which meant he needed to man up and stop yanking Jadyn around. He wanted her, and no amount of heart-clenching when she was in danger should stop him from making that known.

Still, the heart-clenching was pretty damn awful.

He sighed and pulled open the door to the diner.

Jadyn was already seated, and he was happy to see she'd gotten a booth in the back corner, away from other patrons. He planned on asking some of the diner personnel about Clifton but didn't want to start a panic by letting everyone in there overhear. If it turned out Clifton was safe and sound on a bender in New Orleans or offshore fishing for a couple of days, the last thing he wanted to do was scare people.

"Sorry for keeping you hanging," Colt said as he slipped into the booth. "I called Shirley to see if she'd heard anything." He'd actually called while he was driving to the diner, so it wasn't exactly a lie.

"I take it she didn't have anything?"

"No. This lead on Clifton is the only one we've got to work."

A waitress stepped up to the table and took their drink order, then hurried back with sodas. "Y'all wanna eat?" she asked.

"Definitely," Jadyn said. "I'll have the chicken-fried steak with mashed potatoes and gravy."

"I'll have the same," Colt said. "And can we get some Texas toast?"

"Sure thing," the waitress said. "I'll have this right out for ya."

"So to recap," Colt said, "we have a thin lead on this Clifton. His cabin certainly didn't reveal anything, though."

Jadyn frowned. "Yes and no."

"What do you mean?"

"I think the complete lack of information was strange. Not a single postcard, letter, invoice, or bank statement. I found some old receipts, but that's it. Don't you think that's weird?"

"Given that my kitchen counter looks like a file cabinet exploded, yeah, but everyone's not as lax as I am. Maybe he's a neat freak and has everything filed in a storage facility. Maybe he's a computer geek and has all those paperless statements?"

"I didn't see a computer or any computer equipment."

"Maybe he's paranoid and burns everything after reading it."

"Based on Mr. Dagget's description, that's probably the more likely of the explanations, but still. If we didn't have records that said that cabin belonged to Clifton, we would have no way of determining that from what existed inside."

Colt hadn't thought about it to the extent Jadyn had, but it was odd. "You think maybe he's into some shady stuff?"

"I don't know. I guess I was thinking about Marty saying it looked like the boat had been damaged from the inside out. I know crazy things can happen in a storm, but what if Clifton was involved in something illegal? That would explain all the secrecy and lack of personal information lying around."

"True. So we're back to potential crime with shrimp boats. I have to tell you, I don't like the options any more now than I did before."

"Me either."

The waitress returned and placed plates in front of them, then made sure they didn't need anything else before hurrying off across the diner.

"Man, I hope that tastes as good as it smells," Colt said.

"At this point, I'm not even sure I care. It could probably be cardboard." Jadyn grabbed a bottle of ketchup and dosed her chicken-fried steak with it.

Colt grinned. "Did you have a lot of Deep South cooking in north Louisiana?"

"Yes, but it's nothing like it is here. Mother wouldn't allow fried food, so I was in high school before I really got to break out and try new things."

"No offense, but your mother sounds like someone dead set on sucking all the joy out of life."

"That's pretty accurate." Jadyn took a bite of the chicken-fried steak and closed her eyes.

Colt grinned. "How is it?"

"As good as it smells."

He took a bite and had to agree. It was, by far, one of the best chicken-fried steaks he'd ever had. "So how's living at the hotel working out?"

"It's all right. Mildred is great and I can walk across the street for breakfast, lunch, dinner, or beer, but I'll be glad when something comes available."

"I think Marty has a garage apartment that someone just

vacated, but I don't think it has a finished kitchen. Maybe a microwave and cooktop."

"I took a look at the space a week ago. I didn't figure it would work for me, but it didn't hurt to check."

"Too rustic?"

She smiled. "Let's just say it looked more appropriate for one of the fishermen than me. I don't have big requirements, but I'd like two bedrooms and room for a full-size refrigerator and stove. If I have a little lawn space for a grill, even better."

"Back several years ago, you wouldn't have had any trouble finding something like it, but with all the construction guys in New Orleans working on the rebuilding, things came to a stop in the smaller towns. Then the manufacturing plant expanded and we acquired a bunch of employees needing a place to stay, and Mudbug was on overload."

"If something doesn't come up in the next six months or so, I may try to find a builder. I wasn't keen on buying when I first came here. I wanted to see how the job worked out...and the people."

He nodded. "You've fit right in on both counts. Seems like you've always been here."

"Ha. Not if you're a male chauvinist criminal."

"They don't count."

She cocked her head to the side. "You've always gotten a kick out of my being a woman, haven't you?"

Yeah, a mule kick in the heart.

"Let's just say, I have a perverse sense of humor and enjoy watching these hard-core manly men trying to wrangle with you and coming up short."

She grinned. "Well, since I enjoy the wrangling, I guess it's a win for both of us."

They chatted about building houses and the case, and speculated on Maryse's hotel imprisonment over dinner. Colt was surprised to find how easy it was to be with Jadyn, especially when he stopped overthinking things. He hadn't been lying when he said it felt like she'd always been there. Not so much that he felt like he'd known her forever, but that he had a comfort level with her that was reserved only for people he'd known since childhood.

When the waitress came to clear the dishes, he switched back to cop mode. He showed the waitress his badge and explained who Jadyn was.

The waitress's eyes widened. "Have I done something wrong?"

"Not that I'm aware of," he said. "We're looking for information on Clifton Vines. Has he been in here recently?"

"Sure, he's always here for..." She frowned. "That's weird. He's always here for chicken-fried steak night, but he wasn't this week."

"And he's pretty consistent with that schedule?" Colt asked.

"Only missed one day in the twelve years I've been working here, and that was the time he put a hook through his hand and had to go to the hospital and have it removed. Did something happen to him?"

"That's what we're trying to find out. We had a boat wash up in a cove this morning in Mudbug and we're trying to figure out if it belonged to Clifton."

Her hand flew up and covered her mouth. "Oh no! I hope nothing bad happened to him. He's not a big talker, but he's polite, and always leaves a good tip."

Colt pulled out a business card and handed it to her. "If you hear anything that might be of help, please let me know."

She took the card and stuck it in her apron. "Sure." She pointed to a table near the front of the café, occupied by two weather-beaten men. "You may want to ask those two men about it. I think Clifton uses the same dock."

"Great. Thanks."

She nodded and hustled away from the table, her previous smile now replaced with worry.

Colt pulled some bills from his wallet and picked up the ticket. "You ready?" he asked.

Jadyn nodded and they headed for the two men.

"Excuse me," Colt said when they stopped at the table.

The two men looked up, giving him a wary eye.

Colt introduced himself and Jadyn, then explained about the boat and why they were trying to track down Clifton. The two men looked at each other and one of them sighed.

"We tried to tell him not to go out yesterday. I got about fifty yards from the dock before I got hit by wind shear. Can't control a boat well in that kind of weather."

The other man nodded. "And fishing ain't good besides. Clifton and I both got to the dock when Stumpy here was coming back in. He told us how bad it was. Stumpy ain't no girl about things, so I figured it was as good a day as any to watch TV and drink beer."

"But Clifton went out?" Jadyn asked.

"Yes, ma'am," Stumpy said. "I did my best to warn him but he was determined that he wasn't going to lose a day of work to Mother Nature. Can't stop a man from being a fool."

"Unfortunately true," Colt agreed. "Were either of you at the dock today?"

"Sure," Stumpy said. "Today was a great day for fishing. We both headed out early."

"Did you see Clifton or his boat at the dock?" Jadyn asked.

The two men looked at each other and frowned. Then they both slowly shook their heads.

"His boat wasn't there when I left," Stumpy said. "I figured he'd gone out before me."

"Didn't see him this evening either," the other man said.

"And I came in pretty late. Got held up a bit at the shrimp house."

Jadyn pulled out her phone and showed them the pictures of the boat. The men looked at the pictures and their expressions darkened.

"It looks like Clifton's," Stumpy said.

"It's his," the other man said and pointed to the phone. "Look at the net on the right side. That's the one that snapped during the hurricane last year. See the weld midway? Ain't no one else got a weld like that in that location except Clifton."

Stumpy shook his head. "Don't look like the boat fared too well. I guess you ain't found Clifton or you wouldn't be asking."

"I'm afraid not," Colt said. "But at least now we know who the boat belonged to and can launch a search party."

Stumpy gave him a skeptical look. "I hate to say it, but I don't know that you're going to have much luck a day later."

"I know," Colt agreed, "but we have to try."

Stumpy nodded. "I got some time and a good flat-bottom boat. If you need some volunteers."

"Me too," the other man said.

"We can use all the help we can get," Colt said. "Can you meet at the dock at the sheriff's department in Mudbug tomorrow morning at eight? I'll see how many volunteers show up, then divvy up the search areas accordingly."

Both men nodded.

"Thanks for your help," Colt said and headed to the register to pay. As they walked outside, he sighed. "Well, I guess that's that."

"You don't think he's alive," Jadyn said.

"The chances are so slim, they're not worth calculating."

"The chances were slim for Raissa too, but she's safe and sound."

"True, but this is different. One man, alone in that storm... it's a recipe for disaster, and with no one to help."

"We'll hope for the best and prepare for the worst."

"The staple of law enforcement." He stopped with Jadyn at her Jeep. "Hey, be careful. We don't know why someone took a shot at you, and until we know it was random or he mistook you for someone else, we need to proceed as if you were the target."

Jadyn nodded. "I'll be extra watchful."

He stared at her, fighting the urge to gather her in his arms and hold her tight until this case was solved. But that would leave no one on the job. Instead, he leaned down and brushed his lips lightly against hers. Her eyes widened but she didn't move away.

"Call me if you see or hear anything odd," he said. "I'll have my cell phone on me."

He turned around and headed to his truck. He'd just unlocked a can of worms...again. The difference was, this time he was going to leave it open, and consequences be damned.

CHAPTER EIGHT

SABINE TURNED AROUND THE CLOSED SIGN ON THE FRONT door of her shop and joined Maryse and Helena in her corner sitting area. All Maryse had said in the somewhat frantic phone exchange they'd had minutes earlier was that she had an emergency and needed Sabine to let her in the back door of the shop and close down for the day.

Maryse had disconnected before Sabine even had a chance to respond. Her lifelong friend was often short or distracted, but this time it felt abrupt, even for Maryse. She'd barely locked the front door and headed to the back when she heard sharp rapping. She unlocked the door and found herself face-to-face with a walking blanket.

Maryse guided the walking blanket inside and toward the front of the store. Sabine looked down at the feet, trying to get some idea of who was under the blanket, and blinked. Maybe she shouldn't have had that glass of wine with lunch. She bent over a little as she went, trying to get a closer look, but the boots looked the same up close as they had from a distance.

At least that explained part of it. The walking blanket must be Helena.

She waved Maryse toward her reading corner, then drew all the blinds. Mudbug residents wouldn't be able to see whatever was going on under that blanket, but they could see Sabine's reaction to it. And she had a feeling it was going to be a doozy.

"What's wrong?" she asked.

"Helena is having some problems with wardrobe," Maryse explained. "Mildred and I think it's due to stress. Her mind seems to be latching onto things she sees on television or hears someone say, and then when she goes to change clothes, she's frantic and everything ends up a big ole mess."

Sabine tried to process Maryse's words. "Okay, so why the blanket?"

"Because she refused to leave the hotel without cover."

"But no one else can see her."

Maryse sighed. "I know."

Sabine took a breath. Part of her thought "how bad could it be?" and then the other part reminded her they were talking about Helena. "Okay, so what do you want me to do?"

"We figure she needs to learn some relaxation techniques or something. It's not like there's a list for ghost shrinks in the phone book, but we thought since you know hypnosis and yoga and all that Zen stuff, you might be able to help."

Sabine stared, trying to formulate a clear thought. Lord, how things had changed in a year. Back then, she was no more than a fake psychic running a small business with a pleasant repeat clientele. Now she was a fake psychic and about to play mental health professional to a ghost. It was a large leap, and a rather absurd one unless you considered that Helena Henry was part of the equation. Helena had single-handedly redefined absurd.

"I can certainly try," Sabine said finally. "But I can't guarantee anything."

"That's all anyone can ask," Maryse said.

Sabine leaned forward. "Is she drugged or something?"

"No, why?"

"Because it's not like Helena to go this long without talking."

"Oh sure," Helena said, "throw out the insults when I'm at an all-time low. Why don't you go out and kick puppies when you're done with me?"

Maryse rolled her eyes, and Sabine shook her head. This was going to be a handful.

"Well," Sabine said, "I guess the first thing is I need to see her."

Maryse grabbed the blanket on top of Helena's head and tugged it off.

Since she'd already gotten a look at the footwear, Sabine expected bad or crazy or worse, but nothing could have prepared her for the pink-and-black zebra stripes, the turban, or the tennis racket. It couldn't have been more confusing if she'd been trying.

"Oh my." Sabine put her hand over her mouth and took it all in. "Have you figured out from where these items originated?"

Maryse nodded and explained their earlier conversation.

"That seems logical enough," Sabine said.

"I'm glad you think so," Helena said. "Because it seems like a helluva mess to me."

"We're going to try to fix that," Sabine said, with that soothing voice she used on customers. "Why don't you take a seat and I'm going to make you some hot tea. It will help you relax."

Helena flopped in the chair and snatched the blanket from

Maryse to cover herself. She was still grumbling under her breath about "sitting around half-nude" when Sabine headed for the break room, Maryse trailing behind.

Sabine poured water into the pot to heat and turned to face Maryse. "I take it I've gotten the short version. What else do I need to know?"

Maryse told her about a conversation she'd had with Jadyn that morning where Jadyn suggested that a lot of Helena's problems might be boredom. She suggested the ghost needed a purpose for existing, even though she was visible to only a few. Then Maryse explained how Jadyn sent Helena to the beauty shop to eavesdrop.

Sabine frowned. "Didn't a fight break out at the beauty salon today?"

"Yeah, well, I don't think it worked out exactly how Jadyn had in mind, but I still think there's some merit to her idea."

"I agree. The key is figuring out in what capacity Helena can be both engaged and not detrimental."

Maryse turned up her hands. "I got nothing."

"I was afraid of that. While I agree with Jadyn in theory, I think we're going to find it difficult to put in practice."

"Do you want me to stick around or do you think she'll be more cooperative if I'm not here?"

It was a question that didn't have a straightforward answer. *Cooperative* and *Helena* were rarely used in the same paragraph, much less sentence. Maryse and Mildred were probably the closest to the ghost, but then Maryse had an acerbic tongue and sometimes lacked the ability to temper it.

"Let me have a go at her alone," Sabine said. "If I can't get anywhere, then we'll try it again with you or Mildred present."

"You're sure?"

"No. I wouldn't say I'm sure of anything. But I'm going to give it a try."

"Okay. Call if you need me. I'll be at the hotel doing next to nothing."

Maryse looked so down that Sabine gave her a quick hug. "I know it's killing you being locked up inside, but you're doing the right thing."

"I know. I just wish the 'right thing' wasn't the exact opposite of what I want to be doing." She gave Sabine a small smile before slipping out the back door.

Sabine locked the door behind Maryse and prepared two cups of tea, slipping in a little extra root for relaxation. She had a feeling both of them were going to need it.

Helena hadn't moved since they'd left the room, which was almost disconcerting in itself. Normally, unless the ghost was eating, she didn't sit still for very long. Sabine put the tea on the table beside her along with a container of sweetener and a spoon.

"I hope you like green tea," Sabine said as she took a seat across from the ghost.

Helena nodded. "I didn't figure I would because it's supposed to be good for you, but I like the taste. There's a lot of things I probably would have liked when I was alive, but I never would give them a chance."

"Does that bother you?" Sabine asked.

"Of course it bothers me. If you died and found out you'd wasted your life on bullshit that didn't matter and being angry and bitter, wouldn't it bother you?"

"I suppose I would have to take into account why I lived the way I did and make an honest assessment of how easily I could have changed things. Your life wasn't an easy one, Helena. I know most people think because you had money that it was or should have been, but they didn't live with your father. You had that one evil man feeding you garbage from the time you were a small child. Surely you don't blame your-self for his abuse?"

Helena shook her head, a sad look on her face. "No. You can't blame a child for their situation, but my father also died when I was a child. So what was my excuse then?"

"Well, for starters, no one got you the help you needed after his death, and someone should have."

Helena shrugged. "No one knew how it was inside those walls."

"The servants knew. Someone could have spoken up."

"But they didn't. After he died, the only thing people came to see me about was trying to get money."

"Exactly," Sabine said. "Which made you even more cynical and closed to relationships. Why wouldn't you be? You had yet to encounter someone who was interested in you and not your money."

Helena scrunched her brow. "I guess I hadn't looked at it that way. I suppose it explains why I made the decisions I did, but it doesn't excuse them."

"I don't think I'm trying to. You didn't do anything illegal or ethically wrong."

"Tell that to all the people I offended."

"Offending someone is not automatically an ethics issue."

"Even if I mean to?"

"Even if you mean to." Sabine studied her for a moment, then asked the question she'd been longing to. "If your life here was so unfulfilling, then why did you come back?"

"I guess it doesn't make much sense when you look at it that way, does it?" Helena sighed. "I know this is going to sound stupid, but I don't think my life here really began until I died."

"Why do you think that is?" Sabine had a good idea what the answer would be, but she wanted to hear Helena say it—to know that the ghost had processed that emotional information.

"Because I finally cared about someone other than myself. I mean, don't get me wrong, I always looked out for Maryse because I promised her mother I would. Her mother was probably the only person I ever had a semblance of a real relationship with when I was alive. When I came back, things weren't easy, especially with people coming after you, Maryse, and Raissa, but for the first time in my life, I formed relationships with people. Relationships that mattered."

Helena shook her head and gave Sabine a sad look. "Except that it wasn't really the first time in my life, was it? Because I was already dead."

"Is that why you came back?"

"I guess so. I had this overwhelming feeling that I wasn't done with this life. I know I mostly make everyone miserable, but I missed all of you. I thought if I returned, I could help make your lives better...you know, to try to make up for all the trouble I caused. But I just seem to create more trouble."

Sabine raised an eyebrow. She didn't doubt Helena's sincerity at that moment, but the ghost had to know that a lot of her actions would cause trouble. Still, accusing her of being a troublemaker didn't seem like the right course. Helena may be old and dead, but she seemed to have the emotional maturity of a child. Maybe it was as simple as her actions being either those of a bored, spoiled child or a cry for attention.

"I think the problem is an imbalance of assets," Sabine said.

"What do you mean?"

"You came back but you can't have a normal life with a job, or charitable work. Only a handful of people can see you, but we all have our own lives and can't contribute to yours on a full-time basis. There's a lot of weight on a handful of people to provide you with a life, and as they shy away more and more from the pressure of it, you get increasingly pushier."

Helena opened her mouth, then shut it and frowned. Finally, she spoke. "I'm not going to agree with you, but let's just say you were right. What can I do about it?"

"You could start with actually being helpful when people need help. I understand that sometimes the situations get out of control and you panic, but fiascoes like what happened at the beauty shop today could be avoided."

Helena crossed her arms in front of her chest. "They were talking smack about Maryse."

"I understand how that made you angry, but your actions caused problems for Jadyn and Colt. And you know as well as I do that Maryse and Jadyn couldn't care less what those old biddies say."

"That's true. So are you saying I need a job?"

"Maybe not a job in the usual sense, but a purpose. Something to focus your energy and time on. The bottom line is that if you're going to stay here, you've got to get a life—your own life, or you're going to make yourself and everyone else crazy."

"We're all already crazy, but I get what you're saying."

"Good. So I want you to think about what you can do to make a difference. I know you have some unusual limitations, but you also have unusual abilities. Find a way to work around one and use the other."

Helena narrowed her eyes at Sabine. "When did you get so smart?"

Sabine blushed. "I've been taking some long-distance courses in mental health. I thought it would be a good way for me to better understand my clientele."

"Since your clientele is a bunch of crazy people, sounds like a solid plan." Helena hesitated for a moment, then spoke once more. "Thanks."

She looked down after saying it. No surprise there. Sabine knew how hard it was for Helena to admit her flaws, much less thank someone. She'd spent her whole life paying for what she wanted and expecting no blowback. This living-dead thing she had going now was the exact opposite of the way she'd been able to manipulate everything to her advantage before.

"Hey," Helena said, "I don't suppose you've got a snack to go with this tea?"

Sabine smiled.

And she's back.

———

JADYN WAS A MIXTURE OF EMOTIONS AS SHE PARKED IN front of the hotel. Professionally, she was tired, disappointed, and apprehensive. Personally, she was energized, excited, and apprehensive. It was an oddly euphoric and depressing feeling, all at the same time, and both caused by men. Clifton being the depressing one and Colt in charge of the euphoria.

He'd actually kissed her. Just like that. Like they were a regular couple at the end of a date. And he was worried about her. Granted, Colt would worry about anyone he thought was at risk, but she doubted he kissed everyone he thought was in danger. At least, she hoped he didn't. So what did it mean? Or was it another one of his spur-of-the-moment actions that he'd pretend hadn't happened the next time she saw him?

Stupid.

Worrying over romantic possibilities when she ought to be concentrating on her job or the situation with Helena—things she had more control over. Well, maybe Helena didn't fall into that category.

She pushed open the front door to the hotel and saw Mildred sitting at the front desk.

"You working late?" Jadyn asked.

"Just a little. I had some interruptions today and got behind on the pay-per-view billings." She picked up a sheet of paper and grimaced. "You don't even want to know what half of those men are watching."

"You're the one selling it," Jadyn pointed out.

"I buy the service from a provider, but yeah, I see your point. Maybe I'll see if they can offer me a cleaner option. That whole deer steak situation bothers me a bit. I don't want my hotel to get a reputation for being one of those seedy cheat-on-your-wife places."

"I don't think there's any chance of that. It's far too classy and right in the center of Main Street. Only an idiot would carry on here."

"Lots of idiots around."

Jadyn laughed. "Yeah, I guess so."

Mildred waved a hand. "Anyway, never mind my day. Did you find out anything about the boat?"

"Yeah, it appears so." She told Mildred about Clifton, leaving out the part about someone taking a shot at her. That information needed to be kept confidential until she and Colt had a better handle on what was going on, and besides, it would cause Mildred unnecessary worry.

"That's a shame," Mildred said when she finished. "Sounds like he was a stand-up guy. How come a storm can't take a drunk or wife-beater?"

"Maybe because despite being douche bags, the drunks and wife-beaters were smart enough not to go out in that storm."

"I suppose you're right. Still, it seems a waste. I wonder what possessed him to go against good advice and his own eyesight?"

Jadyn shook her head. "We may never know."

"Probably money problems. People will do things they shouldn't over money problems."

"He seemed to live simply, but then so do a lot of people with addictive personalities. We may find out more once we officially declare him missing. People have a tendency to start gossiping then."

Mildred nodded. "Are you putting together a search party for tomorrow?"

"Yeah. Eight o'clock at the sheriff's department dock, and we'll divvy up coverage."

"I'll make some phone calls to help spread the word around. I doubt you'll have any shortage of help."

"I appreciate it."

Footsteps came pounding down the stairs and Jadyn looked over as Maryse jumped the last two steps and landed in the lobby. Mildred shook her head, looking every bit the tired parent she was.

"You working late too?" Jadyn asked.

Maryse rolled her eyes. "If you want to call it work. I haven't had enough plants to work with for well over a week. Luc had to stay late and I figured he'd worry less if I stayed here than if I was home alone."

"She did wonderful things with my almost-dead roses," Mildred said.

"Those were the old ones on the porch?" Jadyn asked. "Wow. They look great. Hey, did Helena make it back here? I couldn't keep her from leaving."

"She made it, all right," Maryse said and told Jadyn everything that had transpired with the disgruntled ghost.

"Seriously?" Jadyn said. "So she asked God for some unholy cosmic do-over and he agreed?"

"I know, right?" Maryse said. "It doesn't seem very nice of him...not to the rest of us, anyway."

"So Sabine played shrink," Jadyn mused. "Do you think it helped?"

"It seemed to. At least Helena managed to get on some decent clothes after she got back to the hotel. And the turban and tennis racket are gone."

"What about the boots?"

Before Maryse could answer, Jadyn heard a squeal of glee and a second later, Helena dropped through the ceiling and landed right on the front counter. The giant dragon boots stared Jadyn straight in the face.

"Never mind," Jadyn said to Maryse.

Helena began to teeter on the platform boots and flapped her arms like she was going to fly. A second later, she lost the battle and pitched off the counter.

"Incoming!" she yelled before crashing into Mildred and sending them both sprawling onto the floor.

Mildred struggled back up and glared down at Helena. "What the hell are you thinking, disrespecting antiques that way? Those boots have sharp edges."

Helena rolled her eyes and pushed herself up to a standing position, clutching the wall to keep her from falling. "And the boots don't really exist in your world, so what can they hurt?"

"They don't exist unless you get solid," Mildred pointed out. "Which always seems to happen at the worst time and to everyone else's detriment, like just now when you tackled me like an NFL lineman. My back will hurt for a week."

"Whatever," Helena said. "I'm in too good a mood. You're not going to spoil it with all that worry over a butt-ugly countertop or your ancient back."

"Why didn't you change shoes?" Jadyn asked.

"I did," Helena said. "But then I was thinking about how

cool the boots were and they're back again. I can't walk for crap in them, though, which is why I came down through the ceiling. I would have never made it down the stairs without falling."

"Yes, that was such a better option," Maryse said. "Helena's always had a problem with shoes."

The jangle of the bells over the front door caused them all to turn. Jadyn was surprised to see Colt holding the door open for a pretty young woman.

"Ladies," Colt said. "I hope we're not interrupting important women business."

"You are," Maryse said, "but we can always get back to it as soon as you're gone."

Colt smiled and pointed to the young woman. "This is Taylor Beaumont, a private investigator from New Orleans. She's looking for a missing husband and a hotel room. I told her I could help her with the hotel room part, but since you're all here, you may be able to help with the husband part."

Colt waved his hand at each of them. "This is Mildred, the hotel owner. If your missing husband has stayed here, she'll remember. Her memory is sorta frightening when you're on the wrong end of it."

"Welcome to my hotel," Mildred said and shook her hand.

"The sarcastic one is Maryse," Colt continued. "If your missing husband spent a lot of time on a boat in the surrounding bayous, she will recognize him."

"You know it," Maryse said.

"And this is Jadyn, our game warden. She's fairly new around these parts but catching on quickly."

"Nice to meet you," Jadyn said.

"What?" Helena said. "No introduction for me? People are so rude."

"If you ladies have it under control," Colt said, "I'm going to head home for a hot shower and a cold beer."

Taylor's eyes narrowed for a split second before she smiled. "Thanks. I appreciate the help."

Colt gave them all a smile, winked at Jadyn, and left the hotel.

"I hope you have a room available," Taylor said. "I think I've driven through ten bayou towns asking for a place to stay. This was the first one that I actually got a positive response in."

"You're in luck," Mildred said. "The last round of EPA inspectors left a couple of days ago."

"Great," she said and pulled out her wallet.

She looked around the hotel, then at each of them, the normal sizing up that someone in her line of work did. But Jadyn got the impression that with Taylor Beaumont, something more was going on than what they could see.

Finally, she cocked her head to the side and said, "So, who's the ghost?"

CHAPTER NINE

THEY ALL FROZE. MILDRED'S EYES WIDENED AND MARYSE sucked in a breath. Jadyn stared, trying to wrap her mind around this strange woman, standing in front of her and calmly asking about Helena.

Even Helena appeared shocked into silence.

Finally, Maryse broke the silence. "You can see her?"

"Yes," Taylor said. "I can't decide whether the boots are awesome or tragic, but I can definitely see her."

Jadyn frowned. "And that doesn't freak you out? Because when I first realized I was seeing dead people, I wasn't nearly as calm about it as you are."

Taylor smiled. "I suppose if this were my first time, it might bother me, but the truth is I always see them."

"Horror story!" Maryse said. "I bet you never get a moment's peace."

Taylor laughed. "They usually don't realize I see them because I no longer react. Some of them look so real, though, that I have to be careful who I speak to, or I'll accidentally address one."

"Helena looks real," Maryse said, "so how did you know she

was a ghost? Does she have some ghost label or aura or something that you read?"

"No. That part was simple deduction. Mildred glared at her when she made the comment about not being introduced. But even though your sheriff seems a nice and mannered man, he didn't introduce...Helena, right?"

"That's me," Helena said, managing to shake herself out of silence. "We're not related, are we? So far, only people related to me somehow have been able to see me."

"If Taylor sees lots of ghosts, she can't be related to all of them," Maryse pointed out.

Taylor shrugged. "I suppose anything is possible. My family ancestors are from Great Britain and Haiti."

Helena frowned. "Probably not related then. So how come you can see ghosts?"

"I was born with a caul."

"That sounds painful," Helena said. "Is it anything like hemorrhoids?"

Taylor laughed. "No, it's a membrane over the face of an infant when they're born. Some people believe it gives them special powers."

"Like the ability to see the dead," Jadyn said, still dumbfounded at the girl's comfort with her lot in life. Helena was the first ghost Jadyn had ever seen, and she prayed daily that she'd also be the last.

"Exactly," Taylor said. "My grandmother had the ability to see glimpses of the future. Her mother could predict the weather with uncanny accuracy, even down to a five-minute shower."

"What about your mother?"

Taylor shook her head. "Grandma says that Mom was a skeptic even in the womb. She became an accountant and doesn't buy into any of this. You can about imagine how horrified she was when I was born. And even more so when I started talking to people who weren't there."

Jadyn cringed. Her relationship with her own mother had been less than stellar, but she couldn't imagine the difficulties Taylor had faced, especially before she managed to sort out the living from the dead. "That sucks," Jadyn said.

"That's a most accurate description," Taylor agreed.

Mildred, who'd been staring at Taylor, almost without blinking, gave a start. "Lord, we're being rude. Grilling you like the police and here you are needing a room and probably some rest."

"It's not a problem," Taylor assured them. "I'm as fascinated as you are by this. I rarely meet others who can see spirits."

"Oh we can't, really," Maryse said. "We can only see Helena, and if it's all right with the universe, we'd like to keep it that way."

Taylor grinned. "I hope I have some time to sit and talk with you while I'm here. If not, I must come back and visit when I'm done with this case."

"A missing husband, right?" Jadyn said. "And you have reason to believe he's been in Mudbug?"

"Or nearby. A witness spotted a man matching his description on one of the docks in a nearby fishing village while she was antiquing in this area."

"I hope it wasn't Deer Killer," Helena said.

"Oh no." Mildred's hand flew over her mouth. "I'd completely forgotten."

"Who's Deer Killer?" Taylor asked.

Mildred gave her the short version of what had transpired. Taylor's eyes widened when Mildred described the whole head-in-the-bed incident.

"You didn't?" Taylor asked Helena.

"Damn straight I did," Helena said. "Those two rotten cheaters deserved exactly what they got."

Taylor reached into her tote bag and pulled out a drawing. "Was this the man?"

Helena and Mildred peered down at the drawing and both shook their heads.

"I've never seen this man in the hotel before," Mildred said.

"Not even close," Helena agreed. "This guy is Christian Bale compared to Deer Killer. Christian Bale was the best Batman ever."

"We know," Maryse said. "You've told us a million times. May I?" She motioned to the drawing and Taylor passed it to her. Maryse studied it for several seconds, then frowned.

"Does he look familiar?" Taylor asked.

"Not really," Maryse said. "I mean, I get the impression that I've seen him before, but I don't recognize him in a way that would be helpful. Sorry."

Jadyn looked at the drawing, but the man didn't resemble anyone she'd met so far. Still, something about it bothered her, and finally it clicked. "How come you have a drawing and not a photo?"

"The man I'm looking for went missing almost thirty years ago. The woman who saw this man is a friend of the wife and also a fairly famous portrait artist. She did the drawing. I know it sounds weird..."

"Not really," Jadyn said. "She saw something similar in the bone structure."

"Exactly," Taylor said. "Being a very accomplished artist, she would see right past the surface things the rest of us see. I'm not saying she's right and that this is the same man, and neither is she, but the wife can afford for me to check it out and so I am."

"You're saying wife," Jadyn said, "like they're still married."

"I guess, technically, they are. He was supposed to have died in an explosion, but his wife saw one of those specials about amnesia and now she thinks there's a tiny chance he could have survived but lost his memory."

"Fascinating," Jadyn said. "Would you mind if I made some copies of this? With my job, I meet new people every day. It doesn't hurt to ask."

Taylor brightened. "That would be great. Thanks so much for offering."

"No problem," Jadyn said and headed to the break room to make some copies. The man in the drawing didn't look even remotely familiar to her, and the story sounded more like the far-fetched fantasy of a long-grieving widow than something that could really happen, but perhaps finding the man in the drawing and seeing that he wasn't her missing husband would finally set the widow on the road to recovery.

Thirty years was a long time to mourn and hope.

———

HE WATCHED FROM THE ALLEY ACROSS THE STREET AS SHE entered the hotel. She'd been at the cabin, the diner, and now at the hotel. He'd seen her and the man talking to fishermen in the café. What had they learned? Apparently, the shot he'd fired hadn't scared her off the job. In fact, she looked completely comfortable having dinner with the man. Not the response he expected her to have when she'd almost been killed.

How much time did he have until she caught up with him? Even though he'd had to put it into action before he was ready, his backup plan was working for now. But he had a month, maybe six weeks at best before he had to make other plans.

Would his carefully created cover hold until then? He hoped so.

But in the meantime, he'd keep an eye on the woman. In case she got closer.

————

JADYN KNEW THAT THE MUDBUG COMMUNITY, ESPECIALLY the fishermen, would rally for the search party, but she was surprised at the number of people at the dock when she pulled up that morning. At least fifty locals as well as the two men from the diner and some others she didn't recognize were huddled by the bayou, sipping coffee and talking.

Colt pulled up beside her while she was exiting her Jeep and gave her a nod. "Good turnout," he said as he grabbed a stack of papers and headed for the group.

"Yeah, it's great." The more people they had, the quicker they could cover the areas the boat may have traversed in the storm and the inlying channels.

"Morning, gentlemen," Colt said as he approached the group.

"And ladies," a woman Jadyn hadn't seen before called out.

Colt smiled. "And ladies. Glad you're here, Tina. One of the main areas is your stomping ground."

The middle-aged Tina, with her weathered skin and ripped forearms, looked as though she could hold her own against any of the men here.

"I assume you've all heard the basics—the boat was found in one of the coves near here yesterday morning, most likely damaged in the storm the day before. We have reason to believe the boat captain is Clifton Vines, a fisherman from Pirate's Cove. We all know that an underwater recovery is an impossibility, so we're concentrating on the possibility that Clifton made it ashore somewhere and is injured."

One of the locals raised his hand. "How well does Clifton know the topography out this way?"

One of the men from the diner spoke up. "I don't think he knew it overly well. He usually fished east of town, not west. But he's got a good sense of things. He'd know to wait for the outgoing tide and follow it out. Assuming he's able."

Colt nodded. "We're going to assume that if Clifton is on the move, he'll remain close to the banks. Get as close to the banks as you can for the search. Given the number of people we have, I'm going to ask you to form teams of two so that one can go ashore in the places where the bank is too high to see over. Does anyone have any questions?"

"What channel are we using?" Jadyn asked. Cell phones were essentially useless in the swamp, so boaters communicated using CB radios.

"Channel 15. My dispatcher will be listening as well, so if you encounter an emergency situation, call out to Shirley and ask her to send help. If you get into trouble or encounter a situation that is more than two of you can handle, call for backup. Whoever is closest to your territory can respond. I know I don't have to tell you all to be careful."

He held the papers in the air. "I have the territories divided out for the most efficient coverage. We have enough people to cover them all today. If you have expert knowledge of any area, let me know and I'll make sure you're assigned to it."

"You and I will work together," Colt said to Jadyn as the men and Tina buddied up and formed a line. He spoke briefly with each duo and gave them a map of the coverage area, indicating their assignment.

When the last of the groups had their maps, Colt went back to his truck to grab his supplies. Jadyn knew she should get her own as well, but instead, she stood on the bank watching the two men from the diner. She had a copy of the drawing of the missing husband in her pocket and couldn't ignore the overwhelming feeling that she should show it to the fishermen. But she had no logical reason why.

Deciding she'd rather be assumed crazy than not have an answer, she called to the men as they climbed into a boat, and hurried down the bank.

"I know this is going to sound strange," she said, "but I have a drawing I'd like you to take a look at. I want to know if you recognize the man in it."

They glanced at each other and nodded.

She pulled out the drawing and showed it to the men. Their reaction was immediate. Their eyes widened and they stared at her.

"This is Clifton," one of the men said. "Where did you get this?"

Jadyn's pulse spiked. What were the odds that the man Taylor was looking for was the same man the search party was looking for?

"You're sure it's Clifton?" she asked.

Both men nodded. "Whoever drew this was good. It looks just like him, down to the crook in his nose. Did someone at the diner draw it?"

"No. A private investigator from New Orleans showed up in Mudbug yesterday looking for this man, but she didn't know his identity, just an approximate area where he was thought to reside."

The men glanced at each other again. "What would a private investigator want with Clifton?"

"I'm not sure," Jadyn said, not comfortable giving confidential information to the fishermen. They may be completely trustworthy, but it wasn't her place to tell them about Taylor's case. "Was Clifton a secretive sort of guy?"

"He was private...kept to himself. But I don't know that I'd describe him as secretive. Always seemed straightforward."

"Thanks," Jadyn said. "I'll let you get going."

The men nodded and climbed into their boat, but Jadyn didn't miss the uneasy glances they exchanged. She'd watched them closely when they'd spoken and she didn't think they were lying about Clifton. So why the worried looks? Were they now remembering things they hadn't noticed before? Or perhaps they were questioning themselves and asking just how much they really knew about the man they considered a friend.

Jadyn folded the drawing and put it back in her pocket, then hurried up the bank to collect her supplies. Colt was already in the boat, storing his duffel bag in the container under the backseat. She handed him her backpack and untied the boat from the pylon. He fired up the engine and she pushed the boat away from the dock with her foot, then hopped inside, taking a seat next to Colt.

She wondered briefly if Colt wanted her working with him because she wasn't familiar with all of the channels yet or because of the shooting at Clifton's cabin, but didn't ask. It made no difference in the big scheme of things. Working with Colt was the best place for her, given either circumstance.

"You know that woman you brought to the hotel last night?" she asked as he started down the bayou.

"The private investigator?"

"Yeah. Did she show you the drawing of the man she was looking for?"

He nodded. "I didn't recognize him, but then the whole story is rather out-there."

"The story is definitely out-there, but the two fishermen

from the diner just gave me a positive ID on the drawing. It's Clifton Vines."

Colt's head whipped around to face her. "You're kidding?"

"Not even. They both agree that the drawing looks exactly like Clifton even down to the crook in his nose. I watched them carefully. They were both shocked when I showed them the drawing. They're telling the truth and I think they're right about the man in the drawing being Clifton."

"What the hell?"

She shook her head. Granted, she thought the chances of Clifton being the long-lost amnesiac husband of a New Orleans widow was the stuff fiction was made of, but she doubted the long-grieving widow would view it the same way.

"I don't think Clifton is the woman's missing husband," she said finally. "The odds of her theory being true are so slim they're almost nonexistent."

"Agreed, but if she thinks Clifton could be her husband, and he's missing again..."

"Yeah. It's not a good situation. If she's locked onto the possibility of him being alive all this time, I doubt she's going to take a second death well."

"Especially when this situation is as unlikely to produce a body as the last one." He ran a hand through his hair. "What a nightmare for Taylor. I hope she's skilled at dealing with hysterics. Sounds like that's the way her case is going."

"It's definitely not a conversation I'd want to have with the wife. I guess I'll fill her in when we get back this evening. Do you have Shirley working on getting us background information on Clifton?"

He nodded. "She started running the usual checks yesterday and will keep digging. Surface-level research didn't produce much. I have to admit, I'm worried there's not much more to find."

"Let's hope she finds enough to prove that Clifton Vines can't be Samuel Perkins. For the wife's peace of mind, anyway, because we both know what the chances are of finding Clifton alive."

"Yeah."

"What section of the swamp are we taking?"

"The area surrounding the cove the boat was in. Unless he bailed before then, it's the most logical place for him to be if he made it ashore. That boat couldn't have traveled very far with the damage it had, even in the storm."

Jadyn nodded and looked down the bayou. The search was a necessary part of the investigation, but she couldn't help feeling it wouldn't turn up so much as a clue. Maybe they'd get lucky and Shirley would turn up some information on the elusive Clifton Vines, but she was starting to wonder how likely it was.

According to the people who knew him, Clifton had lived in Pirate's Cove for decades, yet no one seemed to know much about him. It was especially odd for a small town to know so little about a long-term resident. Granted, small towns and villages usually had their resident hermit, but Jadyn hadn't gotten the impression from anyone they'd questioned that Clifton was eccentric, just private.

How someone could remain an unknown quantity for years was as big a mystery as what had happened to Clifton. And she wanted answers to both.

CHAPTER TEN

TAYLOR TOOK ONE STEP INTO THE LOBBY, AND HELENA jumped up from a chair in front of the picture window and started to wobble toward her. Her progress was so slow and deliberate—one tiny step, lots of arm waving, another tiny step —that it was almost painful to watch.

"Are you looking for that guy today?" Helena asked and clutched the edge of the counter.

"That's the plan."

"I sometimes help with investigations," Helena said.

Mildred, who was sitting behind the counter, snorted.

Helena glared at her. "I help. Just because it doesn't always go smoothly at times doesn't mean I don't contribute to the process."

"You contribute something all right," Mildred said.

"Anyway," Helena said, ignoring Mildred's comment, "I was thinking that I could help you out. I know my way around the area, and if you question someone you think is hiding something, I can always stay behind a bit and see if they say anything after you leave."

"That's not a bad idea," Taylor said. "I take it you've done something like this before?"

"Just yesterday, as a matter of fact, and I got the information that led them to the missing boat captain."

Mildred shook her head. "You also came home in your underwear and holding a scepter."

Taylor's eyes widened. "I don't understand..."

"Helena's having a wardrobe crisis," Mildred explained. "We suspect stress, although the rest of us are far more stressed than she is. But she's having trouble changing things, hence those ridiculous boots that she can't walk in."

Taylor looked down at the boots. "You can't take them off? This is all so fascinating."

"Sure," Mildred said, "until you've been living it every day for months. That takes some of the shine off of it."

"You don't have to be rude about it," Helena said. "I'd much rather a sensible pair of tennis shoes right now."

The words had barely left her mouth when Helena dropped a good six inches lower, losing her grip on the counter and pitching backward into a potted plant. The pot flipped over, breaking and scattering potting soil and leaves all over the lobby rug. Helena sat up and pointed to her feet, which were now clad in bright red tennis shoes.

Taylor took one look at the disaster and cringed.

"Look at that!" Helena said.

Mildred, who'd risen from her chair when Helena fell, stared in dismay at her rug. "I see a huge mess on my new rug, and my steam cleaner is on the fritz. No need to sound so triumphant over it."

"I meant my shoes." Helena scrambled up from the floor. "Look on the bright side—now that I have tennis shoes on again, I won't be knocking as much stuff over."

Taylor frowned. "Is that really a problem?"

"Not very often," Helena said.

"Yes," Mildred said at the same time.

Taylor looked from one to the other, but would bet money that Mildred was the only one telling the truth. She looked back at Helena. "But how can that be? Why don't you just pass right through things?"

Helena shrugged. "It's one of the many mysteries that is me."

Mildred rolled her eyes. "You make yourself sound like a special on the History Channel." She looked at Taylor. "We have no idea why it happens, as it's the most illogical thing ever, but sometimes Helena seems to acquire mass. She's still invisible, but things around her react the same as they would if she were still alive and solid."

Taylor absorbed this information. "So if she say, tripped on the sidewalk, she may pass right through someone, or she may knock them down. But either way, the other person wouldn't see her."

"Exactly," Mildred said.

"That's incredible," Taylor said, then noticed Mildred's exasperated look. "But clearly also troublesome."

"You've never heard of this before?" Helena asked.

"No. I can't say that I have. Quite frankly, you're the first ghost I've engaged with that has been able to carry on a conversation as if you're still alive. Most of them are confused and often incoherent. They speak more with emotions than with words."

Helena looked disappointed. "Bummer."

Taylor gave her a sympathetic look. "I wish I could be of more help, but I've never had a conversation with a ghost about how to be a ghost. Quite frankly, it never occurred to me that the skill would need to be learned. I guess I just assumed you were however ghosts are and that was that."

Mildred nodded. "You'd think so, right? But Helena has presented us with a side of death I'll bet no one ever considered. When Helena first returned, she couldn't touch things. Now she's not perfect, but a lot more reliable, especially if she's reaching for food."

Helena sighed. "More insults."

Taylor stared at the ghost. "You eat?"

"She'll eat you out of house and home, if you allow it, and steal what you don't provide."

Taylor's mind whirled, trying to absorb this absolutely pointless act. "But..."

"I know," Mildred said. "She doesn't need to eat. Her argument is that if you couldn't gain weight—ever—wouldn't you eat anything you wanted?"

Taylor blinked. "When you put it that way, I suppose so, although I'd have problems with the theft part of things. I'm a big believer in karma."

"Me too," Mildred said. "Helena is walking karma, but for the life of me, I can't figure out what I did to deserve her."

Helena shot Mildred a dirty look and crossed her arms across her chest. Taylor held in a smile. Given Helena's extraordinarily bizarre abilities and limitations, coupled with her less-than-responsible attitude, Taylor could only imagine the things the ghost had put the hotel owner through.

"And this wardrobe problem?" Taylor asked.

"Is a doozy," Mildred said. "Everything she's seen on television the last couple days has graced her body at some point, whether it was a good fit or not."

Taylor nodded. "Like the Gene Simmons boots."

"Hey," Helena argued, "the Gene Simmons boots were the bomb."

The words had barely left her mouth when she shot up six

inches in the air and fell backward over one of the lobby chairs.

"And they're back," Helena said, staring at her Gene Simmons–clad feet.

"Oh goody," Mildred said.

"So can I go with you?" Helena asked as she scrambled to get up. "Please? You see what it's like around here for me. While you drive you could tell me everything you know about ghosts, and maybe stop for corny dogs at the diner just up the highway."

Taylor looked over at Mildred. "She's not going to give me a moment's peace if I don't take her, is she?"

Mildred shook her head. "Probably not."

Taylor turned to the ghost. "Then I guess you're coming with me. But I have some rules, starting with nothing illegal. That includes stealing food. If you behave yourself, then I'll get you corny dogs on the way back to the hotel."

"That could take all day. I'll starve to death."

"Clearly, that's not true. Rule number two—no lying, and that includes exaggeration. I understand the Southern flair for the dramatic, but I don't like to deal with it while I'm working. My client wonders if the husband she lost thirty years ago is walking around the swamp somewhere. I need to make sure she gets an answer."

"Your client is a loon," Helena said.

"Regardless of her mental state, she's paying me for answers and she deserves some peace of mind."

"I guess so," Helena grumbled. "Even though no man is worth thinking about for thirty years."

"George Clooney might be," Mildred said.

"Okay," Helena said. "I'll give you George Clooney."

Taylor grinned. "Then if you can manage to walk outside, mine is the beat-up navy sedan parked up front. You might want to start out now. I'm going to bum a cup of coffee from Mildred and then I'll meet you out there."

Helena took a wobbly step toward the door, then stumbled forward three steps and grabbed the coatrack. The rack teetered back and forth with her as she reached for the doorknob. Finally she managed to latch onto it and turn. As the door opened, she released the coatrack and pitched out onto the porch, the door slamming shut behind her.

"Are you sure you want to do this?" Mildred asked.

"Not even remotely, but I've dealt with her type before. She's not going to go away until she gets what she needs out of me. I may as well try to answer all her questions now, and there's always the slim chance she might actually prove useful."

"Sometimes she does, even despite herself."

"Is there anything I need to know about her? I don't expect you to predict her actions, but can you think of anything in particular you need to warn me about?"

Mildred slowly shook her head. "She's not dangerous...not intentionally, anyway. But she manages to get into situations that can cause trouble and attract unwanted attention. Despite your rule, she *will* lift food wherever she finds it, without qualm or thought to how it looks when a roomful of people see a floating pizza."

Taylor cringed. "I hadn't considered that. Things don't disappear when she's touching them?"

"If she created it to begin with then yes, but if she picks up something from this world, it shows. Just looks like it's hovering in midair. Except food, of course. It usually looks like it's either flying as she exits a room or disappears as she crams it down."

"I have a feeling this may be a very long day."

Mildred nodded. "Coffee's in the break room down the

hall. There's a bottle of whiskey in the cabinet above the refrigerator...for when you get back."

"Thanks," Taylor said and headed down the hallway. Usually a good round of meditation and a cleansing candle was enough to rid her of negative energy at the end of a long day, but the more she considered things, the more she wondered if tonight wouldn't find her clutching that whiskey bottle.

———

HE WAITED UNTIL THE HOTEL OWNER PUT UP HER "BE Right Back" sign and walked across the street to the café before slipping down the alley and jimmying the back door. He'd already watched the woman leave with the rest of the search party. She wouldn't be back anytime soon. From watching the hotel last night, he already knew which room the woman was in. Hurrying down the hallway, then up the stairs, he hoped no cleaning crew was in place to take notice of his passage. Other patrons of the hotel wouldn't think twice about him walking down the hallway, but someone who worked there might realize he wasn't a guest.

When he stepped onto the landing, he was pleased to see the hallway clear and quiet. He headed straight for the woman's room, made quick work of the lock, then slipped inside. In the small refrigerator next to the dresser, he spotted a bottle of water and unscrewed the top. He pulled a packet from his pocket and poured it into the bottle, then shook it. The powder swirled around for a while before finally dissolving, then he put the bottle back in the front of the refrigerator.

It wasn't enough to kill her. At least he hoped it wasn't. Her death would only bring more heat, and that was the one thing he couldn't afford. But he needed to buy some time. One day, two at the most, and his backup plan would be in place. He didn't think for a moment the woman would stop poking into things. Women were always that way when they set their sights on something. But if she was too sick to work, that would buy him enough time to cover his tracks.

———

JADYN ROSE FROM THE BOAT SEAT AND PEERED OVER THE SIDE as they neared the bank. Her cheeks stung a bit from too much sun and not enough sunscreen. Despite the decent base tan she'd managed in the past couple of weeks, seven long hours in the direct sunlight and salty winds had taken their toll.

And all for nothing.

She and Colt hadn't spotted anything that might lead them to believe Clifton had made it out of the boat, much less that he was still alive. In fact, they hadn't even located a single piece of debris, and neither had any of the other search volunteers. It wasn't exactly surprising, but Jadyn couldn't help but be disappointed, especially since she had to go back to the hotel this evening and tell Taylor the man she sought was dead. The only saving grace would be finding enough background information on Clifton to ensure that he couldn't possibly be Sophia's missing husband.

"How far away from the wreck location is this cove?" Jadyn asked.

"About a mile as the crow flies. Probably twice that taking the channels."

"Do you think we're too far out now to find anything?"

He shook his head. "It's impossible to say without knowing where the boat sustained the bulk of damage. Until it took on too much water to float any longer, it would still have moved along with the incoming tide. Whether that was five miles or one, we may never know."

"And Clifton could have bailed out or been tossed out anywhere along the path." The man-in-the-swamp hunt was much, much worse than the needle-in-a-haystack.

"Yeah, and he could have floated some distance from where he entered the water. Any of the fishermen would be smart enough to shed the hip waders and float until they hit something solid to grab hold of. The last thing you do in a storm is try to swim against the tide. It will take you right under."

"So he could have floated miles away."

Colt nodded. "Assuming he was conscious when he went in."

"Yeah, assuming." She held in a sigh. Assuming was something she tried to avoid, especially if the question was life or death.

"The bank looks pretty solid over there," she said and pointed to a flat stretch of hard dirt about twenty yards away, and sat back down to brace for landing.

He guided the boat toward the area she indicated, gunning the engine right before they hit the bank in order to drive the front of the boat up onto it. They exited the boat and without speaking automatically walked in opposite directions, searching the bank for any sign of life or debris.

Jadyn scanned the dirt and weeds as she trudged. Her boots were packed with mud, making each step twice the exertion it would have been with a clean pair of shoes, and she found her mind wandering to thoughts of a hot shower, then sticking her feet in a bucket of cold water. She'd thought herself in decent shape when she arrived in Mudbug, but an entire day combing the swamp, much of it on foot, had changed her mind. As soon as she got her own place, she would invest in some free weights and a treadmill.

She'd almost reached the far side of the cove when she saw a piece of wood sticking out of the water. It was about a foot from the bank and she gauged the ground surrounding it. Only one small section looked as though it had the potential to be firm, so she took a step onto it. She held in the curse when her boot sank up to her ankle in the slimy mud. No good options available, she dragged her other leg over and plopped it down in the sticky goo, then went to work on the board.

Her expectations were nil. Already today, she'd pulled at least fifty boards similar to this one out of the water. But as she gave it an initial tug, she looked closer and realized this board wasn't as weathered as the others she'd seen. It hadn't been in the water for nearly as long. She tugged again and it gave a couple of inches. One last good tug and the board came free, setting her off-balance.

Her arms flew involuntarily up, trying to balance her before she pitched backward, but with her feet stuck firmly in the mud, she had no way of shifting her stance to keep herself from falling. She braced herself for the plunge into the stinky mud and stiffened when arms circled around her, breaking her fall.

"Just in time," Colt said as he gave her a tug to free her feet from the mud.

Her boots stuck like glue, the mud creating suction from the bottom that seemed to have an agenda of not letting her go. When they finally broke loose, a popping sound echoed and she scrambled to get her legs underneath her, but Colt's tug was too strong. Both of them went sprawling backward onto the bank.

Mortified that she was quite literally sprawled on top of Colt, Jadyn immediately tried to push herself up from the ground, but Colt's arms were still clenched around her and unless he wanted to release her, no way was she going to

132

budge. After a second of uncomfortable silence, she felt him start to shake underneath her and finally realized he was laughing. Sound followed a couple of seconds later.

Jadyn jabbed him with her elbow, but he still held tight. "You have a warped sense of humor," she said.

He chuckled again and finally released her. She rolled off of him—not the most ladylike action but the most expedient—and rose to glare. He pushed himself to a sitting position and grinned up at her before finally standing.

"I'm so glad my lack of balance could amuse you," Jadyn said, fighting off her embarrassment.

"Oh, it's not that. It's just that the times I've pictured you on top of me, that wasn't one of the images I came up with."

Jadyn's stiffened. Her pulse shot up, and a spike of heat burned from her center and out through her limbs. She felt the flush creep up her neck and onto her face.

He took one step closer to her and locked his gaze on hers. Then he leaned in and whispered, "Most of the positions I imaged were more, um...comfortable...and with a lot less clothes."

Jadyn's voice caught in her throat, but that was probably a good thing. Her brain raced trying to think of something to say but the only thing that came to mind was "Please yes," and that was the last thing she needed to say. They hadn't even officially dated, unless she counted dinner last night at the diner. Surely she wasn't ready to move right past dating and into Biblical knowledge like a teenager in heat.

That wasn't appropriate, right?

Her mind made a feeble argument that a man should at least have a meal with her that wasn't work-related before she lay on him in fewer clothes, but damned if her body could come up with a reason to agree.

He reached one hand up and pushed a lock of hair behind

her ear. "One of these days it's going to be the right place and time. If you're interested, that is."

Jadyn opened her mouth and silently willed something intelligent to come out of it. "I...uh..."

Damn it.

He smiled. "I'll take that as a maybe." He glanced around the ground. "So what got you stuck in the mud in the first place?"

Back to work.

Relief washed through Jadyn. Work was something she was prepared to handle. "It was a board. I think I flung it behind us when we fell. There." She pointed to the plank directly behind Colt.

"Probably nothing," he said as he reached down to grab it, but as he rose, he stiffened.

"What is it?"

He turned the piece of wood around.

Houdini.

The lettering was faded and chipped, but there was no mistaking the word. The plank had been torn off the back of Clifton Vines's boat.

Jadyn's pulse ticked up a notch. "That means the boat was damaged prior to the split to this channel, right?"

Colt nodded. "Yeah, the stronger current carried the boat forward on the larger channel, but pieces could have drifted with the weaker current to this cove."

"And Clifton?"

"Anything's possible."

"I didn't see any footprints. If he was floating this direction until he hit something solid, where do you think he would have made contact?"

Colt scanned the mouth of the channel, watching the water flow past the bank and swirl around the cypress roots.

"Probably there." He pointed to a small jut of land about twenty yards up from them and right at the entry of the channel.

They headed up the channel toward the point Colt had indicated. The ground was thick with reeds and marsh grass, so progress was slow as they scanned the bank for any indication that Clifton had emerged from the bayou. Just as Jadyn was about to decide there was nothing to find, she spotted an indentation in a bare patch between tufts of marsh grass. She squatted and pushed the grass to the side.

"Look," she said and pointed.

A single bare footprint was clearly outlined in the dried mud.

She looked up at Colt. "You said he would have kicked off his hip waders, right? Would he have been wearing shoes underneath?"

"Doubtful."

"Well, then unless we've got a crazy person swimming the bayous barefoot, I think we need to assume Clifton Vines made it off the boat and to shore."

Colt nodded. "The question is, where did he go from here?"

CHAPTER ELEVEN

MARYSE REACHED FOR THE BOTTLE OF WATER ON HER makeshift laboratory table and cursed when she saw it was empty. And it had been the last one in Mildred's refrigerator. She glanced at her watch and cursed again. The general store had closed twenty minutes before and a drive down the highway to Walmart was outside the scope of movement that Luc was comfortable with.

She sat the bottle back on the dresser next to a rack of test tubes and flopped backward onto the bed in the hotel room Mildred had given her to work in. She supposed the bed part was an advantage. It was sort of convenient to be able to flop when she was aggravated. At her real lab, she resorted to pacing. Flopping and lying were better options when one was feeling tired, frustrated, and lazy.

And lately, those three were her standard.

Scientists who were trying to save the world should not have their progress delayed by lack of bottled water. Nor should they be making do with hotel room dressers for laboratory tables. They should be hiding away in dark laboratories, with cool equipment that only other scientist nerds would covet.

"My life sucks," she said to the ceiling.

"You're young, skinny, financially well off, and have the most gorgeous husband in Louisiana," Mildred's voice sounded from the doorway. "If your life sucks, then I should go ahead and take a bullet."

Maryse looked over at Mildred and grinned. "Why? You're not old, not fat, rich as Caesar, and don't want a man messing things up."

"Touché." Mildred smiled. "So what's got you whining like a six-year-old?"

"Besides the fact that it's six p.m., I arrived here at an indecent hour, and I haven't heard from my husband—who was supposed to pick me up at five—since lunchtime?"

"That's a lot of complaints for one sentence."

Maryse sighed. "That's the condensed version. But my current dilemma is that I ran out of bottled water."

"So drink a soda. Problem solved."

"Not for drinking. I need good clean water for my experiment, and I know you're not going to suggest I get it from the tap."

"Heck no. Sometimes the water's such a weird color I think I should boil my bathwater."

"That's all the algae blooms. I suppose I could boil some water."

"Are you able to without burning it?"

"Ha ha. Just because I choose not to cook doesn't mean I can't."

"I know you can cook. You've been burning stinkweed in here all day. I had to close the air registers in my office because of the smell. Thank God the rest of the rooms are on a separate ventilation system."

"Well, the stinkweed burning is over for the day because I don't have bottled water, don't feel like cooking any, and can't go to Walmart."

"If you really want to finish up with whatever that green mess is, check Jadyn's room. She bought a case of bottled water the other day. I'm sure she won't mind you borrowing one. I'm getting a supply shipment tomorrow, so I'll be restocked."

Maryse perked up, the thought of being able to complete her experiment overriding her aggravation and laziness. "Cool!" She popped up off the bed and grabbed the key from Mildred before hurrying to Jadyn's room. Sure enough, the refrigerator was stocked with soda and water. She grabbed the first bottled water, then realized it had been opened. She checked the water level, but it didn't look as if Jadyn had even taken a drink from it. Good enough.

She hurried back to her room, handing Mildred her keys as she walked in. Mildred shoved the keys in her pocket and pointed at the test tubes on the dresser. "So what are you working on?" Mildred asked.

"A topical pain cream," Maryse said as she lifted one of the tubes from the rack and placed it in a holder over her burner.

"Don't they already have topical pain creams?"

"Yeah, but not like this. If I can get this right, it will penetrate enough layers of skin to make minor surgery possible without any anesthesia."

"Hmmmmpff. I don't think I'd even be brave enough to try that."

"If you were allergic to anesthesia and needed surgery, you would be."

"Fair enough."

Maryse removed the cap from the bottled water and poured some of the water into a beaker. She put the water bottle back on the dresser and brought the beaker closer to her face to make sure the measurement was perfect. As she moved the beaker away, a faint odor wafted past her.

She frowned and waved her hand over the beaker, fanning the air toward her face. Sniffing again, her nose wrinkled and she pulled the beaker right under her nose for a big sniff.

"Is something wrong?" Mildred asked.

"It smells almost...well, fishy."

"Maybe you need to clean your beaker."

Maryse shook her head. "I only use this one for water, and I cleaned it this morning with purified water." She sniffed again. "Oh well, it looks clean."

She dumped the water into the test tube and the reaction was immediate. The solution in the test tube bubbled up and over the tube, sending the liquid running across the dresser. Maryse grabbed a towel and wiped up the liquid before any of it ran off onto the carpet.

"I take it that wasn't supposed to happen?" Mildred asked.

"Not even. Nothing I'm working with should react to water that way." She picked up the test tube and shook it. The solution bubbled again, then settled down after several seconds. The color looked normal and the fishy smell was no longer present. She was just about to chuck the whole thing and try again tomorrow when she caught sight of something in the bottom of the test tube.

She lifted the tube up to the light and studied the bottom. "There's something in here. Like tiny grains of white."

"Something in the plant you were using, maybe?"

"I don't see how. I strained the juice myself." She glanced at the water bottle and frowned. "Surely not," she said and lifted the water bottle up to the light. In the bottom, she could barely make out tiny granules. "I'll be damned. It's in the water."

"Isn't that a heck of a note," Mildred said. "You pay a premium for that water because it's supposed to be pure and you're telling me it has strange things floating in it."

"Not floating, sinking." She shook the bottle and the granules disappeared. "And dissolving. This isn't right. Hand me some of those empty test tubes."

The urgency must have come through in her voice because without a single comment, Mildred shut the door and passed her the box of empty test tubes. For the next thirty minutes, Maryse ran tests on the water, making notes as she went. Mildred worked silently beside her until she finished with the last test and placed the tube in the holder. Maryse stared at her notes for a minute, certain that she'd made a mistake somewhere, but she knew she hadn't.

She took two steps back and sat on the bed, completely at a loss. Mildred inched over to her, clearly worried. "What is it?"

"Cocaine."

Mildred sucked in a breath, her eyes so wide Maryse thought they would pop out of her skull. "No. That's not possible. Jadyn would never..."

"I know. But the alternative isn't much better."

"I don't understand."

"The bottle had already been opened, but it didn't appear as if any water was missing from it. I figured Jadyn had opened it, then got interrupted or realized she already had another open—whatever—then capped it and put it back in the refrigerator for later."

"That sounds logical, but what does that have to do with drugs?"

Maryse looked up at Mildred, a wave of nausea passing through her. "Someone must have put the cocaine in her water bottle."

Mildred's mouth fell open and she stared at Maryse for several seconds. Then she turned slowly and dropped onto the bed as if her legs would no longer support her. "But who? Why?"

Maryse shook her head. "I have absolutely no idea."

"Why would someone want to kill Jadyn?"

"Unless she has an intolerance to cocaine, it wouldn't have killed her. But it probably would have made her pretty sick."

Mildred scrunched her brow. "But what would that accomplish?"

"Maybe someone has a grudge. Mudbug has some strange residents, and some aren't walking the right side of the law."

"That seems especially true lately. You're sure it's cocaine? You didn't make a mistake with your tests?"

Maryse shook her head. "I'm positive."

Mildred looked directly at her. "And how exactly are you sure it's cocaine? Why would you even know how to test for that?"

"It was one of the base components for one of my previous trials."

Mildred popped up from the bed. "You what? With cocaine? Have you lost your mind? Your husband works for the DEA. Good God Almighty!"

"Calm down. It's not like that. The drug company supplied the cocaine. It was all completely legal and aboveboard."

Mildred huffed. "That's the most insane thing I've ever heard. What in the world will they think of next?"

"Who knows." Maryse looked up at Mildred. "What are we going to tell Jadyn?"

"The truth. What else can we do?"

Maryse slumped back on the bed. "Tell her. Crap. How do you tell a person that someone is trying to poison them?"

"Carefully?"

Maryse sighed. "This needs work."

———

Taylor trudged into the hotel around 7:00 p.m. It had been a long, frustrating day, with no answers for her client. The longer the day had gotten, the less enchanted Helena had become with investigative work, especially when Taylor refused to buy her hot dogs every time they saw a convenience store. Taylor had barely stopped her vehicle before the ghost fled her car, claiming she needed a hot shower and a good night's sleep. Taylor was so tired she didn't even try to process those comments. In a single day, Helena had given her more to think about when it came to ghosts than she'd considered in her entire lifetime.

And she would have preferred not knowing at least half of it.

Mildred walked into the lobby from the back of the hotel and gave her a wave. "How did it go?" Mildred asked.

"Not very well, I'm afraid. At least not for my client. No one recognized the man from the drawing."

Mildred gave her a sympathetic look. "I'm sorry. Maybe you'll get lucky tomorrow."

"Maybe. I knew it was a long shot when I took the job, and so did my client. As long as both of us remember that, everything will probably turn out all right."

"And Helena? I'd love to imagine it went well, but I can't suspend disbelief long enough to muster up the thought."

"Ha. Yeah, that's a loaded question. She's quite a piece of work."

"That's the polite way of putting it."

"I have to be honest, I don't know what to make of her at all."

Mildred sighed. "Damn. We were really hoping you'd have some insight."

Taylor shook her head. "I've never seen or heard of anything like her. I wish my great-grandmother were still alive. She was a ghost-talker, too."

"Did she teach you?"

"No. I didn't get to spend as much time with her as I would have liked. My mom...well, let's just say she didn't like talking about any of this." Taylor stared down at the floor, the way she usually did when she talked about her mother.

"That's a shame, but it can't be helped now. I hope Helena didn't cause you any trouble at least."

"Based on your comments this morning, I'm going to assume that she was reasonably well-behaved. I did have to cut her off after sixteen hot dogs. I don't have anything personally against gluttony, but my wallet couldn't keep up."

"She'll eat you into bankruptcy if you let her, so don't. She doesn't need to eat, no matter how much she will try to convince you differently."

"Mostly I fed her so that she'd shut up."

"That's how she reels you in. Did she try to help at all?"

"Yeah. She stayed behind and listened to the gossip after I left people. If anyone had known something relevant, it would have been great. Mostly, the women talked about how my jeans were too tight and the men talked about how they liked my tight jeans."

Mildred smiled. "When someone young and pretty turns up in these tired old towns, it tends to bring out the worst in some."

"It sorta grossed me out. Those men were old enough to be my father, some of them grandfather."

Mildred patted her arm. "Honey, in their minds, they're all still eighteen and off to conquer the world."

Taylor grimaced. "Don't they have mirrors?"

Mildred laughed. "Haven't you learned yet—mirrors lie?"

Taylor smiled. The hotel owner was unlike anyone she'd ever met before. She had a way of putting her at ease that she'd never experienced with another person, especially someone considerably older. Mostly, Taylor always felt that older women were mentally tallying all the things she was doing wrong. God knows, her mother always was. But with Mildred, she didn't feel that judgment. It was refreshing and unexpected.

The bells on the front door of the hotel jangled and Taylor looked over to see Jadyn and Colt walk inside. They both looked exhausted.

Mildred, who'd been relaxed just seconds before, hurried around the front desk and Taylor could almost feel her anxiety spike. She knew about the missing fisherman and the search party, but Mildred had never indicated that she knew the missing man. Something else was troubling the hotel owner. Something to do with Jadyn or Colt. It would probably be obvious even to a normal person, but with her special "skills" it was more like a flashing neon sign.

"Did you find anything?" Mildred asked.

Jadyn nodded and they filled Mildred in on their discoveries in the cove. "We called everyone to the area and searched until we started losing daylight. We'll head back out tomorrow."

Mildred nodded, but didn't look more or less relieved.

Jadyn looked over at Taylor. "I'm glad you're here. We need to talk."

"Me?" Taylor didn't bother to hide her surprise. She had no idea what the game warden could possibly want with her.

Jadyn nodded and shot a glance at Colt before stepping over to the front desk. "I think I know who the man in the drawing is."

Taylor's pulse spiked. "You're kidding me. Who is he?"

Jadyn frowned. "He's our missing fisherman."

Of all the things Jadyn could have said, that was one Taylor would never have seen coming. "Wow. That's crazy." She knew she sounded silly and unprofessional, but at that moment, they were the only words that came to mind.

Jadyn nodded. "It's quite an odd coincidence, and I'm not all that fond of coincidences."

"Me either. I mean, I know they exist, but not nearly as often as people think they do."

"Agreed, but in this case, I can't find a strand to connect the dots. And even if we assume our missing fisherman is the man in your picture, there's still no proof that he's your client's husband. Colt's office is tracking down everything they can find on Clifton Vines, the missing man. Hopefully, they can put together a profile that clearly eliminates him as an option for you."

Jadyn frowned. "That sounded harsher than I intended it to. I'm sorry. I'm exhausted."

"No, that's okay," Taylor said. "I get what you're saying. As long as I can prove to my client that the man her friend saw can't be her husband, then she can move on from this."

Jadyn gave her a grateful smile. "Yes, that's it exactly."

"Well, I can't be of any help with local tracking, but if someone's willing to point me in the right direction and keep me from getting lost, I'm happy to help with the search tomorrow."

Colt nodded. "We can use all the help we can get. I'll pair you up with a couple of the locals. We're meeting at the sheriff's department tomorrow morning at eight."

"Great. I'll see you then. If you don't need me for anything, I'm going to have a hot shower and a big dinner."

"That sounds like the best plan ever," Jadyn said. "We'll see you tomorrow morning."

Taylor gave them a wave and headed upstairs. Before she hit the second floor landing, she glanced back down into the lobby. Mildred had been oddly quiet during the entire exchange, but Taylor could tell she was biding her time. Whatever she needed to say to Jadyn, she was waiting to say in private. Taylor knew it was none of her business, but she couldn't help but wonder what had unnerved the seemingly calm hotel owner.

If you weren't naturally curious, you'd make an awful private investigator.

She cast one more glance at them before continuing up the stairs and down the hallway to her room. With any luck, she'd soon have answers for her client. She was 99 percent sure they weren't going to be the answers Sophia wanted, but as long as they were the truth, Taylor would be satisfied with her work, if not necessarily the outcome.

CHAPTER TWELVE

COLT WATCHED AS TAYLOR DISAPPEARED UPSTAIRS, THEN turned to Jadyn. "I'm going to take off. I think Taylor has the right idea."

"Wait!" Mildred grabbed his arm. "I need to talk to you both, in private."

Colt stared at the hotel owner, not bothering to hide his surprise. Mildred was hardly the sort of woman prone to dramatics, but she was so tense it was visibly apparent.

"What's wrong?" Jadyn asked, her voice sharp.

"My office," she said. "We've been waiting for you." She spun around and hurried off down the hallway.

Colt looked over at Jadyn. "We?"

Jadyn shrugged. "Whatever it is has Mildred seriously stressed, and in my limited experience, that's not easy to do."

"No, it's not. We better find out what's going on."

Colt brought up the rear as they filed into Mildred's office. Maryse was already standing there, answering the "we" question, and just finishing up a call on her cell.

"Luc?" Mildred asked.

Maryse nodded. "He'll be here in ten minutes." She looked

over at Jadyn and Colt. "I guess all you law enforcement types had a long day. I'm sorry I'm holding you up even longer, but this can't wait."

"What's wrong?" Colt asked. He knew why Maryse had been sticking close to the hotel during working hours and hoped her situation hadn't gotten more dire.

"I ran out of bottled water today," Maryse said. "I only had one test tube left in my experiment so Mildred suggested I borrow a bottle from you." She looked at Jadyn.

"Of course," Jadyn said. "You're welcome to anything you need. You don't even have to tell me about it."

Maryse waved a hand in dismissal. "That's not what this is about."

"Something was wrong with the water," Mildred interjected, apparently unable to hold it in any longer.

Jadyn stared at Maryse. "What was wrong with it?"

"Well, I thought it smelled slightly fishy," Maryse said, "but I don't think that had anything to do with the real problem. When I added the water to the solution in my test tube it reacted in a way it shouldn't have."

Mildred nodded. "Then Maryse noticed something in the water and started running tests. It was cocaine. There was cocaine in your bottled water!"

Colt stared at Mildred, waiting for the punch line, but one look at the hotel owner's horrified expression let him know this was no joke.

Jadyn's eyes widened. "But how can that be? I bought that case last week at Walmart."

Maryse nodded. "Did you put it in the refrigerator then?"

"No," Jadyn replied. "I wasn't quite out yet. I restocked it last night before I went to bed."

"Did you open any of the bottles?" Maryse asked.

"No. I already had half of one left." Jadyn looked from

Maryse to Mildred. "Are you telling me that someone broke into my room and put cocaine in one of my water bottles?"

Maryse nodded. "We don't see any other explanation."

Colt drew in a breath and slowly let it out. It was a curveball he'd never seen coming, and he had absolutely no explanation for it. Certainly game wardens made their share of enemies, but Jadyn hadn't been in town long enough to create such discord, except with a handful of people who were either dead or in jail.

Colt narrowed his gaze on Maryse. "You're certain it's cocaine?"

"Positive," Maryse said.

"She's worked with it before," Mildred said. "The drug companies gave it to her just like that. Can you believe it?"

Jadyn nodded. "It has certain numbing components for surgical procedures, right?"

Mildred threw her hands in the air. "Am I the only one in the room who finds that insane?"

"It's sorta insane," Colt agreed, hoping to calm Mildred down. "So sometime between this morning and when you took the bottle, someone spiked it. What time did you take the bottle?"

"Around five thirty," Maryse said.

"That leaves most of the day." Colt tapped his finger on Mildred's desk.

"Forget the when," Jadyn said, "I want to know why."

"We all do," Colt said. "You haven't gotten any strange phone calls, seen anyone following you, things like that?"

"No. Everything has been normal. For Mudbug, anyway."

Colt looked at Maryse. "Would the dosage have killed her?"

Maryse shook her head. "Not unless she's allergic. It probably would have made her sick for a couple days."

"So either he didn't know the proper dosage to kill someone or he only intended to make her ill."

"Exactly," Maryse said, "but why would anyone want to do either?"

"That is the real question," Colt said.

"I feel really bad about this," Jadyn said. "Maryse could have drunk that water, or Mildred. Someone could have been seriously hurt because of me."

"Don't even go there," Mildred said. "None of this is your fault."

"To some degree it is," Jadyn said. "Obviously, I've made an enemy somewhere."

Colt had been mulling over the entire situation since Mildred first made her cocaine announcement, trying to make some sense of it. "Maybe it's not an enemy," he said. "Not in the sense we're thinking about it, anyway."

"What do you mean?" Jadyn asked.

"We've been poking around other towns looking for the missing boat captain. And although we haven't started down that path yet, there's still the chance that the damage to the boat was deliberate."

Jadyn's eyes widened. "Which means the footprint we saw in the bank could have been made by the person who sank the boat, and not Vines."

"Assuming that train of thought is correct, then yeah, it's more likely the saboteur went ashore than Clifton."

"And if one of the people I questioned was the saboteur..."

"Then he might not want you taking a closer look at things," Colt finished. He pinned his gaze on Jadyn, whose eyes widened as she locked in on the unspoken thought he had —that someone had also taken a shot at her the day before. Two attacks in as many days.

Jadyn shook her head. "I don't like it, but it makes sense."

She blew out a breath. "If Vines never made it off that boat, the search tomorrow will be a complete waste of time."

"Maybe," Colt agreed, "but we don't know for certain what happened. Until we do, we have to proceed with this as a search-and-rescue mission. In the meantime, I don't think you should stay at the hotel. Whoever spiked that bottle knew enough about the hotel and you to enter without being seen and go straight to your room."

"No," Mildred protested. "There's nowhere else to stay in town. I'm on high alert now. The hotel is safer than anywhere else."

Colt shook his head. "It's not safer than my house."

"What?" Jadyn whirled around and stared at him. "No, I can't stay with you."

"I have a guest room, an excellent security system, and an arsenal of weapons. Anyone who attempts to get to you at my place will be on the receiving end of doom."

"I...but..." Jadyn glanced over at Maryse and Mildred, as if expecting them to offer some sort of argument against his plan, but both women were strangely silent. Colt took that as agreement.

"Just until we figure this out," Colt said. "If he's smart, he won't make another attempt here. We could use my place to draw him out."

"He makes a good point," Maryse said. "Colt's place is fairly remote. Someone would make the mistake of thinking it was easier to make a move on."

He could tell that Jadyn understood the wisdom of what he proposed, but her uncertainty was clear. Was she worried about the potential for another attack, or was her uncertainty due to being alone with him?

Colt looked at Maryse. "I assume you still have some of the contaminated water? I'll need my lab to run tests."

"I'm not an idiot," Maryse said and pulled out a sealed plastic bag with the water bottle inside. "My fingerprints and Jadyn's will both be on there. I figure he was wearing gloves, but you never know."

Colt took the bag. "Thanks. I have both your prints on file, so I'll be able to eliminate them."

Jadyn took a deep breath and blew it out. "Then I guess I better go pack a bag." She hurried out of the room and Colt could hear her running up the stairs.

Mildred locked her gaze on him. "What is happening to this town?"

Colt knew exactly what Mildred was asking. The past year had been an odd and extreme one for the previously quiet Mudbug. "I don't know." He knew it wasn't what Mildred wanted to hear, but the reality was he didn't have a good answer.

Maryse frowned. "It's like Helena Henry's death was a sort of hurricane. Things that have been long buried are starting to surface."

Colt nodded. He wasn't sure what the catalyst was, or if there even was one. But he agreed with Maryse's sentiment. Things were definitely surfacing in Mudbug. And not for the better.

─────────

JADYN PACKED HER TOILETRIES INTO A SMALL BAG AND shoved it and some clothes into her duffel along with spare ammo, her binoculars, and her phone charger. It wasn't much, but she could make do for a day or two before needing more clothes.

He probably has a washer and dryer.

She shook her head. Doing laundry at Colt's house felt

entirely too domestic. Even packing her bag to stay there, despite the completely logical reason for doing so, made her feel a little like a participant in something illicit. She was about to zip the duffel when she realized she hadn't included something to sleep in. In the hotel, she usually wore a T-shirt and underwear, but that would hardly be appropriate at Colt's house.

Or maybe it will be.

Her mind flashed back to the scene at the cove, when she'd fallen on top of him. His words echoed through her mind as if he were standing right there beside her and saying them for the first time.

Most of the positions I imaged were more, um...comfortable...and with a lot less clothes.

A flash of heat ran through her and she grabbed a pair of shorts and a T-shirt from the dresser and shoved them into the bag.

"I hope you're packing something skimpy and lacy." Maryse's voice sounded in the doorway and Jadyn whirled around.

"Sorry," Maryse said. "I didn't mean to startle you."

"It's not your fault," Jadyn said. "I was a million miles away."

Maryse nodded. "Entirely too much to think about for one day. I get it. I've lived it. Still am, a little, although my situation now isn't personal like the stuff that happened before."

"I find it all unnerving, then I get frustrated with myself for feeling that way, because I've always known that part of my job was the potential for danger."

"Yeah, but I bet you never thought about the carnal kind of danger. I saw your face when Colt suggested you stay with him. It freaked you out a little. Are you afraid that if you take things further and change your mind, it might be uncomfortable?"

Jadyn sighed, embarrassed that Maryse had been able to tap directly into her biggest worry. "I'm afraid that if I take things further I will want to run full speed and he won't. Colt hasn't exactly been consistent where I'm concerned. He flirts with me, then he's all business. He kisses me, then acts as if it never happened."

Jadyn couldn't bring herself to tell Maryse about what had happened at the cove. She still wasn't sure what she thought about it and wasn't comfortable trying to translate it to her cousin.

"I almost never gave in to Luc," Maryse said. "And then when I finally decided he was actually into me and not just looking for another notch in his belt, all hell broke loose and I found out he'd been lying to me the entire time about who he really was. After everything that happened with Hank, it was a huge blow."

"I can't even imagine how you must have felt." Maryse's first husband, Hank, had all but turned her against relationships, so finding out that Luc had completely misrepresented himself must have been an enormous blow, especially with everything else happening to her at the time.

"It sucked hard," Maryse said. "But when the emotional shitstorm in my head cleared enough for me to see things as they really were, I knew there was no malice behind his actions. He was just doing his job and felt horrible for the way things went down. He teased me in the beginning, thinking he'd romance my secrets out of me. He was as surprised and as scared as I was when everything got real."

Jadyn frowned. "You think Colt is afraid of something? That's the reason for the back and forth?"

Maryse shrugged. "I don't know. But it's certainly a possibility. Colt doesn't talk much about his time in New Orleans. Granted, he's not exactly a gossip, but it's still strange that he doesn't share detective war stories. I've always wondered if there was a woman there—someone he didn't want to remember."

"Another cop?"

"Maybe. It might explain why he doesn't volunteer anything about his work there."

What Maryse said made a lot of sense. More sense than anything she'd come up with. But if Colt was fighting some memory of the one who got away, did she want to take up with him on any level? Wouldn't it be better to wait until he was sure that the past was really in the past? It was a big decision to make based on speculation, but Jadyn had a feeling she might need to make up her mind soon...like in the next couple of hours.

"What would you do?" Jadyn asked.

Maryse smiled. "If you'd asked me that question a year ago, I would have said run far, far away from temptation."

"And now?"

"Now I'd tell you that you can heal a broken heart, but you can't heal regret."

"So you'd roll the dice?"

"For Colt Bertrand? I think I would."

Jadyn smiled at her cousin. "Thanks. I know neither of us is good at the whole girlie thing, but I want you to know that I love that I can talk to you about this stuff. I've never had that before."

Maryse threw her arms around Jadyn and squeezed. "Promise me you won't let anyone hurt you."

Surprised and moved by her cousin's burst of emotion, Jadyn hugged Maryse and said, "I promise."

Maryse released her and sniffed. "You're in good hands

with Colt...however you choose to use them." She winked and hurried off down the hall.

Jadyn grabbed her duffel bag and headed downstairs. It had been a long day, and she had a feeling it was going to be an even longer night.

CHAPTER THIRTEEN

COLT STARTED HIS TRUCK AS JADYN TOSSED HER DUFFEL BAG in the backseat, then climbed inside the cab. Maryse's discovery had thrown a huge curve into an already-confusing mix, and he was having trouble deciding what direction to take next.

"I know we're both exhausted," he said, finally making up his mind, "but would you mind if we stop by the sheriff's department before heading to my place? Given the new circumstances, I'd like to know everything we can about Clifton Vines as soon as we can get the information."

Jadyn looked almost relieved at his suggestion. "I would really appreciate that. This entire thing has sorta thrown me for a loop."

"Yeah, this one surprised me too. And I don't guess I have to tell you how much I hate being surprised."

"Not on my list of favorites either." She smiled, as if remembering something.

"What's so funny?"

"I was just remembering the one and only time my mother decided to throw me a surprise birthday party. I was twelve and she'd been completely clueless about anything I liked for years already."

"I take it the party was not the success your mother expected?"

"You could say that. When I walked into our house after riding lessons, a clown jumped out from behind the couch and everyone yelled. Before I could even formulate a thought, I clocked the clown with a solid right hook and sent him sprawling backward over the couch. I'm pretty sure he sued."

Colt laughed. Every time Jadyn revealed something about herself, he found more things to like about her. "I would have loved to have seen that."

"I'm sure my mother would have gladly traded places with you. She punished me for embarrassing her."

"No offense, but your mother sounds like a real piece of work." It wasn't exactly what he was thinking. Based on the little she had revealed about her mother, Colt knew for certain he didn't like her one bit, but he didn't want to come right out and call her the first name that had come to mind.

"That's one way to put it."

"Do you talk to her much now?"

"Not unless I have to. Every conversation begins with her trying to push me into marrying one of the eligible bachelors she's selected for me to help 'improve my status.'"

He bristled at the thought of a parent trying to force someone on their child as a means to make them somehow "better." Jadyn didn't need a man to make her something. She was already more than her mother would ever give her credit for.

"Sounds to me like you'd be improving their status," he said. "Not the other way around."

"Thanks," she said and dropped her gaze to the floorboard.

He'd noticed that when he complimented her, she blushed

or looked away. Was it because she was unused to compliments? He couldn't really believe that was the case. She was an amazing woman. Surely others had said so. Selfishly, he hoped she blushed only when he complimented her, because that would mean she was into him as much as he was into her. Unless he'd completely misread her responses to his sporadic advances.

That would suck.

Shifting his mind back to the case, he pulled his truck in front of the sheriff's department and they headed inside. Eugenia, the night dispatcher, was at the front desk, sorting through a stack of paper. She looked relieved when she saw them walk inside.

"I was just about to call you," she said.

"Did we get anything on Vines?" he asked.

"Sort of."

Colt pulled a couple of chairs in front of her desk. "Show me."

"Well, we can start with identification. Clifton Vines owns the house you searched, a shrimp boat, and a 2004 Dodge pickup truck. His driver's license history puts him at the same address for the last twenty-eight years."

"And before that?" Jadyn asked.

"That's the 'sort of' part of the equation. Before that, the only Clifton Vines that existed died in 1975."

"Maybe he came from another state," Colt suggested.

Eugenia nodded. "Shirley thought about that and set to running the name in the national database. Records exist for three Clifton Vines. Our dead guy, a pensioner in Maryland, and a college student in New Mexico."

"You checked on the pensioner?" Jadyn asked.

"Yep. He's in his wheelchair in Foster Assisted Living Center and hasn't left the place for the last six years."

Colt looked at Jadyn. "Please tell me he isn't the missing husband."

She shook her head. "It would be the most incredible thing I've ever heard of, but based on this information, we can't eliminate the possibility."

"But you don't really think he could be, do you?"

"No. Even if the missing husband was knocked out and never remembered who he was, at some point, he would have been issued an identity by the state, right?"

"Yes," Colt said, "and there would be a record."

"So for now, our assumption has to be that Clifton Vines began life as someone else and acquired his current identity around thirty years ago."

"I wish I knew why."

"Me too," she agreed, "but twenty bucks says it wasn't for any good reason."

"Should we tell Taylor what we've discovered?"

"I think so. It's her choice whether or not to tell her client now or wait until she has more information."

He nodded. "Sounds like a plan."

Jadyn pulled her cell phone from her pocket. "I'll give her a call."

———

TAYLOR HUNG UP THE PHONE AND FLOPPED BACK ON THE bed. Never in her life had she been so exhausted by a conversation. It was a total drama fest.

You shouldn't have called her.

"Shut up," she said. As if she needed a reminder from herself that she'd made the decision to update Sophia with the information she'd gotten from Jadyn. She could have left it alone—should have left it alone until they knew more—but nooooooooo, that horrible thing called her conscience has reared its ugly head and she'd spouted off everything.

One of these days, she'd learn and hopefully cultivate the ability to lie by omission. It would certainly make her life easier on both personal and professional fronts. Sophia had been a crazy woman, crying one moment, then demanding that the entire US Navy be sent out to search for the missing fisherman. Taylor did her best to talk the woman back into sanity, but she wouldn't be surprised if Sophia was currently on the phone with the Navy, Coast Guard, or any other agency with a fleet of ships, demanding they all get into the bayou.

She took in a deep breath and slowly let it out. She'd originally thought this case would be a whole lot of nothing, but it was turning into something she hadn't expected or had a plan for. Damned empathy. It totally eclipsed her better judgment every time.

Why do you waste time on others instead of bettering yourself?

Her mother's words echoed through her mind and Taylor clenched her teeth. As though caring about other people was somehow a crime. Maybe to her mother it was. She certainly hadn't shown any care for Taylor, and she was her daughter. Caring for someone she hadn't carried for nine months and birthed herself was probably such a far-fetched idea that it had never crossed her mother's mind.

To hell with her.

Taylor rose from the bed and headed for the shower.

Exactly. To hell with her.

———

JADYN HESITATED A SECOND BEFORE STEPPING INTO COLT'S house. She knew leaving the hotel was the right thing to do, but wished there had been another option. Granted, Colt hadn't downplayed the security system he'd installed, and given the remote location of his house, she was happy he'd gone to such lengths even though he probably never thought he'd need it.

"I can give you the grand tour," Colt said, "or I can point to everything standing right here."

Jadyn smiled as she glanced around the small but neat living room, which was open to a kitchen with a breakfast nook. Large windows graced the walls of both rooms. She figured it was probably quite bright and cheerful when the sunlight was streaming in on the cool blue wall paint in the living room and the bright yellow of the kitchen.

"It's very nice," she said.

"You sound a bit surprised."

"I, uh, most guys' places don't look this nice. Unless they're married."

He laughed. "When I first moved in, I had this old sofa that I'd been dragging around since college and milk crates for end tables. My bed consisted of mattresses on the floor. It worked fine for me, but my mom wouldn't have it. I think she was afraid women would see it and be scared off."

"More likely, they'd see it and want to fix you."

"Ha. You're probably right, but mom didn't give any the opportunity. She swooped down on the place and after a month of telling her I didn't care about fabric and paint swatches, she was finally satisfied with the result."

"She did a great job."

"She thinks so too, but I thought it was painful. Do you have any idea how much furniture costs? I could have bought a really nice used bass boat." He pointed to a hallway at the back of the living room. "There are two bedrooms at the end of the hall. Guest room is on the left. Only one bathroom—it's the first door on the right. Laundry is on the left."

"It's perfect."

"I think so. Mom keeps harping on me to add another bedroom and bath, but I don't see the point as long as it's just me."

"I'd love to have something like this eventually."

He looked around and nodded. "I would never admit it to my mother, but she did a great job." He headed toward the kitchen. "I know I'm tired and starving, and figure you are too. I'm not exactly a chef, but I have a frozen pizza I can pop in the oven. You can take the shower first."

"My mouth just watered at 'frozen pizza.'"

"Always a sign that you're working too hard."

He stepped into the kitchen and opened the freezer. Jadyn clutched the strap of her duffel bag and headed for the bathroom. The thought of standing under a hot stream of water was heavenly. Even her hunger couldn't surpass her desire to shed the layers of mud and salt water that covered her from head to toe.

The bathroom was done in a marine theme with white walls and navy accents, which looked both masculine and tasteful. Jadyn closed the door and turned on the shower. Colt's mother had really good taste.

I wonder if she will like me.

The thought rocketed through her mind so unbidden that she froze in place. Where in the world had that come from? Colt had made some suggestive statements...a couple of advances that were never followed through. They'd never even been on a date. Certainly, they were nowhere near the meeting-the-mother part of things.

She shed her clothes and stepped into the hot stream of water, still pondering her odd thought. Never had she considered herself a traditional sort of woman. She had nothing against marriage, and always assumed she'd get there someday, but she'd never had the desire to pursue it like her contempo-raries. Her career had always been more important.

That's because you never met the right man.

She leaned back and let the water cascade through her hair. Maybe it was that simple—she'd never met a man who made her think long-term. But why in the world would the thought enter her head now when she had nothing to base it on?

Maybe because you're naked in his shower.

Okay, so there was that. Her current situation was far from normal, and being closed up in an intimate space in an isolated area had her on edge for more reasons than the attempted attack she'd narrowly escaped.

Focus on the work.

She sighed. How come her mind always went back around to logic? The last thing she needed right now was distraction, and Colt was the biggest distraction she'd ever known. Her focus should be on Clifton Vines and why someone tried to poison her. That was plenty to think about. She didn't need to cloud things with thoughts of Colt and possibilities that might never be.

She finished up her shower, slipped on shorts and a T-shirt, and pulled her long wet hair into a ponytail, then headed back to the kitchen. Colt was sitting at the breakfast table, typing on his laptop. He rose from the table as she entered the room.

"The pizza has another ten minutes. There are sodas, water, and beer in the refrigerator. Take your pick."

He gave her a smile and headed off for the bathroom. Jadyn opened the refrigerator and stared at the selection. A cold beer was so tempting, but who wanted to stop at one, especially with pizza? Finally she settled on a diet soda, checked the pizza, then sat at the breakfast table.

Colt's laptop was still open and she stared at it for several seconds before pulling it over in front of her. Surely if he were working on something confidential, he wouldn't have left it open. She found herself somewhat relieved when she saw that he'd been checking the weather for tomorrow.

She accessed her own e-mail and cleared through the junk. The last one remaining was an e-mail from her mother. Her finger hovered over the touch pad, but she couldn't bring herself to open it. Finally, she closed the e-mail page. With everything she had on her plate, she didn't need aggravation, and contact with her mother was guaranteed to provide just that.

On a new page, she opened a search for Taylor's client. It wasn't any of her business, but she found herself oddly fascinated by a woman who would carry a torch for a man for so long. Thousands of hits returned from her search and she started reading. When the timer went off on the stove, she jumped.

Colt, who'd just walked back into the kitchen, gave her a look of concern. "You need to try to relax."

One look at him and her heart went fluttering all over again. His hair was still damp and hung in a slight wave. His athletic shorts and T-shirt were modest but revealed enough of his ripped body to make her momentarily speechless.

Finally she recovered use of her mouth. "I am relaxing. I mean, I will. The buzzer just startled me is all. I was caught up in what I was reading."

Colt pulled the tray with the pizza on it out of the oven and grabbed a knife to cut it. "And what was so interesting that you attempted to burn our dinner?"

"I was reading up on Taylor's client."

"Any particular reason why?" He pulled two large slices of pizza onto plates and slid them onto the breakfast table.

Jadyn shrugged as he took the seat next to her. "I guess I

just wondered what kind of woman would still be looking for her missing husband almost three decades later."

"It's definitely a level of dedication you don't see often today. Did you find anything interesting?"

"No. Just more detailed information of the things Taylor already told us. Sophia Lambert is a very wealthy woman who inherited the family empire and by all accounts, runs it with a firm grip. She's clearly intelligent, has more money than Donald Trump, and recent pictures show her to be quite a beauty. I guess I wonder why she never remarried."

"Probably no man could handle her," Colt joked.

"True," Jadyn said as she reached for the slice of pizza. Her mouth started to water as she lifted the slice to her lips. That first bite was pure heaven. A tomato sauce and melted cheese heaven.

Colt frowned. "I would say maybe she's protecting her money, but she was already set to inherit when she married Perkins. Who knows? Maybe she loved her husband so much she doesn't want to replace him. Maybe no other man ever measured up to her standards—I'm betting they're high."

She swallowed her bite and chugged some of her soda.

"Maybe," she said. "The only takeaway I got was that Taylor's probably going to have her hands full dealing with her, especially if she decides to tell her about the Clifton Vines situation."

"Yeah, I wouldn't want to make that phone call. What about the water bottle situation? You have any breakthrough thoughts on that?"

"Nothing that really stands out. If we assume I got on someone's shit list while we were trying to identify Clifton Vines, then that limits the suspects to the shrimp house owners and workers that I spoke to. For now, I'm leaving out people we talked to together since no one came after you."

"That we know of. I'll be checking the tabs on my water bottles pretty closely until we figure this out. But yeah, we should probably focus first on the places you visited alone. You mentioned before that something seemed off at one of them, right?"

Jadyn set her slice of pizza back on her plate. "I think I arrived in the middle of a disagreement between the owners. That could be all there was to it, but something didn't feel right. And then there was the situation with the fish." She described in detail what had happened at Vincent Brothers Shrimp House from the time she arrived and including helping with the scattered fish. She left out Helena's part in it all.

When she finished, Colt nodded. "Might be something. Might be nothing. But it's as good a place to start as any. I'll get Shirley and Eugenia started checking backgrounds on the owners and the two dockworkers."

"Do you think they could have had something to do with Clifton's boat sinking?"

"At this point, I've decided that anything's possible."

"If someone deliberately sank Vines's boat, that would be all the more reason for him to stay hidden in the swamp, assuming he's still alive. But how long could he survive out there?"

"Plenty of camps are empty most of the time. He could find shelter and probably enough food to keep him going for a month or more if he moved around. Lots of people leave fishing tackle at their camps too. Worst case, he could fish after dark."

Jadyn nodded, remembering her and Colt's impromptu stay at one of the camps during their last investigation. "Bottom line is he probably wouldn't starve."

"No. If he's not injured, he could survive quite well for a while."

"Do you think we should let the rest of the search party cover the bayou and we should start checking the camps in the area?"

"It sounds like a plan."

Jadyn polished off her piece of pizza and leaned back in her chair.

"You want another piece?" Colt asked.

"Nah. That was practically a third of the pie."

He glanced at the remaining pizza. "I admit, I'm tempted, but I shouldn't load up this late."

"I hear ya," Jadyn said, although she didn't think for a moment that the additional calories would hurt one perfect inch of Colt's body. She rose from the table and put her plate in the dishwasher. When she turned around, Colt was right behind her. She took his plate and put it beside hers in the rack. When she straightened back up, she expected that he would have moved, but he was still standing there, not six inches from her.

His gaze locked on hers and she felt a tingle run through her body. She knew that look. She'd seen it when they were trapped in a camp together, hiding from a shooter. And she knew the kiss that had followed—had thought about that kiss a million times since then.

He was also hesitating, which she supposed made sense. Colt was a good guy and probably felt he would be taking advantage of the situation if he made a move. But Jadyn couldn't help wishing he'd abandon logic and simply go with instinct. She had no way of knowing what the next day would bring, but right now she knew someone was out to get her.

You can heal a broken heart, but you can't heal regret.

Before she could change her mind, she took a tiny step toward him. That step was all the invitation he needed. His hands clasped around her and he drew her in for the kiss. His lips brushing against hers set her heart beating so fast it felt as if someone were beating a drum in her chest.

The kiss deepened and Jadyn pressed her body against Colt's, running her hands across his body and leaving him no doubt what her intentions were.

He paused for a second. "Are you sure?"

"Right now, this is the only thing I'm sure about."

CHAPTER FOURTEEN

THE SECURITY ALARM'S SOUNDING startled COLT OUT OF A deep sleep and a great dream. In a split second his trained mind processed everything—the attempted attack on Jadyn, her staying at his cabin, the alarm blaring. In that split second his mind processed the situation, his body went on autopilot. He bolted out of bed and grabbed his pistol from the nightstand, then hurried to the security panel next to his bedroom door.

By the time he reached the panel, Jadyn was already beside him and armed as well. If he hadn't been so worried, it might have been amusing, both of them standing there naked except for their firearms.

"What is it?" she asked.

"One of the cameras on the back of the house picked up motion."

"Could it be an animal?"

"Only if it's as tall as a human. The alarm only goes off if the motion is above five feet from the ground." He grabbed his shorts and tennis shoes and pulled them both on before dashing to the back door.

Jadyn was only seconds behind him and clothed when he peered out the back window and scanned the yard. The floodlights on the edges of the roof had automatically flipped on when the alarm sounded, giving him a good field of vision all the way to the tree line. Nothing moved. Nothing in the light, anyway.

"I don't see anything," he said. "Most likely, he was scared away by the alarm. I'm going to see if I can find footprints."

"I'm going with you."

"No. If he's positioned at the edge of the swamp, you're an open target."

"So are you."

"But he's not after me."

"That you know of."

He shook his head. "This isn't up for discussion. I'm going outside and I need you inside covering me in case things go south. Go into the guest room and raise the window enough for you to get a good shot off if needed."

He slipped outside, pulling the door shut behind him before she could reply. Scanning the tree line, he listened for any sound that was out of place, but the noisy night creatures were all he heard. He hurried down the steps into the lawn and headed for the left side of the house, where the camera that had tripped the alarm was mounted. Starting close to the house, he scanned the soft ground for any sign of passage. With the recent rain and his lawn's lack of good drainage, anything of size would leave an impression.

About ten feet out from the corner of the house he spotted the footprints. They were large—a man's prints—and made by rubber boots. The tracks led out of the swamp to the left and retreated back in the same direction. Automatically, Colt reached back for the small flashlight that was usually attached to his belt and cursed when his hand brushed against bare skin and the cotton waistband of his shorts.

The foliage of the swamp was thick and the trees so close together that not a sliver of moonlight entered the area where the man had made passage. Without a good light, no way could he track him. Frustrated and more than a little concerned, he made his way back inside his house.

Jadyn met him at the back door, her anxious expression a dead giveaway to how she felt. "Anything?" she asked.

"Footprints leading out from and back into the swamp. The footprints leading into the swamp were farther apart than the ones leading into my yard."

"He was running when he left."

Colt nodded.

"What is going on?" Jadyn asked. "I don't understand any of this."

Colt's heart broke a little at the tiny sliver of fear that made it through Jadyn's words. A stalker was every woman's worst nightmare, and this one was more brazen than most. He'd entered the hotel in broad daylight to poison her water. Now he'd approached a house belonging to a law enforcement officer.

"Let's check the camera footage. Maybe we'll get lucky."

They hurried to the kitchen and Colt accessed the security footage from his laptop, rewinding to a couple of minutes before the alarm tripped. They both leaned forward in their seats, staring at the screen, and after thirty seconds or so, they saw him creeping out of the swamp where Colt found the footprints.

He wore jeans, rubber boots, a long-sleeved flannel shirt, and a ball cap. Jadyn squinted, trying to catch a glimpse of something that might tell her who the man was.

"Damn it!" Colt swore. "He's got his hat pulled down so far that we can't see his face."

He saw Jadyn's hands clench as she watched the man inch closer to the house. Suddenly, the man froze.

"That must be when the alarm went off," she said as he whirled around and hurried back into the swamp.

Colt reversed the footage and froze it in frame. "He doesn't move like a young man."

"No, and his neck has thickened. He's definitely older."

"What about height and weight? I'm thinking six foot, give or take an inch or two, and maybe two hundred pounds."

Jadyn studied the man and nodded. "That looks about right."

"Does it match the description of any of the shrimp house people you talked to?"

"Yeah. All of them."

"Of course." He sighed. "I'm going to send this footage to my office. Maybe a specialist can do more with it than us."

"It doesn't hurt to try," she said, but Colt could tell she was as disappointed with the lack of solid leads as he was.

She rose from her chair and glanced at the kitchen clock. "It's almost six. Might as well get dressed for work."

Colt watched as she shuffled off down the hall. This wasn't even close to his thoughts of how the morning would go. Last night, he'd thought it impossible to get enough of Jadyn, and he was right. Any doubt he'd had about her attraction to him and their potential together had flown completely out the window. Jadyn St. James was the most perfect woman he'd ever met, and he was going to do everything he could to make her part of his everyday life.

Last night had been incredible and he'd never wanted it to end.

Unfortunately, the mind was willing but the body was no

longer sixteen. After hours of incredible lovemaking, they'd collapsed in each other's arms. He couldn't remember the last time he'd slept so soundly.

Until the alarm went off.

He opened his e-mail and sent the file to the sheriff's department. The man had made a bad mistake coming after Jadyn. And if it was the last thing Colt ever did, he would hunt him down and make him pay.

————

JADYN PULLED ON HER CLOTHES, THEN SAT ON THE EDGE OF the bed to pull on her work boots. Before she reached for a boot, she lifted the pillow to her nose and inhaled.

It smelled like him—spicy and masculine.

She put the pillow back on the bed and ran her hand over the rumpled sheets. If anyone had told her that making love to a man could be like what she and Colt had last night, she would have called them crazy. Now she was a believer. Her night with Colt had been mind-blowing, earth-shattering, and a whole bunch of other adjectives she couldn't think of at the moment.

You're falling for him.

Her hand flew up to cover her mouth. No. That couldn't be. She barely knew him.

She shook her head. That wasn't really true. Granted, she hadn't known Colt for very long, but she was pretty sure she knew what kind of man he was. What he stood for and believed in. Was that enough to fall for someone? That and a compatibility in bed that boggled the mind?

She reached for her boots. This was not the time to get ahead of herself. They had to find Clifton Vines and figure out who was stalking her. Both of those were potentially life-threatening issues and besides that, it was their job to fix things. Colt wasn't going anywhere. They had plenty of time to work out what was between them. There was no need to rush.

No need to deal with all the feelings she'd been throttling for weeks now.

She pulled on her boots and exited the room. The bathroom door was closed and she could hear water running in the sink. She headed into the kitchen and dug around for coffee to brew, then located a couple of thermoses in the kitchen cabinets. Colt's laptop was open on the kitchen table, so she sat down in front of it to check her e-mail.

The browser was open to Colt's e-mail and she glided her finger over the touchpad to close the window. But before she reached the X, her eyes caught sight of the words "Hey Sexy" from someone named Maria. She glanced at the hallway but the bathroom door was still closed.

She knew she shouldn't open it. Whatever was in the message, it was private and intended only for Colt. But for the first time in her life, she threw logic and ethics both right out the window. She hovered for several seconds and finally clicked. The e-mail opened and she began to read.

HEY SEXY,

I know you said when you left NOLA you were done with big-city crime, but I'm hoping I can change your mind. Our old boss Captain Franks is creating a task force specializing in special victims of violent crimes. I know how much you valued your work on those types of cases and always wished there was a special division for them. Well, now there is. Ace and I have already been accepted into the unit, but there's one more space.

It's yours if you want it.

It's the job you always wanted, and it couldn't be offered under *better circumstances. Franks practically foamed at the mouth at the thought of getting you back on his team. And he's not the only one who feels a little weak at the thought of you returning.*

I miss you, Colt.

I know I didn't do a good job showing you how important you were to me, and it's my biggest regret. When you left, I thought I'd be able to handle it, but I was a mess. And you know me. I don't do sentimental.

I guess that means I care for you. A lot.

We were great together once before—on the job and off. I know we can be great together again.

Maria

JADYN FELT AS IF SOMEONE HAD REACHED INTO HER CHEST and squeezed. Of course, she'd known Colt had other women in his past. How could he not? But it sounded as though whatever he'd had with Maria was far more than a passing fling. Maryse had hit the nail on the head with her call that Colt's failure to expound on his New Orleans time was due to a woman. Jadyn had called the law enforcement part.

Colt had told Jadyn he left New Orleans because he was weary of seeing the horrible things people did to each other, but if the past months were any indication, he hadn't gotten the respite he was looking for in Mudbug. And if a job he'd always wanted was on the table and all he had to do was ask, what was stopping him from leaving?

Unable to stop herself, she opened another window and Googled Maria. News stories of the very accomplished detective flooded the screen. She clicked on one of them and her heart fell even more. The woman was so gorgeous she didn't even look real. If Jadyn hadn't known any better, she would have thought it was a photo of an actress playing a cop on a

Hollywood movie set. She closed the window without reading any of the articles. The headlines alone let her know that Maria was not only beautiful but a total badass at her job.

She switched back to the e-mail and marked it as unread, wishing she'd listened to her conscience and never opened it in the first place. She jumped up from the kitchen table and turned to stare out the front window at the sun coming up over the bayou.

What have I done?

She'd given her body and a good chunk of her heart to a man who had never given her the first indication that he was interested in anything long-term. With the job he'd always wanted and the stunning, accomplished woman he'd once cared for waiting for him in New Orleans, Jadyn couldn't help feeling she would be a distant second.

"Are you ready?" Colt's voice sounded behind her, causing her to jump.

"Sorry," he said as she turned around. "I didn't mean to startle you."

"I guess I was lost in thought," she said.

He circled his arms around her and pulled her in for a soft kiss. "We're going to figure this out. No one is going to get to you. Not on my watch. Not ever."

He squeezed her in closer and she buried her head in his chest. She knew he meant every word he said. Now.

The question was, would he feel the same way after he read the e-mail?

CHAPTER FIFTEEN

"WAKE UP!"

Taylor bolted upright in bed just as Helena dropped through the ceiling and slammed into the mattress, sending her vaulting off the bed and onto the floor. She was still only half-awake when she struggled up from the floor and glared at Helena over the edge of the bed. She was almost sorry she did.

The ghost wore a flight suit, but Taylor was fairly sure a person of Helena's size had never been in the cockpit of an airplane. Her head was covered with what looked like the helmet from a space suit, and she wore a backpack that looked as though it contained a parachute. Mildred and company hadn't been kidding about the wardrobe thing. She hadn't seen anything this out-there since she'd last visited Aunt Freda in the mental hospital.

"Sorry," Helena said, at least having the decency to look a little sorry.

"If that's the way you wake people up, I can see why someone killed you."

Helena rolled her eyes. "Like I haven't heard that insult before. You're really not a morning person, are you?"

Taylor rose from the floor and checked her arms and legs for potential future bruising. "I hate mornings, actually. They always come too early."

Helena looked up at her. "What time do you go to sleep?"

"It varies. Three, sometimes four."

"In the morning?"

"No, in the afternoon."

"What do you do all night?"

Taylor shrugged. "Sometimes I work on a case. Sometimes I read."

"No television? I've been watching a lot of television lately."

"Yeah. I heard about the deer head."

Helena waved a hand in dismissal. "She deserved it."

Taylor glanced at the window and realized the sun was just beginning to peek over the bayou. She looked at the alarm clock and groaned. "It's not even six a.m."

"I know, but Mildred said to get you, so here I am."

"Mildred? Is something wrong?"

Helena nodded. "There's some crazy weepy woman in the lobby asking for you. Says her entire world is on the line and she's not leaving until she speaks with you. She has good taste in handbags, though. Her purse cost at least a thousand bucks."

Taylor groaned. The only thing worse than being awake at a completely indecent hour was dealing with an emotional client before she'd had a decent night's sleep and at least one pot of coffee.

Helena's eyes widened. "She's not your mother, is she?"

"No! She's my client." Taylor turned to grab a brush from the dresser and attempted to tame her bed hair.

"Thank God. I usually don't start insulting people's parents until I've known them for at least a week."

"Well, if you ever have the misfortune to meet my mother, you have my permission to forgo your week rule."

"That good, huh? So is the client the missing husband woman?"

"The one and only."

"I guess you called her last night and told her about Clifton Vines. Probably not the best idea if you don't like mornings. All it takes is ten seconds in the same room with her and you know everything about her is drama. She got a flat driving into town and had an entire weeping session about her car as soon as she walked in the door."

Taylor held in a sigh, wondering just how much Sophia was going to make her regret taking this case. "How did you know about Vines?"

"Mildred told me. She's worried about Jadyn on account of someone trying to poison her."

"What?" Taylor whirled around to face Helena. "What are you talking about?"

"Someone sneaked into the hotel yesterday and spiked Jadyn's water with cocaine. Lucky for Jadyn, Maryse needed bottled water for one of her stinkweed experiments and she realized something was wrong with it and tested it. Maryse said it wasn't enough to kill Jadyn unless she was allergic or something, but it would have made her pretty sick."

Taylor tried to process this information, but was having trouble absorbing it all. She'd had little interaction with Jadyn, but from what she could see, the game warden was honest and capable, and cared about the town she served. "Why would someone want to hurt Jadyn?"

Helena shrugged. "No one knows, but Colt will figure it out. He's got the hots for her. I see the way he stares at her when she's not looking." Helena grinned. "She stayed at his house last night."

Taylor knew she shouldn't encourage the ghost to gossip, especially about a law enforcement officer's potential sex life, but she couldn't help but be interested in the people she'd met here. She'd never met other people who could talk to ghosts, but here in Mudbug, she'd found not one but three women who did so every day and didn't think anything of it. Well, except for thinking about the aggravation that Helena brought, but that was a whole other thing.

"Why did she leave the hotel? Wouldn't she be safer here?"

"Maybe, but she said by her staying it put others at risk."

Taylor began to understand Jadyn's train of thought. "Like Maryse could have drunk the water rather than using it in an experiment."

"Exactly. And Colt has this badass security system at his house, probably because it's in the middle of the swamp. He claims he's better suited to protect her, but I bet he just wanted to get her naked."

Taylor tried not to smile. She was firmly in the hetero-sexual camp, but only a blind person would fail to see how attractive Jadyn was. As far as she could tell, Colt's vision was just fine. "Maybe he was using her as bait," she suggested.

"Bait? Is that some new sex game you young people are playing?"

Taylor laughed. "No. I mean since the stalker was unsuccessful the first time, he might try again. And if Jadyn was in a more isolated location than the hotel and with good security, it could give Colt an opportunity to catch him if he made a move."

"That's pretty smart. But I still think he wanted to get her naked."

"The two are not mutually exclusive."

Helena's eyes widened. "Ah, I get it."

Taylor placed the brush back on the bathroom cabinet and

pulled her hair into a ponytail. "I guess I better get downstairs and absorb some of the crazy and drama before Mildred charges me extra."

She looked over at Helena, but the ghost didn't respond. Instead, she sat stock-still, her eyes still opened wide and now her mouth wide open as well.

"Helena?" Taylor took a step closer to her.

"Can't breathe." Helena huffed out a breath and the glass front of her space helmet fogged over.

"Crap!" Taylor rushed over and reached out to pull the helmet off Helena's head, but her hands passed right through it. A spike of panic rushed through her. "I can't touch it."

"Starting to lose consciousness," Helena said, her voice starting to drift off.

"Stay awake, Helena! You have to change clothes. Concentrate on changing clothes now!"

Helena's eyes had started to close but popped back open when Taylor yelled. "What? Oh, yes, clothes change."

"Something simple, and hurry."

Helena lifted her arms and Taylor could tell the ghost was weak by the effort it took to get them off the bed. She waved them a bit in the air and clenched her eyes shut. A second later, the paratrooper-with-space-helmet outfit was gone.

Now, Helena wore a wet suit complete with diving tank and mouthpiece, firmly affixed in her mouth. She'd gone from having no air to having air shoved directly into her mouth. The entire thing boggled Taylor's mind.

Helena dragged in huge gasps of air, and Taylor could see some color returning to her face. She lifted one hand to pull away the mouthpiece, but no matter how many times she popped it out of her mouth, another appeared in its place. Her aggrieved expression left Taylor with no doubt how Helena felt about it.

"Are you all right?" Taylor asked. "I mean, considering? Just nod if it's okay for me to leave."

Helena gave her a begrudging nod and Taylor headed for the door. "I'll send Mildred up to help. Or...something."

She closed the door behind her and hurried downstairs. What the hell had just happened? Could a ghost die twice? Did Helena actually experience the symptoms of lack of air, or was she just being a drama queen? As soon as this case was behind her, she was going to spend some serious time picking the ghost's brain. Somewhere in the mess that everyone put up with had to be logical, consistent reasons for things. If she could figure out how to help Helena control her more random and hysterical impulses, it would make life easier for all those who could see her.

Sophia was standing in the lobby, wringing her hands and staring out the picture window. Mildred looked a bit worse for the wear, and Taylor felt instantly guilty for exposing the hotel owner to her over-the-top client. Life with Helena was difficult enough without adding another crazy female to the mix.

Sophia looked up when she heard Taylor's footsteps and rushed over to her as she stepped into the lobby. "After what you told me last night, I couldn't stay away. I spent hours tossing and turning in my bed and finally I couldn't stand it anymore. I have to talk to you, and I think it's best that I say what I have to say to the sheriff as well. That way, I don't have to repeat anything."

Taylor glanced over at Mildred, who shook her head. Whatever was up with Sophia, she hadn't shared it with the hotel owner. Looking at her client now, Taylor could tell she was agitated but something else was present—fear, anticipation—she couldn't put her finger on it any more than she could in her first meeting with Sophia. Whatever it was, maybe she'd find out when she put Sophia in front of Colt.

"I talked to Jadyn a couple of minutes ago," Mildred offered. "They were on their way to the sheriff's department. Might even be there already."

"Thanks. I guess we'll head that way then." She started for the front door, then remembered Helena. "Oh, I almost forgot. There's an issue with my room."

Mildred frowned. "What's wrong?"

"A...uh, leak, I think. A particularly *loud* leak."

Mildred's expression cleared in understanding. "I'll go check it out right now."

"Thanks," Taylor said as she opened the front door and gestured Sophia outside. "The sheriff's department is at the other end of Main Street." Taylor glanced over at the flat tire on Sophia's pristine Mercedes. "I don't think your heels will appreciate the sidewalk or the brick road much, so I'll drive us over." She gestured to her vehicle.

Sophia looked at the car and wrinkled her nose for a moment, then glanced down at the end of Main Street. A second later, she headed for the passenger door and slid inside. Taylor managed to hold in a smile as she climbed into the driver's seat and headed down Main Street.

The heiress was oddly quiet during the ride to the sheriff's department. Granted, it took ten seconds or less, but it was still the longest stretch of time Taylor had seen her client go without speaking. She hoped Sophia wasn't going to waste Colt's time, but she wasn't counting on it. Given what Sophia had told her before about her missing husband, Taylor couldn't see anything requiring law enforcement involvement.

Taylor's anxiety ticked up a notch when Colt's truck pulled in next to hers and parked in front of the building. She stepped out and waved.

"Morning," he said. "Is something wrong?"

Sophia climbed out of the passenger's seat and extended

her hand to Colt. "You must be the sheriff. I'm Sophia Lambert and it's imperative that I talk to you before you begin your search."

Colt shook her hand and looked over her shoulder at Taylor. She shook her head and shrugged, feeling bad that Colt had to deal with her client when he needed to be doing his job.

"Then let's head inside. I can put on some coffee and we'll all talk." He waved a hand at Jadyn as he unlocked the door. "This is Jadyn St. James, our game warden. She'll be partnering with me today, so anything I need to know, she'll need to know."

Sophia glanced at Jadyn and nodded. "Of course."

Colt motioned them inside and to his office at the back of the building. Two chairs sat in front of Colt's weathered desk and Sophia perched on the edge of one of them. Jadyn moved to the back wall of the office and sat on a window ledge near Colt's chair, so Taylor took the seat next to Sophia. A minute later, Colt walked in and took a seat behind the desk.

"I put on a pot of coffee," he said. "Can I offer anyone a glass of water until then?"

Sophia shook her head and Taylor noticed her knuckles were white as they clenched her purse.

"No, thank you," Taylor said.

Colt looked at Sophia. "How can we help you, Ms. Lambert?"

Sophia glanced at Taylor, then looked back at Colt. "Ms. Beaumont informed you of my situation?"

Colt nodded. "We're aware of the circumstances surrounding your husband's disappearance."

"Then you understand how overwhelming this is for me."

"I can see how it would be, but I have to be honest with you. Just because it's not impossible that the fisherman we're searching for today is your husband doesn't mean it's likely."

Sophia nodded. "I'd feel the same way if I had only the knowledge you do." She looked over at Taylor, a guilty look on her face. "I'm afraid I owe Ms. Beaumont an apology. I wasn't completely honest with you."

Taylor straightened in her chair and looked down at the floor. Whatever Sophia had neglected to tell her during their interview, Taylor had the uncomfortable feeling that she wasn't going to like it at all. Every single time she ignored that voice in her head, it caused her problems. She already knew this time would be no exception.

She looked back up at Colt, expecting to see a look of disapproval, but only the barest hint of curiosity showed on his face. Jadyn, who was still perched on the window ledge, hadn't changed expressions at all during the entire exchange. Taylor decided right then and there that when she grew up, she wanted to have the composure of Jadyn St. James.

Finally Colt spoke. "Ms. Beaumont is a professional and I'm sure, not interested in holding grudges. Please tell us what is so important that it had you driving here in the middle of the night."

Sophia took a deep breath and began. "I understand why, despite no evidence to the contrary, you don't feel your missing fisherman is my missing husband, but I think the odds are far higher than you think. You see, this wouldn't be the first time my husband disappeared into the water and never returned."

"According to the reports," Colt said, "your husband either died in the explosion or drowned and was swept into the Mississippi River."

Sophia leaned forward in her chair and nodded. "That's exactly what the police report said. But if my husband died in that explosion, then who removed two million dollars from our joint bank account the next day?"

Taylor whipped her head around to stare at Sophia. It took

a couple of seconds to realize her mouth was hanging open, and she clamped it shut and looked at Colt. He glanced over at Jadyn, who raised an eyebrow but was otherwise still as cool as a cucumber.

"Who had access to your accounts?" Colt asked.

"My accountants control many of my accounts, but this one was our personal checking. No one had the ability to transfer money except Samuel and me."

"Was the bank able to trace the money?"

"As far as Brazil, and then they lost it."

"And you made the police aware of this?"

"Yes, of course. But given my family's um...status in the community, only two detectives knew the entire story and they were sworn to secrecy. We were poised to acquire a competitor, and a scandal, particularly one concerning money, could have cost us the deal."

Colt nodded. "Our missing fisherman's standard of living is meager at best. Hardly indicative of a large pool of funds at his disposal."

"That doesn't surprise me," Sophia said. "Working with my father was an enormous amount of stress. Samuel had developed a bit of a gambling problem and before the explosion, I'd noticed changes in his behavior. He was forgetful and seemed to easily lose focus when working on a project. I found several mistakes in the last software conversion he worked on."

"Drugs?" Colt asked.

"Maybe. He was running through quite a bit of cash at the time with nothing to show for it. I suppose anything is possible."

"It seems a big stretch," Taylor interjected, "to go from tech genius at the top of a major corporation to bayou fisherman."

Sophia looked excited. "But you see, that's exactly why I

think the man you're looking for is my husband. He was working construction when I met him, but he'd worked the family business before that. His entire family are fishermen."

Taylor looked at Colt, who frowned. She could tell he wanted to continue to believe Clifton Vines was not Sophia's long-lost husband, but everything Sophia had told them leaned more toward that likelihood rather than away from it.

Colt looked straight at Sophia. "Someone took a shot at Jadyn at Clifton Vines's house. Was your husband a violent man?"

Sophia pursed her lips before replying. "At one time I would have said it was impossible. But the investigators never determined the cause of the explosion. I've often wondered..."

Colt glanced at Jadyn, then back at Sophia. "I see."

Sophia nodded. "I think you actually do. Can you imagine the difficulty of living all these years without answers? Wondering if my husband not only stole from me but caused the explosion that killed my father? The guilt crippled me for years. After all, I brought him into my family—lied to do it even." She sniffed as tears began to form. "And damn it, the worst part is that I still care for him. How does that make any sense?"

Taylor assumed the question was a rhetorical one, which was a good thing. Because she had zero idea why Sophia would still care for the man she'd described. Taylor was fairly certain that if a man had put her through all of that, the only thing she'd care about was throttling him to death.

"I appreciate your taking the time to come here and explain your situation in person," Colt said. "If we locate Mr. Vines, I will place him in custody until his background can be sorted out. If he is your husband, then he'll be turned over to the New Orleans police so that they can conduct an investigation."

"Thank you," Sophia said. "And I would appreciate your discretion in this matter. If this Clifton Vines is my husband, it will all come out soon enough."

"Of course," Colt said and rose from his desk. "Unless you have anything else, Jadyn and I need to coordinate the search parties."

Sophia rose. "I don't suppose I could tag along?"

"No, ma'am," Colt said. "We're not going on a vacation tour. No offense, but you'd only be in the way."

"I understand," Sophia said, but Taylor could tell she was disappointed. "I don't feel like driving back to New Orleans, so I think I'll get a room at the hotel. Maybe I'll be able to get some rest."

Colt nodded. "If we find out anything, I'll contact you there."

Sophia looked at Taylor. "I'm sorry for not telling you everything in the beginning. I was afraid I'd sound even crazier than I already did. If you don't mind, I think I'll walk back to the hotel. I'd like some time to process all of this."

"Sure," Taylor said and watched as she walked out of Colt's office. When she heard the front door of the sheriff's department close, she looked at Colt. "I'm so sorry. In hindsight, I shouldn't have called her last night."

"No," Colt said, "calling her was the right thing to do. If she hadn't shown up, we would be treating Vines as an innocent victim. Now we know there's a possibility he could be dangerous. We'll be better prepared for anything that might occur."

A wave of relief washed over Taylor. "I appreciate it, but I still feel silly for not questioning her more in the beginning. I had a feeling she wasn't telling me everything but I didn't pursue it." She sighed.

"Don't be so hard on yourself," Jadyn said, finally breaking her silence. "If you thought something was off after your initial interview, you have good instincts. Learning to trust them and the actions to take because of them are things that come with experience."

Colt nodded. "She's absolutely right."

"Thank you both," Taylor said. "I want so badly to be good at this. I study investigative techniques all the time, but I guess there's no replacement for experience. I would offer to help with the search, but I know I'd just be in the way as well. If there's anything I can do here, please let me know."

"I think keeping an eye on Sophia is the best thing for you to do for now," Jadyn said. "I don't want her getting any ideas about renting a boat or chartering a fisherman to take her around."

"Oh, I hadn't even thought of that," Taylor said. "You're right. I'll get back to the hotel and watch her like a hawk. And thanks again."

She headed out of the sheriff's department and hopped in her car. She could see Sophia ahead of her entering the café. Breakfast sounded like a good idea. Coffee sounded even better.

And both allowed her to keep an eye on her less-than-forthcoming client.

CHAPTER SIXTEEN

MARYSE BOLTED OUT OF BED AND STOOD IN THE MIDDLE OF the bedroom, trying to figure out what had caused her to leap out of bed, wide-awake. She glanced at the clock and groaned. Six a.m. She was convinced the entire world was conspiring to keep her from sleeping.

The next-door neighbors had bought one of those giant bouncy jumpy castle thingies for their kids and installed it the day before. The entire evening and night—going well past midnight—all she could hear was the sound of kids screaming and screeching. She would have given darn near anything for a pair of noise-canceling headphones.

Finally, the parents had ended the fun and after much whining and griping, the outside returned to its normal state of quiet. She'd fallen asleep almost immediately, only to be awakened an hour and a half later when Luc received a work call. Maybe it was being in the house alone at night, or the attempted attack on Jadyn, or maybe she was on edge from all the noise she'd listened to that day, but for whatever reason it had taken her hours to get back to sleep. And now, she was wide-awake again and with no idea why.

The sound of glass breaking outside drew her back into the moment and she peered out between the blinds, scanning their backyard to find the source of the noise. It couldn't be a window. Their alarm system would have gone off, and Luc set it before he left. It had to be something outside, but the yard appeared clear from the back of the house all the way to the fence.

The shed had small windows on each side, but the side she could see showed no sign of damage. She reached for the nightstand and pulled out her nine-millimeter.

You should call the police.

She shook her head. It would end up being a raccoon and she'd look like one of those hysterical, incompetent women. It would take her family three generations to live it down and since she wasn't sold on the idea of kids, that meant she'd get the brunt of it forever. Besides, it was daylight. A person wouldn't be stupid enough to break into her shed in daylight.

She headed to the kitchen and looked out the back door window. Still nothing.

Before she could change her mind, she punched in the code to disarm the alarm and slipped out the back door, clutching her pistol. She paused on the back porch and listened, but only the sound of morning insects surrounded her.

"Helena?" she called out. "That better not be you."

Nothing.

She took a deep breath and took one step down from the porch, then another, until she made it to the lawn. She'd just lifted her foot for the next step when a voice boomed behind her.

"What the hell are you doing?"

Maryse screamed and tried to spin around, but her foot lodged in a hole and she twisted her ankle and lurched sideways. Her flailing about caused her to fire her pistol and a second later, she crashed to the ground.

She rolled over to see a raccoon shoot out from behind the shed and Luc staring down at her as if she'd lost her mind. And if she was so wound up that she hadn't even recognized her own husband's voice, then maybe she had.

"I heard something in the shed," she said, "so I came outside..."

Suddenly she heard a loud hiss and stopped talking. "Oh my God. Is that a snake?"

Luc glanced around, then reached down and pulled her up from the ground. "Inside and make it fast."

He held on to her hand and practically jogged into the house, dragging her behind him. Once inside, he shut the door and peeked out the blinds.

"What the hell!" Maryse heard her neighbor yelling from his yard.

"It's a snake, isn't it?" Maryse asked. "It's the mother of all water moccasins. I need a bigger gun."

Luc looked over at her, his lips quivering for a second before he broke into a grin. "You shot the neighbors' jumping castle."

"Really?" Maryse perked up. "Do you think it can be patched?"

Please say no. Please say no.

"Probably. But maybe we can list our house and move before they get it done."

Maryse smiled. "You're not going to yell at me for shooting it?"

Luc shook his head. "I'm not overly pleased you accidentally discharged a weapon. You could have killed someone or even yourself. But I'm not about to complain about the unintended target in this matter. In fact, you've given me an idea for the future."

"Maybe it would be safer to move."

Luc grabbed Maryse and pulled her in for a kiss. When he released her, his grin was even bigger than before. "Besides, nothing can upset me this morning."

"Why? You're usually not this enthused when you get called into work in the middle of the night. What...did something happen with Rico?"

"Something happened all right. He got into a mess with some Colombians and there was a shoot-out in Florida. Rico and six of his top men are all dead."

Relief flooded through Maryse so powerfully that she felt dizzy and her legs felt weak. "So it's over. I mean, my life can go back to normal?"

"Yes." He leaned down and kissed her again. "Whatever normal is."

———

Jadyn hopped off the window ledge as Taylor exited Colt's office. "That was weird," she said.

"Oh yeah."

"She's still not telling us everything."

Colt frowned. "I know. But is she leaving out something we need to know, or something embarrassing that she wants to keep a secret?"

"I'm hoping it's the latter if she wants us to bring her husband back, assuming he is her husband."

"It would be nice if we could get that information up front."

"You thinking of lifting a print from his cabin?"

"Yeah, but everything has to be by the book. If he stole the money and caused that explosion, we can't give a defense attorney any reason to get the case thrown out."

"How soon can you get a search warrant?"

"Probably by this afternoon. I'll stop on the way out and have Shirley get the warrant over to Judge Miller. Once it's executed Deputy Nelson can get the prints."

Jadyn nodded. "Sounds like a plan."

Colt shook his head. "If you'd told me two days ago that these two cases might be related, I would have called you crazy."

"But now you think they might be?"

"As incredible as it sounds, I do. And you know what cinched it for me?"

Jadyn shook her head.

"The name of his boat."

"Oh!" Jadyn gave a single laugh. "The *Houdini*."

"Master escape artist."

"I thought it was an odd name for a boat, but in this context, it would make perfect sense. I guess all that remains is proving it out." She glanced out the window again. "The search parties are all waiting at the dock. We best get moving."

Jadyn headed out of the sheriff's department and around back to the dock. Sophia's revelation had been unexpected and more than a little strange, but neither that nor the impending search was what worried Jadyn. Instead, what kept playing through her mind was the e-mail she'd read.

Colt hadn't had a chance to read it yet and probably wouldn't until tonight, so his behavior toward her hadn't changed. But what about after he read it? It sounded to her as though Maria was offering him everything he'd always wanted, and at a time when he was frustrated with the way things were going in his hometown. And that was just the job part. The second part of her offer worried Jadyn even more. Was there really a man alive who could refuse a woman who looked like Maria? If so, Jadyn wasn't sure she'd met him yet.

If only she'd seen the e-mail before she'd slept with him. Maybe then she wouldn't feel as if someone were stabbing her in the heart. And she could have escaped with a little dignity and self-respect. But now...if Colt left for the job in New Orleans, she'd be the woman he'd left in his wake. Someone to be pitied.

And that sucked.

Even worse, she had to spend an entire day in the boat alone with him, trying to pretend everything was normal when absolutely nothing was normal anymore. Not her life. Not her future. Not even the Clifton Vines investigation.

It was going to be a very long day.

As she approached the dock, she caught sight of a man fiddling with his cell phone and drew up short.

"What's wrong?" Colt stepped up beside her and followed her gaze. "Do you know him?"

"Yeah. That's Peter Vincent."

Colt's jaw twitched. "I thought he didn't recognize Clifton's boat."

"That's what he said."

"Then let's go find out why he's here."

They walked toward the dock, Jadyn watching Peter the entire time. As they drew closer, he looked up from his phone and his gaze locked on Jadyn's.

"Mr. Vincent," Jadyn said as they stepped in front of him. "I'm surprised to see you here."

"Some of the fishermen were talking yesterday about the search party. Finances prevent some of them from helping, but I don't have the same restrictions. Bobby's handling things back at the shrimp house."

"I didn't think you knew Clifton," Jadyn said.

"I don't. I mean, I checked the records and we've bought from him before, but I don't know him by sight. Still, I make a good living off the hard work of these men. I don't like to think about one of them stranded somewhere in the swamp."

"It's nice of you to help," Jadyn said and waved a hand at Colt. "This is Colt Bertrand. He's the sheriff here."

Peter's eyes widened just a tick. If Jadyn hadn't been watching him closely, she wouldn't have caught it. Colt shook Peter's hand, and Jadyn could tell the two men were sizing each other up.

"Thanks for volunteering," Colt said. "We can use all the help we can get. The knowledgeable kind, anyway."

Peter nodded. "The swamp is no place for the inexperienced."

"I'm going to get this started," Colt said. "Since you're probably not overly familiar with the area, I can pair you up with one of the locals."

"Nah, that's all right. Just give me a rudimentary map and I can find my way around most places."

"All right then." Colt headed to the dock where most of the volunteers had gathered. Peter set off behind him as Jadyn hung back and watched. Peter was lying. Jadyn hadn't liked the feeling she got from him at his shrimp house, and she liked it even less now. No doubt he knew Clifton Vines. The question was, why lie about it?

She had a feeling if she knew that answer, then some of the mystery surrounding Clifton Vines would start to unravel. She waited as Colt handed out maps with the assignments for each search party and gave them instructions for CB usage. As the groups began to head for their boats, Colt motioned to her and called out to the two fishermen they'd questioned in the diner.

The men stopped and turned around as Colt and Jadyn

approached them. Colt shook hands with both men and thanked them again for joining the search.

"We've received some strange information," Colt said. "I'm not at liberty to go into it as it's related to an ongoing case, but I was hoping you could help."

The two men looked at each other and nodded. "Anything we can do to help," the first man said.

"Did Clifton have a camp?"

"Not that I ever heard of," the first man said as the second shook his head.

"Did he borrow anyone's camp?"

"I suppose he could have," the first man said, "but I don't know of any in particular or on a regular basis. Clifton didn't take a day off very often."

"He usually went fishing when he did," the second man said.

The first man grunted. "So he always said, but I think he just took his bass boat out and slept. He never caught much, and had no tales about the one that got away."

The second man shrugged. "You're probably right. I never saw him at the hot spots."

"Did you see him fishing anywhere?" Colt asked.

"Saw him coming out of channels in the evening several times recently," the second man said. "Two were regular fishing locations that most of us know about, but the other one doesn't make much sense now that I think about it."

"Why not?"

"It's a small channel with a lot of cypress trees making up the bank. The hurricane did a pretty good number on the older trees. I don't think you could get very far back, and the channel's too narrow to have much good fishing."

The first man nodded. "Sleeping. I told you."

Colt smiled. "You're probably right."

The second man narrowed his gaze at Colt. "You don't think Clifton is off somewhere in a camp, letting us all run around like fools, do you? Because I can't see him doing something like that."

Colt shook his head. "He doesn't sound like the kind of guy who would let everyone worry for no reason, but like I said, I got some information that I have to check out or I wouldn't be doing my job."

"I guess not," the second man said, but he still looked confused.

"Would you mind pointing out the channel with the hurricane damage?" Colt asked.

"Sure." The man took the map from Colt and pointed to an area a good bit north of the search area. "You used to be able to access it from Bayou Bend, but I don't think you can get through anymore."

Colt folded the map and nodded. "I won't hold you guys up any longer. Thanks for the information."

The two men gave him a nod and headed for their boat. Jadyn fell in step with Colt as they walked toward the dock.

"What do you think?" Jadyn asked.

"At this point, I don't know what to think. He may have a hideout back off that channel or have just been sleeping. Still, there's no way he got that far north without a boat. Clifton's bass boat was parked on the side of his house, and I haven't had any theft reports."

"So if he was hiding out, you think he'd be using the camps closer to the wreckage site."

Colt nodded as he untied his boat from the dock. "Easier to get to. Easier to get away from. To get that far north, he'd have to swim several channels as there's no logical walking path around that wouldn't take him hundreds of miles out of his way."

Jadyn stepped inside the boat and took the seat next to the driver's seat. "Then I guess we should start with the camps. What about the Peter Vincent situation?"

Colt frowned. "I don't believe for a moment he's here out of the goodness of his heart."

"Neither do I, and I think he's lying about knowing Clifton."

"So what's his angle?"

Jadyn shook her head. "Maybe he's the one who damaged Clifton's boat. Maybe Sophia's opinion on what happened isn't the answer to all this."

"Maybe." Colt sighed. "This mess has more layers than my mom's ice cream sundae cake."

"I bet they're not nearly as pleasant."

"Not even. Well, I assigned Peter to the area farthest from us. Right now, I'd like to keep you as far away as possible from anyone we suspect could have poisoned your water."

"Fine by me. I never liked the guy. Something about him is off."

Colt tossed the rope into the boat and climbed in. As he guided the boat down the bayou, a flood of thoughts ran through Jadyn's mind, but no matter how hard she tried to focus on Clifton Vines, the mystery surrounding him, her attacker, and who he might be, she couldn't stop herself from going back to the e-mail.

When they returned home tonight, Colt would have a chance to read it. And then everything she hoped would happen between them was over. She didn't think for one moment that Colt would turn down the job opportunity he'd always wanted.

And even if the job didn't hold the same glitter that it once did, she had no doubt that Maria would.

CHAPTER SEVENTEEN

COLT CLOSED THE DOOR ON THE LAST OF A STRING OF CAMPS along their current stretch of bayou and pushed the dead bolt back into place. It had been a long and completely fruitless day. They'd spent five hours searching camps that morning, then returned to the sheriff's department for gas and lunch before heading out again. Now, six hours later, they were out of camps and no closer to finding answers than they had been that morning. None of the other search party participants had gotten lucky either, and many had finished their areas and were loading up their boats to leave.

"Is this the last one?" Jadyn asked as they headed back to the boat.

"Yep. And we've accomplished a whole lot of nothing."

Jadyn shook her head. "You realize we may never get answers for this, right? Vines might have drowned and the chance of finding evidence of that is slim to none. And if he is Sophia's disappearing husband, he could have vanished again."

"Not knowing doesn't sit all that well with me."

"Me either, especially as I picked up a stalker while investigating this case. I'm hoping finding nothing will be enough reason for the stalker to cut his losses."

Colt stepped into the boat behind Jadyn, his frustration mounting. Jadyn's stalker was the primary reason he needed answers. No way did he want something like that hanging over her head. It was no way to live. Look at how crazy it was making Maryse, and Jadyn could hardly be expected to stay out of the swamps unless she resigned from her position. So until they had a motive or name assigned to her stalker, they had to assume she was still at risk.

Colt had been invested in Jadyn's welfare almost since the moment she'd set foot in Mudbug, but after last night, he wasn't even going to try to deny that everything concerning her had become incredibly personal. This morning, he'd fought the urge to suggest she stay behind. He knew it was a completely illogical suggestion. First off, there was no way she'd agree to it. And second, finding Vines was her job and she took her job seriously.

But it didn't stop him from wishing he could handcuff her to his desk.

"What now?" Jadyn asked. "Should we check out that sketchy fishing place the diner guy told us about?"

Colt glanced up at the sky. "We've got about another two hours of sunlight, but I don't think I know a way through there that's not currently blocked with debris. The direct route is definitely a no-go. A huge cypress tree is blocking entry to the channel. I was going to talk to you about getting a crew out there to move it, as one of the ponds off that channel is a favorite fishing hole for the locals. They've been bitching."

"Is there any way around?"

"I'm sure there is, but offhand, I don't know it."

"Would Maryse?"

Colt nodded. "Probably. No one knows these channels as well as Maryse."

Jadyn motioned to the CB. "Give her a shout and ask. Last night, she offered to listen in on the search talk in case she could help."

"Great," Colt said and picked up the CB. "Maryse, this is Colt. Are you out there?"

"My husband says I am," Maryse replied, "so it must be true."

Colt smiled. "I need your expertise." He gave Maryse coordinates for the area they wished to search. "The hurricane blocked the normal access points but we were hoping you knew a way around that wouldn't take hours."

"Sure. Let me check my phone. I made some notes the last time I was harvesting in that area."

Colt looked over at Jadyn, who lifted her hand with her fingers crossed. He nodded. If Maryse didn't have a workaround, then he didn't know who would. As the minutes ticked by, he started to lose hope, but finally the radio screeched and Maryse came back on.

"I've got a way around for you. Shouldn't take you more than a mile out of the way of the main channel. Are you ready to write?"

"Go ahead."

Colt hurried to make notes as Maryse provided directions and coordinates. At first he thought she'd missed the mark completely, but then he saw the logic of the path she'd given him. It wasn't the most direct route, but they shouldn't have any problems running around in the channels she'd chosen.

"This is great," he said. "Thanks!"

"No problem. Hey, will you do me a favor?"

"Of course."

"I know it's a pain, but can you check in every hour? I've

got a hotel full of worried people, and I'd feel better if I knew my directions hadn't gotten you stranded."

"Will do."

Colt looked over at Jadyn. "Between Mildred worrying about you and Taylor and Sophia worrying about finding her husband, I bet Maryse hasn't gotten a moment's peace all day."

"You know it," Jadyn agreed. "I'm glad I'm out here with you sweating and itchy."

He handed Jadyn the map. "Do you mind navigating?"

She scanned the map. "Looks simple enough. As long as things haven't changed since the last time Maryse was out here."

Colt started the boat. "Let's find out."

Jadyn folded the map so that she could see the notes and the area they were traveling and held it behind the column to avoid the wind. A second later, Colt took off down the bayou. This was the last card they had to play. Either they found something, or they had to deal with the fact that they may never know more than they knew right now.

Thirty minutes later, he cut the engine and the boat glided to a stop in front of a dam of cypress trees. He cursed as he scanned the trunks that completely blocked the last channel they needed to traverse. Another hundred feet and they would have been in the area the other fishermen had seen Clifton exiting.

"I guess this is new," Jadyn said.

Colt nodded. "Maryse said there were a couple of trees down here but there was still enough room to pass on the left side." He looked at the huge trunk that now covered the previous entry point. "It hasn't been in the water that long."

"It might have happened during the storm that sank Vines's boat."

"Probably."

Jadyn walked to the side of the boat and peered over the barricade. "Looks fine on the other side. I don't suppose we could pull one of these out of the way?"

Colt shook his head. "It would take more than this boat to move a tree that size. And the last thing we want to do is risk the motor when we're out here alone."

And with someone stalking you.

He didn't say it, but he knew Jadyn was well aware of the risks.

Jadyn frowned and leaned over the side of the boat, peering at the trunk. "There's a rope here, tied around a big branch."

"Could have been a snare someone set before the tree fell."

Jadyn shook her head. "The rope's too thick and rough for a snare. Something looks weird."

She reached out and pushed the trunk. Colt stared in amazement as the enormous tree glided easily a couple of inches away from the boat. Jadyn glanced back at him, then rapped on the trunk. There was no mistaking the echo.

"It's hollow," Jadyn said. "Could insects have done this?"

"No, or we'd see damage on the outside. And insects certainly didn't tie a rope to it. The other end is tied off behind one of the trees that were already here."

Her eyes widened. "Very clever."

He leaned over the side of the boat and released the rope from the old fallen tree. Afterward, he gave the trunk a good shove and it glided across the water. He started the boat and eased through the opening, stopping on the other side to push the log back into place and toss the rope over the connecting log.

"Shouldn't you leave it open?" Jadyn asked. "I mean, in case we need to get away quickly."

"I thought about that, but if he's not back here and approaches, he'll know someone untied the trunk. If we have to make a run for it, I should be able to strike the trunk with the boat to get away."

Jadyn didn't look completely convinced that his idea would work, and he didn't blame her. He wasn't a hundred percent sure it would work either, but it was the best thing he could come up with that wouldn't blow their cover if Vines had left the channel.

He pulled his firearm from his holster and placed it on the dashboard of the boat. Jadyn removed her pistol from her holster and clutched it as she scanned the banks on both sides of the boat. The channel was a good twenty feet across at first, but narrowed as they progressed deeper into the swamp. Finally, they reached the end where it dumped out into a small pond, maybe one hundred feet across.

"Look," Jadyn said and pointed to a pile of brush on the far left side of the pond. Colt studied it for several seconds and finally made out the back of a boat, hidden by the brush. "He acquired a boat somewhere."

He retrieved his binoculars from the storage bench and looked past the hidden boat and into the trees. "I don't see a cabin," he said and passed the binoculars to Jadyn.

She looked for a bit, scanning the trees from left to right, and finally lowered the binoculars. "I don't either. But there has to be something back there, even if it's just a tent."

"If Vines spent time back here, I'm willing to bet it's more than a tent. It's probably just set far enough back that it can't be seen from the pond."

"You know what that means?"

"That Vines was building a hideaway before his boat sank."

Jadyn nodded. "I'd love to know why."

Colt lifted the CB and called Shirley, giving her the code phrase to change to another channel. "Has everyone in the search party checked in at the dock?" he asked once they'd both switched channels.

"Everyone but one," she said. "One of the volunteers came across Peter Vincent on his way in and said Vincent wanted to continue searching other areas. He tried to talk Vincent out of it, but he wouldn't hear it."

Colt clenched the CB with his hand. "I'm going to switch back to the regular channel. Let me know if Vincent turns up."

"You got it."

Colt hung up the CB, not at all happy with this new bit of information. "I don't like it."

"Me either, but it plays right into our theory that Vincent is hiding something and Vines may know what it is. Maybe Vincent sabotaged his boat and Vines managed to make it to his hiding spot."

"Or Vines had a backup boat ready and faked the accident hoping that he'd be declared dead."

"Either way, it appears he's trying to get away from something."

"And that something has to be big. Otherwise, why go to all this trouble?"

Jadyn nodded. "So how do we approach this? If we're to believe Sophia, he may have already killed one man in an explosion and stolen a stack of cash. How do we know the swamp isn't set with trigger devices or other security measures?"

"We don't know."

"So what's the plan?"

Colt scanned the bank to the right, looking for a safe place to dock. "I'll pull up to the bank over there next to those cypress roots. We can traverse the swamp straight back, then make our way to the left. Hopefully, if Vines set up any security measures near the bank, they'll be where he docked his boat."

Jadyn nodded and Colt started the boat and directed it toward the bank of cypress roots on the opposite side of the pond from where the boat was hidden. He secured the boat to the roots and pulled two shotguns out of the back bench, handing one to Jadyn. He stepped out onto the bank and remembered he needed to check in with Maryse. He turned around and was about to ask Jadyn to make the call when he heard a twig snap behind him.

Before he could react, a rifle shot boomed and he heard the bullet whiz past him, then the sound of plastic breaking. Instantly, he dived back into the boat, crouching on the bottom next to Jadyn, who'd dropped the instant the shot rang out. He looked up at the console and cursed when he saw that the shot had taken out the CB radio.

No chance of calling for backup.

————

MARYSE SAT IN THE HOTEL BREAK ROOM WITH MILDRED, Taylor, Helena, and Sophia, all of them staring at the CB as if their attention alone would cause Colt to check in. Maryse glanced at her watch for the tenth time in as many minutes and felt her frustration tick up another notch.

"How long?" Taylor asked.

"Ten minutes overdue," Maryse said.

"Maybe they forgot," Taylor suggested.

Maryse shook her head. "They both know we're waiting to hear from them." She picked up the CB and called for them again, but the only reply was light static.

Sophia jumped up from her chair and paced the tiny room. "I just know something's wrong," she wailed.

"Good God," Helena said. "That woman is driving me insane. I haven't seen such dramatics since I was married to Harold."

Maryse struggled not to reply. It had been easier to navigate conversation before Sophia showed up thirty minutes ago, hand-wringing and woe-is-meing. But since Sophia couldn't hear or see Helena, the rest of them had switched to stealth mode. Except Helena, of course. Helena was her usual brash, loud self. The fact that she was clad in the Hello Kitty pajamas and the diving mask, which she still hadn't managed to remove, made her even harder to ignore.

"Let's not get ahead of ourselves," Maryse said. "They could be having problems with the CB."

"But if that's the case," Mildred said, "they wouldn't be able to call for help either. More than a couple of people have gotten into a bind with their boats back in those less traveled channels."

Maryse bit her lower lip, a flood of possibilities racing through her mind. What Mildred said was 100 percent true. She'd been left stranded herself so many times she couldn't even count them, but at least her radio had worked and she'd been able to call for help. If she assumed their CB was disabled, then that left two choices—waiting, potentially hours, to see if they turned up or heading into the bayou to see if they needed help.

It took her only a second to know which option was the right one.

"I know exactly where they were going," Maryse said. "I'll head out there and see what the situation is, then radio back for help if it's something we can't handle."

"You're not going out there alone," Mildred said.

"It's safe for me now," Maryse reminded her.

Mildred shook her head. "*One* bad guy has been eliminated.

We have no way of knowing if Clifton Vines is dangerous or not, but I'm going to err on the side of caution."

"I'll go with you," Taylor said. "I don't know the swamps, but I have a pistol and I know how to use it."

"I'm going too," Sophia said.

Maryse shook her head. "I don't think that's a good idea."

"He's my husband," Sophia said. "If anyone can talk some sense into him, it's me. Please. I feel responsible for putting all of you in this position. I don't want things to go badly."

The last thing Maryse wanted was Wailing Sophia in the boat, but the woman did have a point. If Clifton Vines was her missing husband, then she was the only emotional connection available. She might be able to talk him out of actions he'd regret later.

Assuming things hadn't already gone south.

She took in a breath, forcing that thought out of her mind. She wasn't willing to go down that path. Not yet. She grabbed a pad of paper and wrote down the coordinates for Mildred. "Call Shirley and tell her to send Deputy Nelson to this location."

Mildred looked a bit relieved at the thought of backup, but Maryse could tell she still hated their plan. Mildred leaned behind Sophia's back and glared at Helena. The ghost was doing her best to appear nonchalant, but Maryse could tell she was worried.

"Fine," Helena mumbled through the diving mouthpiece. "If it will make you happy, I'll get in a boat with the drama queen and traipse around the swamp. But I want an entire tray of cinnamon rolls tomorrow morning. *Fresh* cinnamon rolls."

Maryse glanced at Mildred, who gave her a barely impercep-tible nod. Leave it to Helena to capitalize on the situation by adding food bribes to the mix. Her ex-mother-in-law was nothing if not predictable. Of course, she was going to have a hard time eating if she couldn't get that mask off, but Maryse couldn't be bothered to worry about it. Helena hadn't eaten all day and Maryse hadn't noticed her energy for complaining waning one bit.

Maryse pointed at Sophia's Prada-clad feet. "You look like a size eight. I only have one pair of work boots, but I can lend you tennis shoes."

Sophia grimaced, probably at the thought of sliding her high-dollar feet into someone else's shoes, but five-inch stilettos weren't optimum for anything as far as Maryse was concerned, much less a trip to the swamp. Before Sophia could get in a word, Maryse hurried upstairs to her makeshift lab and snagged a spare pair of tennis shoes, then scavenged yoga pants and a T-shirt from Jadyn's closet.

Sophia wrinkled her nose as she took the clothes and headed off to her room to change, but she was smart enough to know that Maryse wouldn't let her in the boat with her linen suit and heels.

"Do we really have to take her?" Helena asked as soon as Sophia was out of earshot.

"It's not like I want to," Maryse said. "I'm out of patience for drama, but if she can defuse a potentially dangerous situation, then it's worth the aggravation."

Helena sighed. "Since it's for Jadyn's and Colt's safety, I guess I'll have to deal with it."

Mildred rolled her eyes. "Yes, it's such a strain dealing with an irrational, dramatic person all day long. I can't imagine how you'll manage."

Helena glared.

"I'm really sorry about this," Taylor said. "She seemed so together at our first meeting, but she's starting to look frantic."

"I guess that's to be expected given the situation," Maryse said, "but it sure doesn't make her any easier to tolerate."

"No more rich clients for me," Taylor said. "They're too high-maintenance."

"Probably true in a lot of cases," Maryse agreed, "but not all. Mildred is rich. So am I if you're talking assets."

"Really?" Taylor looked back and forth between the women.

Maryse nodded. "We're both worth millions and you don't see us flailing and pearl-clutching all over the place."

"True," Mildred said, "but we also came into our money recently. Sophia was born into wealth. That's a totally different thing."

"Like Helena," Maryse pointed out.

"Fine," Helena said. "I see where the two of you are going with this. So we're both used to people doing things for us, and we don't like to be told no. What person would be opposed to that lifestyle if they could get it?"

"Me." Maryse and Mildred sounded off at once and Taylor laughed.

"Whatever." Helena flicked her hand at them in dismissal. "I'm heading down to the dock. With any luck, I'll be able to figure out how to get this mask off on the way. Maybe Princess Sophia will finish changing sometime this century."

The ghost stalked out of the break room.

"There's too many odd things about this case for my liking," Mildred said. "The two of you need to be very careful. Don't let your guard down for a second."

Taylor nodded. "I feel an imbalance between what we think we know and what we need to know. I just wish I could pin down where the feeling is derived from."

"Keep thinking about it," Maryse said. "Maybe it will become clearer."

Maryse knew exactly what Taylor felt, because she'd had the same feeling all day. Something was off. The dots didn't connect, but she couldn't fight the overwhelming feeling that somehow they should.

They were all missing something. And it was big.

She just hoped it didn't get them all killed.

CHAPTER EIGHTEEN

JADYN DIDN'T EVEN TRY TO CONTROL HER DISMAY WHEN SHE saw the shattered CB.

"Stupid," Colt berated himself. "I should have called for backup when we saw the hidden boat."

"No use dwelling on it now," Jadyn said. "Could you tell what direction the shot came from?"

"Directly behind me."

"I guess any chance of Vines being the injured party in this just got more questionable."

Colt frowned. "Yeah, except, I was thinking...Vines isn't from Mudbug so he probably wouldn't know either of us, especially by sight. What if he thinks we're someone else?"

"Who? He couldn't mistake either of us for Peter Vincent or his brother."

"I don't know. I was just thinking that maybe we should tell him who we are and see if he surrenders."

Skeptical didn't begin to describe Jadyn's opinion of Colt's plan. "And if he keeps shooting?"

"Then we'll hope we're better shots than he is."

Jadyn didn't bother replying. Being a better shot wasn't the real advantage. Knowledge of the landscape was the big advantage, and it all weighed in on Clifton Vines's side.

"Mr. Vines!" Colt yelled out. "My name is Colt Bertrand and I'm the sheriff of Mudbug. The woman with me is Jadyn St. James, our game warden. We just want to talk to you."

Colt looked at Jadyn and they waited. As the seconds ticked by in absolute silence, Jadyn figured Vines had merely used Colt's speech time to get a better line of sight at them.

"We can't stay here," Jadyn whispered. "We're sitting ducks."

Colt nodded and scanned the bank for a possible escape. Trying to get away in the boat would only make them a more viable target. Retreating on foot was the only option at this point. "Maybe if we skirted that bank of cypress roots to the edge of the bank, then we could make a run for the tree line."

Jadyn studied the path he'd suggested. It wasn't a great option. In fact, it sucked fairly big, but it was also the best one they had.

"How do I know you're really a sheriff?" A man's voice boomed out from the trees and they both froze.

"My boat indicates it," Colt said, "and I have a badge. I can throw it onto the bank if you'd like."

Jadyn stared at Colt, waited for a response. Several seconds later, he said, "Do it."

"It could be a trick," Jadyn said. "If you stand up to throw it, he can pick you off."

"I'm not going to stand completely." Colt removed his badge from his jeans, crouched at the edge of the boat, then threw the badge as hard as he could into the trees. He dropped back down beside Jadyn and they waited again.

Several agonizing minutes later, they heard footsteps coming toward them.

"Please don't shoot me," they heard him say.

Jadyn raised an eyebrow. She'd been under the impression that she and Colt had been at a disadvantage, not the other way around. They both slowly rose from the bottom of the boat to peek over the side. A thin man with silver-and-black hair stood on the bank, holding a rifle. There was no mistaking his exhaustion.

"Clifton Vines?" Colt asked.

The man nodded. "You're really the sheriff?"

"Yes. Who did you think we were?"

"It's a really long story."

"Maybe you can come back with us and tell me everything," Colt suggested.

Vines shook his head. "I don't think so. Not yet, anyway. I'll talk to you here, but I can't risk going back yet. Maybe if you believe me and can do something..."

"If you'll tell me what's going on," Colt said, "I'll see what I can do."

"Okay," Vines said. "But not here. Not out in the open. I have a place just back in the trees. It's safer."

Colt looked over at Jadyn and she nodded. There was always the risk that Vines wasn't alone, but based on everything they knew about him, she felt it was a slim chance. And if the two of them couldn't take one clearly stressed-out man, then they both needed to turn in their credentials.

They climbed onto the bank and Vines waved at the swamp behind him. "This way. It's not far."

They had followed him in silence about fifty yards into the swamp when they stepped into a tiny clearing that contained a tiny cabin. It wasn't much to speak of—mostly a framework of wood and some tarps over the roof, but Jadyn could tell the construction was fairly recent and reasonably sound. Apparently, the time Vines had spent back here hadn't been for fishing or sleeping. What had prompted him to spend his money and time crafting a hideout remained to be heard.

Vines opened the door to the cabin and motioned them inside. It was one big room with a cot covered with a quilt on one wall, a makeshift table and chair in the middle of the room, and a shelf with a small burner on it in the corner. Jadyn's mind flashed back to the conversation she'd overheard in the café and Marty's mother complaining about theft—tarps, a quilt, food—and she had a really good idea where those things had disappeared to now.

Vines sat the rifle on a shelf on the wall and sank onto the cot. Jadyn hopped up on the table and Colt took the chair. The three of them clustered in the tiny space made it feel even smaller. Vines looked at them and shook his head. "I don't even know where to start."

"I'd start with who you're hiding from and why?" Colt said. "Everything else is only details."

"That makes sense," Vines said. "I don't expect you'll believe me, but I'm hiding from the Vincent brothers."

"Peter and Bobby?" Jadyn asked.

"Yes." Vines looked a bit surprised. "You know them?"

"I met them when we were trying to identify your boat wreckage," Jadyn said. "Why are you hiding from them?"

"About a week ago, I saw something I shouldn't have. At first, I thought they didn't know, but someone must have told them I was close enough to witness everything."

"Witness what?" Colt asked.

Vines shrugged. "I'm not sure exactly. What I saw was a fisherman meet another boat out in the Gulf. I didn't know the other boat or the captain, but he didn't look like no fisherman. The other guy exchanged ice chests off his boat for a duffel bag from the fisherman I know. Then they both took off."

"Sounds like a drug drop," Jadyn said.

Colt nodded. "It's definitely an odd place to buy seafood. Why do you think someone saw you?"

"Because the fisherman stopped me on the docks the next day, quizzing me about how my catch was the day before. He was definitely trying to pin down my position. He must have seen my boat well enough to identify it. Then a couple of dockworkers said Peter was asking about me. He claimed it was because he wanted to get me on his supplier list, but he's already got more suppliers than he can process product from."

"I agree that sounds suspicious, but it's a big leap from Vincent suspecting you of something to making a move against you."

"I thought so too until I saw someone prowling around my cabin that night when I got home. I'm too far out to have trouble with theft or vandalism, and not far enough to be in hunting territory. I have no doubt why he was there, and knew it wouldn't be long before he made his move."

"Was Vincent responsible for sinking your boat?" Jadyn asked.

Vines shook his head. "But I figured if he was going to try something, he'd go for my boat first. Less chance of anyone suspecting something that way. The next day, after I docked for the evening, I circled around after dark and hid on a shrimp boat across the pier from mine. Close to midnight, a man showed up and climbed onto my boat."

"One of the Vincent brothers?"

"No, which is why I was suspicious of you two at first. But I know whoever it was, he worked for the Vincents."

"What did he do?"

"Attached explosives to my engine compartment. It was wired into the ignition setup, but set on a timer. Starting the engine would have started the timer. Thirty minutes later, when I would likely be several miles offshore, the engine would have exploded."

"You didn't recognize the man?" Colt asked.

Vines shook his head. "I'd never seen him before, but I got a good look at him when he stepped off my boat. I'd recognize him again if I saw him."

"And there's no one else who might have it in for you?"

"No," Vines said, but Jadyn noticed the slight hesitation in his answer. She wondered if Colt had noticed it as well.

"All the years I've been here, I've never had so much as a cross word with someone. Until now. I know I can't give you definitive evidence, but there's no doubt in my mind that the Vincent brothers are behind it all." Vines rubbed the back of his neck, clearly agitated. "If you could have seen the way that fisherman quizzed me..."

"I understand," Colt said. "And I'm sure you're right. We already suspected the Vincents were up to something. We just didn't know where to start looking."

Vines's relief was apparent. "You believe me?"

"I believe that the Vincents are up to something and they think you saw something they didn't want seen."

"But you can't do anything about it, can you?" Vines asked. "I mean, not without more evidence?"

"I have a friend with the DEA," Colt said. "Let me start there. He'll know how to handle this."

"Did you take a shot at me when I was at your house?" Jadyn asked, unable to contain the question any longer.

Vines flushed and looked at the ground, leaving no guess as to his guilt. "I thought you were working for the Vincents. I wasn't trying to kill you. Just scare you off. I'm really sorry I frightened you."

"You didn't frighten me," Jadyn said. "You pissed me off.

Normal people don't enjoy being shot at...or poisoned, for that matter."

Vines frowned. "Poisoned? I don't understand."

Jadyn stared. "You didn't sneak into the Mudbug Hotel and dump drugs into my bottled water? Another move to scare me away?"

Vines eyes widened so big Jadyn thought blood vessels would start popping. "Good Lord, no! I wouldn't poison anyone. Jesus. And I've never gone anywhere near the Mudbug Hotel."

He was so flustered at the suggestion that Jadyn had no doubt he was telling the truth. But if not Vines, then who?

Then the answer hit her like lightning.

The handoff Vines had witnessed. The frozen fish that Helena had fallen in and how upset Peter had gotten before he was assured they'd recovered them all. Maryse's comment that the water smelled slightly fishy.

"Vincent," Jadyn said. "They're smuggling cocaine in the fish."

Colt frowned for a moment, then everything she'd just put together must have come together for him as well. His eyes widened and he nodded. "That's it. Everything fits."

"Except," Jadyn said, "why poison me only enough to make me sick? Maryse said it wasn't a high enough dosage to kill me."

"Most likely to buy him time," Colt said. "Maybe he had another drop coming up and was afraid you'd be watching too closely. Maybe he was going to change the way he did business and needed the time to make it happen. Killing you would have brought the FBI here. And the first thing they would have done was retraced your steps for the last week or two."

Jadyn nodded. "You're right. Killing me would have

brought more heat. Getting me out of the way for a couple of days was the safer route."

"I guess a lowly fisherman's boat explosion wouldn't have brought the FBI to town," Vines said.

Jadyn glanced over at Vines and frowned. Although she believed his story, a lot about it bothered her. For starters, they still didn't know how Vines came to have a hideaway or how he escaped his sinking boat.

"Should we assume," Jadyn asked, "that you built this cabin, then faked your boat wreck to hide from the Vincents?"

Vines hesitated a moment before nodding. "I know it sounds extreme, but after I saw the explosives, I panicked. I figured if the Vincent brothers thought I was dead then I could hide out until they got caught. I removed the explosives and went out the next day, figuring I would sink my boat in the storm. I'd already acquired a spare bass boat to use for my getaway and stashed it close to the channel where I sank my boat."

He looked down at the floor a moment, his face flushed. "I didn't have time to get all the things in place that I needed, so after I sank the boat..."

"You stole things from Mudbug residents."

His eyes widened. "Yes, but only minor things like tarps and food. I swear I was going to pay them all back."

"If you lived," Jadyn said.

Clifton swallowed and nodded.

"So you were going to send an anonymous tip to the police?" Jadyn asked.

"Uh, yeah, that was the plan."

Jadyn watched his expression carefully. He was an accomplished liar, but not good enough to avoid tells completely. He was lying. Which sent her right to another thing that bothered her. For a fisherman, Vines knew an awful lot about explosives.

And given that Sophia's father had been killed in one and Vines might be Samuel, it didn't leave her with a comfortable feeling.

"How is it," she began, picking her words carefully, "that you know all that stuff about explosives? It seems a strange thing for a fisherman to have in-depth knowledge of."

Vines stiffened and stared at her. He was trying hard not to let his panic show, but her question had unnerved him. He didn't have a good answer, and was struggling to come up with something. Before he had a chance to fabricate something, Jadyn moved in for the kill.

"Are you Samuel Perkins?"

CHAPTER NINETEEN

MARYSE DIRECTED HER BOAT DOWN ONE OF THE MANY channels she needed to traverse to get to Jadyn and Colt's destination. She had pushed her speed as much as possible, but a storm was moving in and the strong gusts of wind blowing against the incoming tide had made the water so choppy that she found herself decreasing her speed the more time that passed.

Sophia sat on the seat next to her, clutching the side of the boat and the console in front of her so tightly that her knuckles were white. Her face looked a bit pale as well, and Maryse hoped she wasn't going to get sick. Taylor was perched on the bench in front of them, scanning the banks as they went. She didn't appear to have any issues with the rough ride, and Maryse felt her respect for the young PI tick up a notch. She'd really been thrown a curveball with this case, but she hadn't backed off for a minute, insisting that she'd taken the job and would see it through to the end.

Her sheer stubbornness on the matter reminded Maryse a lot of herself, which was probably why she liked her. Not to mention they had that whole "I see dead people" thing in common, although Taylor saw a lot of dead people, not just Helena. Maryse wasn't sure how she stayed so calm about it all.

Unfortunately, the last occupant of the boat wasn't as quiet as the other two.

"All this bouncing is killing me," Helena complained. "Can't you slow down?" The fact that the ghost was sitting on the back bench of the boat—the least bouncy spot in the vessel— only made her complaining more annoying. Even more frustrating was the fact that Maryse couldn't turn around and yell at her without looking like a crazy woman.

"I'm sorry about the rough ride," Maryse yelled into the increasing wind. "I want to get there and back before this storm hits or we're going to be far worse off."

She shot a glare at Helena, who looked up at the darkening skies and clamped her mouth shut.

"It's okay," Taylor shouted back.

Sophia gave her a nod, which Maryse took to mean keep going, so she pushed the accelerator just a bit more. As she rounded the corner to the channel where she thought they would find Jadyn and Colt, a wall of trees appeared in front of them. She cut the speed on the boat to nothing, sending Helena sprawling into the bottom of the boat. Taylor and Sophia braced themselves and managed to maintain their seats as Maryse let out a string of cursing.

Taylor stood up and looked at the tree trunks that completely blocked the channel. "Are you sure this is the right place?"

Maryse nodded. "Positive. I mean, I'm positive this is where they asked directions to, but if they couldn't get past..."

She didn't finish her sentence, but she didn't have to. Everyone in the boat knew they had reached a literal dead end. If Jadyn and Colt weren't where they indicated to Maryse they were going, they could be anywhere.

"How come this trunk is bouncing up and down with the waves?" Taylor asked.

Maryse looked at the trunk, then frowned. She walked to the front of the boat and pushed the trunk, then stared in surprise as a rope slipped off the adjacent trunk and the bobbing trunk floated away. "It must be hollow."

"But it was tied to that other trunk," Taylor said. "Why would anyone do that unless they were trying to prevent people from getting back there?"

"Exactly," Maryse said. "This must be where Vines is hiding. He blocked the entrance so that people would pass on by."

"Do you think Colt and Jadyn are back there?"

Maryse nodded. "They're smart. I think they would have seen through this."

"Then I guess we should go in, right?" Taylor asked.

"Actually," Sophia said, "this is as far as either of you will be going."

Maryse and Taylor whirled around and saw Sophia standing in the middle of the boat with a pistol trained on them. "Both of you, jump in and head to the bank. Follow my instructions and no one has to get hurt."

"What the hell are you doing?" Maryse asked.

"I'm going to settle a really old score," Sophia said. "But none of that is your concern."

Maryse shot a look at Helena, who was staring at Sophia in shock. Maryse widened her eyes at the ghost in an attempt to prompt her into action. Helena jumped up from the bench and swiped at Sophia's hand. Maryse sucked in a breath, not sure whether to hope Helena would be successful or be afraid that she'd make things worse. But her worry was wasted when Helena's hand passed right through Sophia's arm.

"I don't have all day," Sophia said and gestured to the bank.

"Get moving and you have a chance. Stand there three more seconds and I start shooting. Your call."

"You're not going to get away with this," Taylor said.

Sophia smiled. "Yes, I will. My company just opened a new facility in Madagascar, selected exclusively for beauty and the lack of extradition laws. When I leave this bayou, I'll be long gone and untouchable."

Taylor looked at the water and then Maryse. "Are there alligators?"

"Not here," Maryse said, lying through her teeth. She had no way of knowing what lurked beneath the surface of the water. Usually, alligators dived for the bottom during a storm, but that wasn't a guarantee.

"Now!" Sophia yelled.

One look at the gun-toting heiress and Maryse could tell she wasn't in her right mind. Whatever had been holding Sophia together all this time had completely vanished. Maryse lowered herself over the side of the boat and motioned to Taylor to do the same, then started swimming for the bank that was about ten feet away.

As she used the cypress roots to pull herself onto the embankment, Maryse looked back to see Taylor right behind her. Sophia was starting the boat with her right hand and still clenching the gun with her left. Helena stood at the back of the boat, clearly terrified with the way things were going. Maryse waved at her and crossed her fingers, hoping to convey that she was counting on Helena to figure out a way to prevent Sophia from killing anyone.

Helena nodded and gave her a thumbs-up. A second later, the diving mask disappeared and the ghost was decked out in full military gear—camo, boots, painted face, and Holy Mother of God, an assault rifle.

As Sophia guided the boat away, Taylor looked at Maryse,

her eyes wide. She didn't have to say a word. Maryse was already praying.

"Come on," Maryse said and motioned Taylor into the trees. "We've got to get to the far side of that pond. That's got to be where Vines's hideout is."

Taylor lifted a mud-clad foot. "This is going to suck."

"Yeah, but we can't depend on Helena."

Taylor nodded and Maryse set off at a quick jog through the swamp. The trees provided cover from Sophia's prying eyes, but also slowed progress more than running on the clear bank would have.

Dead brush and weeds scratched her bare arms as she pushed through the swamp as quickly as her heavy boots allowed. All the time she hoped that Colt and Jadyn were in a position to defend themselves against Sophia. Maryse had no idea what was going on in the woman's deranged mind, but she'd managed to fool them all. That was disconcerting enough.

Waiting for thirty years to settle a score was just plain insanity.

―――

ALL OF THE COLOR WASHED COMPLETELY OUT OF VINES'S face, leaving Jadyn no doubt as to what the answer was. He looked back and forth between her and Colt, and she would have given anything to know what was roaming through his mind, but he appeared to be struck silent.

"It's a yes or no answer," Colt said. "Are you Samuel Perkins?"

"Why...why would you ask me that?"

"I take that as a yes," Jadyn said.

Finally, he nodded. "In another life—a life that went

horribly wrong—I was Samuel Perkins. I suppose you ran my fingerprints when I came up missing. It was the one catch in my plan, but I hoped I'd have other options before it got that far with law enforcement."

It hadn't been a fingerprint that had identified him, but for now, Jadyn was content in letting him believe that's how it happened. "You intended to disappear again, didn't you?" she asked. "All that talk about hiding out until the Vincent brothers were out of business was just talk. You were waiting until things cooled down and then you would reappear in another place with a new identity."

Vines stared down at the floor.

"What I don't understand," Jadyn said, "was why you didn't just leave in the first place? You have millions. Why go through this elaborate plot to make everyone think you're dead? Do you really think the Vincents have the capability to track you to another state or country?"

Vines frowned. "I don't have millions. I have fifty thousand in a 401(k) account and a couple thousand in checking. That's everything I have to my name besides my house and boat."

"Then what happened to the money you transferred from your joint bank account when you disappeared after the explosion in New Orleans?"

Vines eyes widened. "I don't know anything about missing money. The only thing I escaped New Orleans with was my life, and I was lucky to have that. If I had millions of dollars, why would I have spent the last thirty years breaking my back as a fisherman?"

It was the question that Jadyn had most wanted an answer to, and now she found herself somewhat deflated. Every indication pointed to Vines telling the truth, but if he didn't take the money, then who had?

"Do the New Orleans police think I stole the money?" Vines asked. "Are you supposed to arrest me?"

"According to information we received," Colt said, "you're suspected of stealing the money and causing the explosion that killed your father-in-law. And given your knowledge of explosives, I don't think that's a stretch."

Vines jumped up from the cot. "I never killed anyone!"

The door to the cabin flew open and Jadyn jerked her head around to see Sophia standing in the doorway, a pistol leveled at them.

"Hello Sammy," Sophia said. "Did you miss me?"

Jadyn's blood ran cold. They'd been wrong about everything.

Horribly wrong.

CHAPTER TWENTY

Maryse slid to a halt where the tree line turned into a huge span of marsh grass. She frowned, estimating the distance between where they were and the next available set of trees. The two-foot-high grass that covered the half acre gap between their current position and where the trees began again offered no cover at all unless you were one of the lower-stature swamp creatures.

"Do we make a run for it?" Taylor asked.

Maryse looked to the left to see how far out of their way circling around the marsh grass would take them and blew out a breath. It would be a minimum of ten minutes to circle around. Only ten seconds to run across. Assuming, of course, that no one shot them before they got to the other side.

Taylor pointed to the bank on the opposite side of the pond. "There's your boat."

Maryse squinted, trying to locate Sophia and her pistol, but didn't see the psycho anywhere. "Looks like Colt's boat is on the other side but I can't get a good look through these bushes."

She poked her head out of the trees for a better look and

saw Helena disappearing into the swamp. "Helena just went into the trees right behind where the boat is docked," Maryse said.

"Far less chance Sophia will see us now."

"True. But you don't need to do this. Why don't you wait here and flag down Deputy Nelson when he shows up?"

Taylor shook her head. "I brought that crazy woman here. I'm not about to let everyone else clean up my mess."

Maryse recognized the determined look on the young investigator's face. She'd worn it many times herself. She nodded. "On three."

Maryse counted off and they sprang in unison from their hiding spot and sprinted like cheetahs across the open field. They slowed a bit when they reached the tree line but only in order to traverse the thick foliage. The boats were a good quarter mile away, and Sophia already had the jump on them.

With every step Maryse prayed that either Helena figured something out or Jadyn and Colt had the reaction time they needed to stay alive. They wouldn't be expecting an ambush.

Sophia had fooled them all.

———

JADYN SUCKED IN A BREATH AS SHE STARED UP AT THE heiress. Both she and Colt had holstered their pistols when they'd entered the cabin. Vines had placed his rifle on a wall shelf. None of them had a chance of gaining access to a weapon before Sophia opened fire. And given the crazed and evil look Sophia wore, Jadyn had no doubt not only that she knew how to use the gun she held, but that she'd also enjoy it.

"What's wrong, Sammy?" Sophia asked, her cloying tone sending shivers up Jadyn's spine. "Aren't you happy to see me?"

"Sammy" looked more on the verge of a heart attack than

anything. His face was so white there couldn't be more than a drop of blood remaining. His eyes looked as if they would pop out of their sockets, and his hands shook as they clenched the edge of the cot.

"I know you're upset, Ms. Lambert," Colt said, "but this isn't the answer. I will take Mr. Vines...er Perkins into custody and the New Orleans police will sort everything out."

Sophia laughed. "You fool. There's nothing to sort out. Sammy didn't steal my money or kill my father. He doesn't have the backbone for such things."

"I had the backbone to leave you," Samuel said quietly.

Sophia flushed and she pointed the gun directly at his head. "You dare insult me, when I control everything?"

He shook his head. "You don't control me now and you never will again. Kill me if that's what you want to do. But you'll never again get the satisfaction of forcing me to cover for you."

Sophia stared. "You'd rather die than be with me."

He nodded. "Every single day."

Sophia's expression contorted into a rage that Jadyn had never seen the likes of. Her finger whitened on the trigger and Jadyn watched closely, waiting for her to squeeze off the shot. That split second of distraction may be the only chance she and Colt had for accessing their weapons, and even then, it was likely only one person was walking out of the cabin.

The rest would be leaving in body bags.

As Sophia's finger squeezed the trigger one millimeter more, then another, Jadyn prepared to spring. Just two more seconds and it would be time to make her move. She had no doubt Colt was thinking along the same lines.

One second.

But before Jadyn could spring, she heard someone yell "Rambo" and Helena Henry crashed into Sophia, knocking her away from the doorway and into the brush at the side of the cabin. Jadyn and Colt both sprang up at once, accessing their weapons in a flash, then Colt hurried to the door to see where Sophia was.

As he peered around the doorframe, a shot ricocheted off the door hinges only inches from his head and he ducked back inside and crouched down. "What the hell happened?" he asked.

"Thorns!" Helena screamed somewhere outside the shack. "I fell in thorns. Oh my God, it's a snake!"

Jadyn shook her head. "It's like she had a spasm of some sort."

A second shot tore through the wall of the shack, grazing Samuel's shoulder. His hand flew up to cover the injury and Jadyn pushed him off the cot and onto the floor before she dropped down beside him. "Stay low," she whispered. "How many shots is that?"

"Two that we know of," Colt replied. "That magazine holds fifteen rounds but she could have backup."

"Someone shoot that crazy bitch!" Helena yelled. "I accidentally touched a snake. I need therapy."

"We have to do something," Jadyn said.

Samuel pointed to the corner where his makeshift kitchen was located. "Under that shelf, there's a section of the wall that comes off. I won't stay somewhere with only one way out. I have this...thing."

"Small wonder," Colt said and reached under the shelf to remove the wall panel. "I'm going to circle around her. Stay low." He locked his gaze on hers. "If you get her in your sights, take her out."

Jadyn nodded. The time for talking things through was over. All of them weren't leaving the swamp on their own accord. She just hoped Sophia was the only casualty. She crouched on the floor next to Samuel, giving her a clear view of the doorway.

Footsteps sounded outside and her hand tightened on the trigger. A second later, Helena came to a sliding halt in front of the door. The outfit that she'd been wearing when she tackled Sophia was gone. In its place were jeans, a checked shirt, and boots. A pink fluorescent cowboy hat completed the outfit.

"I'm going to round her up," Helena said. "I've got rope."

Jadyn's eyes widened when she saw that Helena was clutching a snake in her right hand and not the rope she thought she had, but before she could say a word, the ghost dashed off.

"Hi-yo, Silver! Away!" Helena yelled and bounded off into the swamp.

Jadyn inched closer to the door, straining to hear what was going on outside. It seemed as if every second that ticked by took an hour as she waited for any indication that Colt had found Sophia, or Helena had discovered she was holding a snake, but the swamp had gone oddly silent.

She looked over at Samuel, who stared back at her, his fear apparent. "Hand me that pillow." She pointed to a travel pillow on the back of the cot.

Samuel passed Jadyn the pillow and she leaned as close to the door as possible, then tossed the pillow out the door. A second later, a shot rang out and foam from the pillow scattered on the ground outside of the cabin.

"She shot me!" Helena yelled. "I'm going to lasso her. Holy shit, I'm holding a snake! I hit her with the snake."

Sophia let out a bloodcurdling scream and Jadyn knew Helena's ghostly snake had transformed into the live version when she'd tossed it at the insane heiress. A second later a shot rang out, then another.

"Help!" Helena yelled. "They're shooting everybody out here!"

Jadyn stressed over her options. Did she risk leaving the cabin by the front door? Or maybe she should head out through the wall panel and follow Colt's path. But that left Samuel alone, and that wasn't the best idea either. The man had a way of disappearing and he still had a lot to answer for.

"All clear!" Colt yelled and Jadyn jumped up from the floor and dashed out of the shack, pulling Samuel along behind her.

She spotted Colt in the swamp about twenty yards from the shack and hurried over. He stood above Sophia, who was prone with a single hole through the center of her head. The back half of a water moccasin was trapped beneath her and struggled to get loose. Colt holstered his gun and motioned to Jadyn, who grabbed Sophia's hip and pulled her up as Colt pulled from the shoulders. The snake shot off into the swamp, apparently having no desire to mix with crazy humans.

"Is she dead?" Samuel asked.

"Oh yeah," Colt said.

"Thank God," Samuel said and collapsed down on a log.

Jadyn looked over at Colt and realized blood was seeping through his shirt on his right side. "You're shot." She leaned over as he lifted his shirt. Relief washed over her when she saw it was a surface wound. It would sting like heck for a while, but he would live.

"It only grazed you," she said.

"Only? Says you." Colt grimaced as he dropped his shirt back into place. "That smarts."

"We need to get back to Mudbug," Jadyn said.

"We won't all be going back to Mudbug." Peter Vincent's voice sounded behind them and they whirled around to find him standing about twenty feet away, holding a shotgun.

CHAPTER TWENTY-ONE

Before Jadyn could even register the danger, the words "not again" ran through her mind. Then she processed their huge disadvantage and her heart fell. Everything they'd endured today had been for nothing. They would all die in the swamp and no one would have any idea what happened.

"Throw that pistol on the ground, honey," Vincent said.

Jadyn clenched the pistol, not wanting to part with it, but also knowing there was no way she could get a clean shot before Vincent did. As she started to lift her arm to throw the gun, a shot rang out.

A wave of dizziness passed over her and she waited for the pain to come. A split second later, she realized she hadn't been shot at all. Vincent's eyes widened and the blood rushed out of his face, and a second later, he dropped like a stone to the ground. In a flash, Jadyn lifted her pistol, ready to take out whoever had shot Vincent.

"Don't shoot, Ms. St. James!" Deputy Nelson stood about twenty feet behind Vincent, holding his arms in the air.

Relief washed over Jadyn and she lowered her arm. "Jeez, Nelson. I'm not going to shoot you."

She looked over at Samuel, who was hunched over on the stump, propping his head up with his hands. He looked like a running year of bad weather. But he probably wasn't a flight risk now that everyone who wanted a piece of him was out of commission.

Deputy Nelson dropped his arms and hurried over to Vincent. Colt was crouched beside him and had already tossed his shotgun to the side.

"Did I kill him?" Deputy Nelson asked.

"No," Colt said. "He passed out. But he's going to be thinking about you for a while every time he sits down." Colt pointed to the bloody hole in Vincent's pants.

Deputy Nelson's eyes widened. "Wow! I can't believe I shot someone."

Colt rose from the ground and patted him on the back. "The first one's always the hardest. I'm happy to get you some counseling."

Deputy Nelson frowned. "I was thinking you should buy me a beer."

Colt grinned and Jadyn laughed. "It's a deal," Colt said. "How did you find us, anyway?"

Deputy Nelson opened his mouth to reply but before he got out a single word, Maryse and Taylor burst through the brush and into the clearing. Maryse took one look at the scene and rushed over to Jadyn, throwing her arms around her.

"I'm so glad you're alive," Maryse said.

Jadyn smiled as Maryse released her. "Me too."

"I am so sorry we brought that crazy psycho woman out here," Maryse said, huffing to catch her breath. "If she had killed you and Colt, I would never have forgiven myself."

Things Jadyn hadn't understood—like how Sophia had found them and how Helena had gotten there—now started to make sense. Speaking of which, she wondered where the ghost had gotten off to. She glanced around but couldn't see hide nor hair of the galloping ghost. "You came looking for us?"

Maryse nodded. "When Colt didn't check in, we got worried. I was going to come alone but Mildred pitched a fit, and Taylor insisted she come since she brought Sophia to town. Then Sophia convinced us that she was the only person who could talk Samuel out of hurting anyone, so...shit. Really bad call on that one."

"We found the fake entrance to the channel," Taylor continued, "and then Sophia pulled a gun and made us get out of the boat and swim to shore."

Jadyn stared. "And you ran all the way here? No wonder you both look ready to drop."

"Yeah," Taylor said. "Maryse had Mildred call the sheriff's department and ask them to send backup, but we didn't know how long he'd be."

"And that's how Deputy Nelson found us," Jadyn said. "Well, you saved the day with your backup call."

"Least I could do since I brought the enemy here." Maryse stared down at the unconscious Vincent. "Who the hell is he?"

"That's what I was wondering," Helena said as she staggered into the clearing. She was still wearing the cowboy gear, but had replaced the snake with a hot-pink whip. The cowboy hat had taken a beating and was all crumpled and cockeyed on her head.

Jadyn held in a grin. "It's a long story. One we don't have all the answers for ourselves."

Maryse glanced at Helena and flinched. "If it's all right by you, I'll wait until you've sorted it out and I've had a shower and at least two beers—maybe therapy—then you can tell me all about it."

"And cinnamon rolls," Helena threw in. "Damn it. Someone owes me an entire tray of cinnamon rolls."

"It's a deal," Jadyn said to Maryse.

"Uh, guys," Deputy Nelson broke in. "If we want to get this party back to Mudbug before that storm hits, we need to get a move on."

"He's right," Colt said. "Maryse and Taylor can take Maryse's boat back. Jadyn and I will take Samuel and Sophia's body. Deputy Nelson can take Vincent, and he goes straight to the hospital with a set of handcuffs attached to the gurney."

"Yes, sir," Deputy Nelson said.

"If you're all done jawing," Helena said, "would someone please get me the hell out of here?"

Jadyn couldn't agree more.

————

IT TOOK THEM A BIT OF TIME AND A LOT OF EFFORT TO HAUL Sophia and the still-unconscious Vincent to the boats, Vincent being the majority of the effort due to his size. Deputy Nelson handcuffed him to the boat in case he woke up and decided to make a dash for it, but Colt doubted he would be dashing anytime soon with that bullet in his rear.

The paramedics from the hospital picked up Sophia's body at the sheriff's department and hauled it off for processing. Colt was not even ready for the hailstorm of shit that was coming over his killing one of the richest and most influential women in the state. Maryse and Taylor had drifted off to the hotel as soon as they hit the dock, both talking about long hot showers as though they were better than winning the lottery. At the moment, Colt agreed with them.

But first, he and Jadyn needed answers from Samuel.

He brewed them a pot of coffee and everyone took a seat in his office. Before he could even start with the questions,

Samuel, who'd been silent the entire boat ride back to the dock, began to talk.

"I'm so sorry," Samuel said. "You don't deserve everything that happened today. Neither of you."

"And you do?" Colt asked. "I'm going to go out on a limb and guess that you faked your death to get away from Sophia."

Samuel nodded. "She was brilliant and beautiful and I was a lowly construction worker with humble beginnings. She enchanted me. It wasn't until after we were married that I saw the cracks in her armor."

"I assume she's disturbed," Jadyn said.

"Oh no," Samuel said, "disturbed is far too light. Sophia was a sociopath. She was just a very skilled one."

"How did you figure it out?" Jadyn asked.

"The first thing I noticed was the cunning with which she dispatched anyone at the corporation she considered a threat to her own promotion. Her father didn't believe in giving family something they hadn't earned, and that included his daughter. She did completely unethical things to rid herself of some of her competition."

"Did you confront her about it?" Colt asked.

"At first, but when I realized she was actually gleeful over how her victims had suffered, I knew I was wasting my breath."

"Why didn't you just leave her?" Jadyn asked.

"Don't you think I would have if I could? You don't understand. People like Sophia don't care about anything but the game. And for Sophia, the game was controlling anything she wanted to control. That included me. When I started pushing back, she told me that if I ever left her, she'd have my entire family killed."

"And you believed her?" Colt asked.

"Wouldn't you?"

Colt nodded. "I guess I would have."

"Wow," Jadyn said. "That's a living nightmare. So did you rig the explosion to fake your death, not knowing that Sophia's father would be in that building?"

"No!" Samuel plopped his coffee mug down on Colt's desk, sloshing the dark liquid onto the desktop. "It wasn't me who rigged the explosion. It was Sophia. I knew she was up to something. She'd been spending a lot of time in one of the units I was working in. It focused specifically on excavation, which is where I learned about explosives. I was programming the software to handle their tolerance calculations."

"And Sophia worked with you on that programming?" Jadyn asked.

"Yes. I knew she had an ulterior motive, but at the time, I took it as her keeping an eye on me. I didn't think...and then all the pieces began to fall together."

"Like what?" Colt asked.

"I found parts for explosive devices in a box in the back of our bathroom cabinet. It was Sophia's space and I usually didn't go into it, but that day I was out of shampoo. I recognized the box as one our explosive parts were delivered in and checked the contents. She had everything she needed to build a bomb that could easily level a small office building."

"What did you do?" Jadyn asked.

"I watched her as closely as possible. What else could I do? If I went to the police, they would have thought I was crazy, and even if they took me seriously enough to question her, it would only have made things worse for me."

Colt shook his head. "You would have had an almost impossible time convincing them that someone of Sophia's wealth would be involved in such insane behavior. And the cops would have trod lightly because of her influence in the city."

"Exactly," Samuel said. "So I watched and waited, hoping that I could figure out what she was up to before she put something into action. But I was too late." He shook his head. "The box went missing from the bathroom cabinet one morning and the maid informed me Sophia had left for the office an hour before. I'd slept so soundly that I never heard her leave and I dressed in a panic and set off for the office."

"Maybe she drugged you," Jadyn suggested.

Samuel's eyes widened. "I hadn't thought about that before, but you could be right. Anyway, one of the executives pulled me aside as soon as I entered the building to give me a warning about Sophia. Apparently, her father had informed her that morning that he was giving the chief operations officer position to one of the older male vice presidents in the company. He'd made the decision and told the top executives the night before."

"Did one of them tip off Sophia?" Colt asked.

"Maybe," Samuel said. "Or maybe she had his office bugged. I'd always wondered. Regardless, I knew it was going to be bad."

Jadyn drew in a breath. "Are you saying Sophia killed her father?"

Samuel nodded, clearly miserable. "I think so. When I reached her office, she was sitting there studying her nails and smiling, as if nothing negative had happened to her that morning. I pretended I hadn't heard anything and greeted her as I always did, then said I needed to speak with her father about some hardware upgrades and left."

Samuel drew in a huge breath, then blew it out. "As soon as I was out of her sight, I practically ran to her father's office, but his secretary said he'd stepped out to one of the power buildings to meet with me as I'd requested. But I hadn't requested a meeting at all."

"Sophia," Jadyn said and shook her head.

"I ran across the facility until I was out of breath, then slowed to a fast walk and jog when I could manage it. I was just about to turn the corner to the power building when it blew. I dived behind a metal storage container that was sitting close to the building. Between the two, I was sheltered from the blast."

"And when it was over," Colt said, "you just walked away?"

"I guess I went into shock. Debris covered the container completely, so I was hidden from sight, and there was no reason for anyone to look for me there. I just sat there, my mind racing so fast it made my head hurt and my body so weak I couldn't even work up the energy to try and escape."

Samuel shook his head. "I sat there so long my legs went numb. I heard the sirens and screaming around me but I just sat, completely silent. I didn't know how long it had been before I finally got the strength to dig my way out of the debris. When I did, I discovered it was pitch black and the facility was empty, and that's when it hit me."

"Everyone thought you were dead," Jadyn said.

"Yeah. It was the perfect opportunity to be rid of Sophia forever and still protect my family. So I dived into the bayou and swam away. Then I hacked myself a new identity and created a new life." He put his hands over his face and sobbed. "All this time, my parents thought I was dead. They buried an empty coffin. And I've been afraid to contact them all this time because I knew Sophia would be watching. And she almost won. What I don't understand is how she found me. Was it the fingerprint?"

Colt shook his head. "There was never a fingerprint." He told Samuel about Sophia's artist friend and how Sophia hired Taylor.

"It's all so unbelievable," Samuel said. "No one will believe it."

"People will believe," Jadyn said. "You have my word along with Colt's, Maryse's, and Taylor's. All of us saw what you saw. They can't call us all liars."

Colt blew out a breath. "I have to be honest. I don't know what to do about all this. I have no intention of asking the prosecutor to pursue identity theft charges. You've been punished enough already and no one was harmed by your actions, as the real Clifton Vines was deceased. The New Orleans police don't have a warrant out for your arrest, but I'm certain they'll want to talk to you."

"Can you put me in jail for the night?" Samuel asked.

Colt stared. "You want me to lock you up?"

Samuel nodded. "It will probably be the best night's sleep I've gotten in twenty-nine years."

CHAPTER TWENTY-TWO

JADYN PUSHED HER UNTOUCHED COFFEE ASIDE AND GRABBED a bottled water from the refrigerator in Colt's office. It had been an incredible, satisfying, yet equally horrifying day. She couldn't remember a time she'd had that many guns pointed at her and hoped to never beat today's record.

She slumped back in her chair and sipped on the water. Colt had left a couple of minutes before to set Samuel up with the promised shower. She supposed she could leave and head for a shower herself, but her bathroom things were at Colt's house.

You can borrow some shampoo from Mildred. You're stalling.

She sighed. Leave it to her never-exhausted conscience to weigh in on her current state of flux. Her entire body ached. Her feet were actually throbbing with desire to be loose of the tightly laced boots. And she probably smelled. But none of that outweighed the one unresolved thing.

The e-mail from Maria.

She wished she could walk out of the sheriff's department, head to the hotel for a shower, and sleep until she couldn't sleep any longer, but Jadyn knew herself better than that. No way could she go about her normal life without knowing where she stood with Colt. And no way was she waiting for him to read the e-mail, then lounge around if he didn't immediately make up his mind.

It would drive her crazy. She'd be watching his every move, looking for a sign that he had made a decision to return to New Orleans. Or worse, taking every positive sign as an indication that he had decided to stay in Mudbug, but never knowing if that decision was permanent.

Like it or not, she had to come right out and tell him what she'd read.

The door opened and Colt walked back in. Jadyn sat upright and took another swig of her water, trying to grasp the words she needed to start the conversation. But nothing sounded right.

"Some day, huh?" Colt said as he leaned against the desk in front of her.

"Oh yeah."

"I'll be doing paperwork and answering questions for a month. I'm glad there are plenty of quality witnesses to back me up on the 'Sophia Lambert was a crazy person' thing."

"It definitely helps, but I have to believe that others saw the real Sophia. Even a sociopath can't hold their cover every minute of every day."

"Poor Samuel. What he went through to get away from her and protect his family. I hope the New Orleans police release him while they investigate. I want him to see his parents."

"It's going to be quite a shock for them, but it's a good one." Jadyn couldn't even begin to imagine what the now-elderly couple would think when they saw their long-lost son at their front door. It was movie-of-the-week material.

"Well, I guess we are clear to get out of here. I'm sure you want a shower and food as much as I do."

Jadyn studied him for a moment. Was he suggesting she return to his place for a shower? Eat dinner together? Or was he suggesting she go to the hotel and resume her regularly scheduled program?

Unable to stand all the unanswered questions any longer, Jadyn burst out, "I read your e-mail this morning. It was wrong, but I did it."

"Okay. Unless you deleted my renewal notice for *Popular Mechanics* I doubt we have a problem." He smiled.

"The e-mail came after you got in the shower. It was from Maria."

Colt's smile faded to a frown and he stared at Jadyn for several excruciating seconds before responding. "What did it say?"

Jadyn told him about the new division with the New Orleans Police Department and the job offer that was his if he just said the word.

He shook his head. "I pushed for that division years ago but no one would listen. I guess it had to be someone else's idea. Typical bureaucratic crap."

"That's not all," Jadyn said, her voice barely a whisper as she relayed Maria's personal message to Colt.

She watched him closely as she talked, looking for any indication that let her know where he stood, but his face may as well have been a block of stone. He looked directly at Jadyn the entire time she spoke. When she finished, he stared out the window at the bayou for what seemed like forever.

"Shit," he said and looked back at her. "I never intended to tell you about Maria—never intended to tell anyone. And she goes and sends that e-mail the morning after we..." He shook his head. "Years later and she's still making a mess of my life."

He reached his hand out for hers and pulled her up from the chair to stand in front of him. Still holding her hand, he looked her directly in the eyes. "Maria is part of my past. A past I have zero intention of revisiting. Not the job and certainly not my relationship with her, or whatever it was."

"She seems so perfect. Did you love her?"

"I thought I did, but getting tangled up with Maria was the worst decision I ever made. She's beautiful and smart and an excellent detective, but she cares for herself first, her job second, and everything else in life falls far short of those two."

"She said she misses you."

He shrugged. "And maybe she does, but wanting me around when it's convenient for her is as deep as Maria goes. That's how I know now that I couldn't have been in love with her. The idea of Maria, sure, but the person wasn't available."

He reached his hand up to stroke her cheek. "I planned on avoiding women the rest of my life. Then I met you. You are the perfect one."

Jadyn's breath caught in her throat, almost choking her. She sniffed and rubbed her nose with one finger, completely overwhelmed by his words. Words she never expected to hear.

"I want you, Jadyn St. James," he said. "I fought it as hard as I could and I know I confused you in the process, but all of that was my issues to work out. I was letting my past control my future, and that was stupid. You're not only perfect. You're perfect for me."

He lowered his lips to hers for a gentle kiss and Jadyn wrapped her arms around him, dizzy from the euphoria. Colt wanted her. He'd finally said the words she'd wanted to hear.

And she knew he meant it.

No more guessing about where they stood. No more wondering if there was a future or if it was only temporary heat. As she tightened her arms around him and deepened the kiss, Jadyn felt she'd finally found the place where she'd always belonged.

EPILOGUE

Two weeks later

Maryse and Mildred stood next to Taylor's sedan, looking down at Helena Henry, who occupied the passenger's seat. "Are you sure about this?" Maryse asked.

Ever since the ghost had declared her intention to move to New Orleans and assist Taylor with her investigations, Maryse had worried about the plan. Part of her mind yelled at her to celebrate the future lack of uninvited guests, particularly when Luc was showering, but then her conscience weighed in and she felt guilty about the trouble Taylor was most certainly in store for.

"I'm sure," Helena said. "I need something to do, and Taylor wants to explore her abilities with ghosts. Maybe we can both learn more about how ghosts work, me especially. And besides, I'll have a new grandbaby soon, and I don't want to bother you guys to make trips to New Orleans all the time."

Maryse glanced at Mildred, who didn't look any more convinced than she was that this was a good idea, but both of them knew there was no changing Helena's mind when she caught hold of an idea.

"Okay, then," Maryse said. "I'll be in New Orleans in a couple of weeks for a meeting with a pharmaceutical company. I'll drop by and see how you're doing."

"You're fussing like an old woman," Helena said. "Close the damn door. The air-conditioning is getting out and it's not all that great to begin with."

Maryse grinned and closed the car door. "I guess that is that," she said.

Mildred nodded as Taylor walked out of the hotel, carrying her overnight bag.

"It was great talking with you guys again," Taylor said.

"I'm sorry you had to come all the way out here for more police reports," Maryse said.

"No worries," Taylor said. "It was a final sign-off, and I am happy to put all of that mess behind me."

Maryse nodded. The fallout from Sophia's crazed rampage and the revelation of Samuel's thirty-year plight had made national news. The New Orleans police scrambled to tie everything up in a neat, inarguable package. They'd found unexpected allies in Sophia's family, domestic help, and coworkers. As Jadyn had suspected, Samuel hadn't been the only person to witness Sophia's evil insanity.

Since no one with wealth or power stepped up to defend Sophia and insist that the legal system put the screws to Samuel, the district attorney's office was more than happy to stay out of the mess entirely. It would have been a no-win situation and they knew it. The entire case had already played out in public opinion, and the public was solidly behind Samuel Perkins.

Colt had insisted on personally delivering Samuel to the New Orleans police, but had deviated on the way and taken the man to see his parents. He confessed to crying at the reunion. Maryse would have paid money to see that.

The final nail in the coffin had been when the DEA seized the Vincent Brothers Shrimp House and arrested several fishermen for drug trafficking. Luc said the case was as solid as they came, and no doubt Peter and Bobby would spend the remaining good years of their lives in federal prison.

"I'm glad it's behind all of you," Maryse agreed. "And it was nice getting to visit with you again."

Taylor nodded. "I really appreciate all the information you've given me. I have a ton of questions, but I also have a ton of ideas about research. With Helena to help, I think I may finally get the answers I've always wanted about the spirit world."

"I hope she's not too much trouble," Mildred said. "Oh hell, who am I kidding? She's going to be a whole mess of trouble. I hope it's not more than you can handle."

"And if it is," Maryse said, "don't hesitate to bring her back here. Even if you need a temporary break, we're happy to take her on again. Well, maybe *happy* is an overstatement."

Taylor smiled. "I know full well what I'm taking on, and I have zero expectation that Helena will make it easy on me. But I have the overwhelming feeling that it's what I'm supposed to do. And after the fiasco with Sophia, I'm no longer going to ignore my feelings."

"Well, good luck," Maryse said and gave Taylor a hug. "And keep in touch. We'd love to hear about your research."

Mildred hugged Taylor as well. "And stay safe with your investigations. No more working for sociopaths."

"I promise," Taylor said and headed around her car to the driver's side. "I'll call you soon," she said and hopped into the car.

Maryse and Mildred waved as she drove away.

"I don't know whether to be worried or relieved," Mildred said.

"No doubt. But I am hungry, and Luc said the burgers were almost ready when I called earlier."

"Then what are we standing here for?"

———

THE BARBECUE IN MARYSE AND LUC'S BACKYARD WAS IN full swing when Mildred and Maryse arrived. Maryse stepped onto her back porch and paused, taking in the scene in front of her.

Her incredible, sexy husband was at the grill, arguing with Beau, Sabine's incredible and sexy husband, over whether the burgers were ready or not. Raissa and Zach, who were packed up and ready for their own move to New Orleans the following week, sat in lawn chairs, drinking beer and grinning about the burger argument. Jadyn and Colt sat in lawn chairs on the other side of the grill, holding hands and whispering to each other. Maryse had little doubt what all the whispering was about. Both of them looked happier than Maryse had ever seen them.

"It doesn't get any better than this," Mildred said quietly.

Maryse squeezed the hotel owner's hand. They'd been through so much together, but it had all been worth it.

"No. It doesn't."

For more hilarious mysteries, check out Jana's Miss Fortune series.

Visit her website at janadeleon.com.

Made in the USA
Middletown, DE
17 January 2022